Highland Alliances

Convenient marriages to save their clan!

Neighboring Scottish clans must form alliances to defeat a dangerous common enemy. New clan leader Ross MacMillan is prepared to enter into a marriage contract to safeguard his people. His brother and sister are under orders to marry strategically as well. Is there a way for love to flourish amid the battle for land and castles in the Highlands?

Read Ross's story from Terri Brisbin in
The Highlander's Substitute Wife

Fergus's story from Jenni Fletcher in
The Highlander's Tactical Marriage

And Elspeth's story from Madeline Martin in
The Highlander's Stolen Bride

All available now

Author Note

I've always enjoyed writing in the medieval period, so when I was first approached about participating in a connected medieval project for Harlequin Historical with talented authors Jenni Fletcher and Terri Brisbin, I jumped at the chance. We were a great team with a lot of laughs between us and finally settled on going with a tale inspired by Neil Oliver's *A History of Scotland*.

One of my favorite things to write about in medieval history is strong women. I've always been inspired by women like Joan of Arc, who rode into battle with French forces; Joanna of Flanders, who held off besiegers of her castle in her husband's absence; and Eleanor of Aquitaine, who remained duchess in her own right and even led her sons in a rebellion against their father. There are many more, but I am so fascinated by women who broke the proverbial mold of the time and like to celebrate their efforts with strong women, like I did in this book with Elspeth.

I hope you enjoy the Highland Alliances series and enjoy the collaboration between myself, Jenni Fletcher and Terri Brisbin.

MADELINE MARTIN

The Highlander's Stolen Bride

HARLEQUIN
HISTORICAL

Recycling programs for this product may not exist in your area.

ISBN-13: 978-1-335-40773-3

The Highlander's Stolen Bride

Copyright © 2022 by Madeline Martin

Harlequin Enterprises ULC
22 Adelaide St. West, 41st Floor
Toronto, Ontario M5H 4E3, Canada
www.Harlequin.com

Printed in U.S.A.

Madeline Martin is a *USA TODAY* and *New York Times* bestselling author of historical romance novels filled with twists and turns, steamy romance, empowered heroines and the men who are strong enough to love them. She lives a glitter-filled life in Jacksonville, Florida, with her two daughters (known collectively as the minions) and a man so wonderful he's been dubbed Mr. Awesome. Find out more about Madeline at her website, madelinemartin.com.

Books by Madeline Martin

Harlequin Historical

Highland Alliances

The Highlander's Stolen Bride

The London School for Ladies

How to Tempt a Duke
How to Start a Scandal
How to Wed a Courtesan

Visit the Author Profile page
at Harlequin.com.

To all the strong women in history
who have inspired the heroines
I love to write.

Chapter One

Argyll, Scotland, October 1360

The air crackled with tension. Perhaps the start of a storm. Perhaps a warning.

Elspeth MacMillan was locked in place between four armed guards en route from Castle Barron, their horses clustered together as tightly as possible in the dense forest lining the path to Castle Lachlan.

She wished she didn't have to rely on these men, that she too could wear a sword slung easily about her waist instead of her paltry dagger. But a woman's place was in the keep, seeing to linens and housemaids and servants while men saved lives and put food into empty bellies.

A low rumble sounded overhead, but it did not allay the tension gripping the back of Elspeth's neck. Something was amiss.

She glanced over her shoulder at the surrounding forest, holding the edge of her hood back to offer her better visibility. Nothing appeared out of place. The scent of damp earth mingled with the musty sweat of the horses as the thud of their hooves in the soil remained steady.

'Do you need to take a break, mistress?' The youngest man asked.

She shook her head and slowly turned her attention forward once more. 'I thought I sensed something in the woods.'

The young guard looked about, but the man at the lead scoffed. 'It's nothing to fret over, mistress. Women oft see things that aren't there when frightened.'

Ladies have grace and patience.

Elspeth gritted her teeth despite the reminder to herself. At least the internal recollection of her duties were enough to help her bite back her sharp remark.

After all, there was nothing she could cite to justify her unease. There had been no movement between the narrowly spaced trees, no snapping of twigs. Nothing except the nagging sensation that left chills prickling over her skin.

The young guard glanced at her. 'If it pleases you, mistress, I can search—'

Thunder cracked overhead, a bang so loud it nearly made Elspeth part with her skin. The lead guard laughed aloud. 'You see? It's only a storm. We'll be there by late afternoon.'

His reassurance did nothing to bring her peace. Even if it were not for the uneasy sensation she could not set aside, their arrival would still bring an unwanted wedding.

Leith MacLachlan waited to marry her. No doubt with scarcely enough time to rest after her travel. They had grown up together, thick as thieves. Their fathers had been close friends and so Leith and Elspeth saw one another with great regularity. So much, in fact, that she considered him to be one of her brothers. But the kind boy she'd known had become an entitled man who expected the world to bow at his feet. And while he was indeed a handsome man, Elspeth regarded him more with sisterly affection than with the passion of a wife and would not want a man so spoilt to contend with.

No, she was not anticipating her imminent union with any eagerness whatsoever.

Rain spit down on them from the sky and popped against the leaves. It was said that rain on one's wedding day brought good fortune.

But she knew better. There would be no love between her and Leith like there was between Elspeth's brother, Fergus, and his new wife Coira. In truth, witnessing the glow in Coira's eyes when Fergus was in the room and the way she made Fergus grin in return had made Elspeth long for the same.

The very thought of Leith looking at her in such a way made Elspeth's stomach clench with distaste.

All three MacMillan siblings had been forced into marriages for alliances with the surrounding clans. Their eldest brother, Ross, the new Chieftain of the MacMillan clan after their uncle's death, had wed one of the MacDonnell daughters, though Elspeth had departed Castle Sween before having met her. Fergus had sealed the alliance with the MacWhinnie clan with his union to Coira at Castle Barron where Elspeth had just been staying.

And Elspeth would bring the MacLachlan clan with her union to Leith.

While Fergus's union had worked out well for him, none of the siblings had wanted the marriages from the beginning. But it was necessary to join together with their allies in an effort to stave off the attacks from the Campbell clan who had swept in from Ireland with a series of violent attacks in an effort to regain their land in Scotland.

Elspeth would rather die than see the Campbell clan in Scotland once more. Especially after Alexander Campbell had killed her father years ago.

A twig snapped in the woods. Her head whipped towards the sound, her gaze darting among the slender trees with their peeling bark, seeking out any unnatural colour in an effort to identify a tunic or a gambeson or even a bit of chainmail.

The lead guard laughed once again, a rough bark of a sound as unpleasant as his disposition. 'It's a forest. Sounds occur regularly, mistress.'

Elspeth gripped her reins harder until her icy fingers ached with the effort. If she was a man, she would have punched him for his insolence.

Suddenly, the hair at the back of her neck prickled. Before she could place the cause of her unease, an arrow shot out from the forest and plunged into the neck of the lead guard. His body jerked back with the impact, blood spurting from the wound.

Elspeth froze in place, her gaze fixed on the gore. Everything in her screamed to run, yet all she could do was remain as she was, sitting atop her horse, gaping in horror. The man pitched backwards, falling from his saddle and into a puddle, his eyes staring up at nothing.

He didn't move or rise.

Dead.

He was dead.

Fear clawed at her, bringing a scream up her throat where it stuck fast.

'Get behind me, mistress,' the young guard said as the

other two closed in more tightly around her, filling in the space the riderless horse had left open.

A roar sounded from the trees and five men rushed from the foliage, their deep blue gambesons similar to the shade of the surrounding forest. The insignia stitched on their padded armour was one Elspeth immediately recognised as it had been the same as those worn by the curs who had attacked the abbey she'd previously been sent to for her safety, causing her to flee to the safety of Castle Barron and Fergus. The Campbells.

They had come for her then, attacking the nuns in their effort to steal her away.

And now, they were here for her again.

This was how it had gone in her life time and again, with her crouched behind men, helpless and unarmed. It was why she wished someone would put a blade in her hand and offer proper instruction on its use.

The marauders clashed with her remaining guards in a clang of metal on metal and grunts as each man struggled to not only kill their opponent, but also emerge alive and unscathed.

Elspeth had once harboured grandiose ideas of bravery in a scenario such as the one she now found herself. The idea of lifting a sword and wielding it expertly, cutting her own way to freedom. Now she remained in place where she hid behind the guards, uncertain what she could possibly do with only her simple dagger and haunted by memories of similar situations.

The guard to her left was knocked from his horse.

His beast tore off at the first opportunity of freedom, leaving a gap in her wall of protection.

One of the Campbells filled the gap immediately and reached for her. 'I have her, Calum.'

The name struck fear through Elspeth as surely as lightning did when it connected with the earth, but she did not let her terror hinder her with immobility. Not again.

No, she lashed out with her foot, thrusting it towards the man with all her might.

Her shoe was a dainty leather thing, meant more for traipsing about a castle as its mistress than for fighting in a battle, but she put every bit of her strength into that kick. Whether it was the force of the blow or the surprise that a lady would so readily attack, the man fell back.

But the man's determination to claim her only confirmed what she suspected. They wanted her. To use her against her brothers, knowing full well she was Ross MacMillan's weakness.

On the road between Castle Barron and Castle Lachlan, she was vulnerable.

'Run,' the young guard said as he fended off the attacker. 'Run.'

Though fleeing went against everything in Elspeth's spirit, she knew the best thing for her people would be to avoid capture, to keep from becoming their enemy's pawn. She snapped her reins and did exactly as the guard ordered, running from a battle she knew they could not win. Rain stung at her face and left her hair clinging to her skin like cobwebs, but she ignored it all as she hugged her body to the horse's powerful neck and fled.

No sooner had she departed from the two remaining guards, than another horse thundered behind her. Her heart caught in her chest, but she didn't dare look behind her.

She didn't have to, not when she already knew exactly who was there.

A man rumoured to be immeasurably cruel, one who took innocent lives and burned the homes of peasants, the son of the very man who had killed Elspeth's own father.

As the ominous pounding of horse hooves rumbled closer, she gripped the reins with one hand and slid free the dagger with the other, locking it in her fist. For she would rather die than be taken by the likes of Calum Campbell.

Calum Campbell was closing in on the fiery haired woman, who could be none other than the MacMillan lass. The only one who might allow him the chance to bring an end to the battle without more violence.

With a savage cry, he pressed himself lower on his horse's powerful neck and surged forward in a burst of raw energy. That surge was all Calum needed to throw himself onto the back of Elspeth MacMillan's steed.

She whipped around, her face a mask of fury as she swung her hand towards him. Before she could land a blow, the jostled gait of the horse upset her balance and sent her flying from the saddle. Calum stopped the beast and leapt from its back.

He couldn't let her go. Not when she was so important.

Rain drove from the heavens at them, leaving Elspeth's hair wild and matted where it had stuck across her face in the fall. He didn't need to see her to abduct her. Whether the rumours of her homely appearance were true or not, he had only to keep her for barter, to reclaim his lands without more bloodshed.

She leapt up suddenly and with a swirl of her sodden cloak, she began to run. Her pace was not swift, no doubt hindered by the bulk of her wet skirts, and how her feet slid about in the thick mud. Calum caught up with her with little effort.

'Come with me,' he said over her rain. 'And I'll see you're not harmed.'

'Nay,' she cried and quickened her pace.

It was as he figured. 'I don't want to use force,' he continued.

She said nothing as her feet slipped again in the sucking mud.

He would have to do as he had threatened. The idea rose like bile in his soul. How he hated the idea of having to overpower her until she submitted. It made him feel like his father, brutish and wrong. The thought squeezed at Calum's chest in a mix of emotions about the old man's recent death.

But it was nothing worth focusing on at present. The safety of the Campbell clan fell solely to his shoulders now, thanks be to God, and Elspeth would be the only key to getting them off Irish soil and back home.

'You're coming with me now.' The harsh voice he used seemed to belong more to someone like his da than to him. He shoved aside his revulsion and lunged at Elspeth.

As expected, her footing was not sure enough to keep her upright. With a cry, she pitched to the ground and he swiftly laid his body atop hers, trapping her without harm.

She snarled with rage and swung at him as she had on the horse. This time, however, he caught the glint of a dagger in her fist. He dodged the blow, but even as he did so, she attacked again, thrusting it towards him.

The thickly padded gambeson he wore would prevent him from being stabbed, especially against such ineffective attacks, but he still would take no chances. He shoved her arm down, carefully twisting her wrist to loosen her grip and plucked the dagger free.

'You cur.' Elspeth glared up at him through the curtain of wild red hair tangled over her face. 'I'll never willingly surrender to a Campbell.'

'I don't want to hurt you,' Calum protested.

'I want to hurt you.' Her knee jerked upward.

Calum flinched backwards before her knee could drive home into his groin. Her blow landed just above it, at his lower stomach. With his body flexed in anticipation of the impact, he hardly felt the hit.

She writhed and cursed with vigour beneath him in her desire to be free. Her efforts were undisciplined, expended out of sheer desperation and entirely without precision. Despite her determined spirit, her slender form was no match for his strength, honed through years of hard living and preparing for battle. Eventually, her efforts lost their potency as she tired. Exactly as he expected she would.

Panting with her exertions, the power drained from her limbs and her feeble hits told him it was time.

Holding her now with only one hand, he was able to dislodge the rope from his belt, glad he had taken Bram's advice on bringing it. Clearly Calum's right-hand man had more experience with feisty woman than he did.

Then all at once, Elspeth screamed and squirmed with renewed struggle, her legs kicking fruitlessly beneath her heavy skirts. The lass didn't go down easily, Calum would give her that.

The fight didn't last as long the second time, sapping out of her within seconds and leaving her body in an angry, frustrated sob. The pathetic sound of it lodged like a splinter in his heart.

He hated what he was doing. What it made him.

But it had to be done. For his people.

Quick as lightning, he bound her hands and curled the rope about her torso to secure her arms to her body. He left her legs unbound, unconcerned with the risk as he knew she would not get far without the use of her arms.

He pushed off the ground and tried to help her upright. She offered no aid and instead lay like a sack of grain.

The rain had begun to ebb, but it did not matter when he was already soaked through to the bone and miserable with the frigid bite in the air. Hunger gnawed at his belly, the way it so often did, exacerbating his irritation.

Still, he was careful as he lifted her from the ground and carried her in his arms. He didn't blame her for fighting back. It was what he would have done, and he refused to fault her for her efforts. Indeed, he was rather impressed.

She shifted in his arms. 'Put me down.'

He didn't reply as he carried her back to where his horse had stopped beside hers, the two lazily grazing in the rain-soaked field.

'Did you hear me?' she demanded.

Again, he did not reply as he draped her over the back of his steed, then took the reins of her horse and secured them to those on his. It would slow their travel, but there were not enough of the beasts to go around with his men. They would put this one to good use.

Before Elspeth could attempt to wriggle from the saddle, he mounted behind her and held her in place with one hand while he took the reins in the other and made way for the shoreline where the boat would be waiting to transport them back to Ireland.

There she would be safely held until the Chieftain of

the MacMillan clan agreed to end this war between their clans and allow Calum back onto Scottish soil. For until they were free from the barren land they had been banished to, his people would continue to die.

Their afflictions were ones which should never have plagued them. Starvation and illness brought on by weakened bodies. The latter of which had claimed Calum's own mother several months before. Their poverty was a fatal blow, one he was determined to put to an end.

Elspeth's horse followed, as well-trained beasts did, and the gentle pace made for an easier ride for the lass who lay face down with smouldering rage across Calum's saddle. All her efforts to free herself as they rode were in vain as he held her carefully but firmly in place.

The ship came into view along the coastline. Around it, the sea shifted slightly, the subtle waves without white caps. It would be a smooth ride back to Ireland.

Bram put a hand on his hip as Calum approached, a knowing smirk spreading over his lips. 'It appears the lass gave you a wee bit of trouble.'

Calum threw him a withering look as he leapt from his mount. 'You have the missive?'

Bram patted the leather pouch at his side where the letter Calum had carefully scribed to Ross MacMillan lay within. While Calum whisked Elspeth to Ireland, Bram would see the message safely delivered.

Calum carefully eased Elspeth from the steed. She staggered as her gaze darted about beneath the mass of her tangled hair, evidently seeking where she might run to, where she might hide.

But on the open coastline, there was nothing.

Even she must have realised this for she spun about and glared at Calum. 'You're a vile creature,' she said vehemently. 'To take an innocent woman. To attack nuns as you did before in your attempt to reach me.'

Bram raised his dark brows and shot Calum a bemused smile that bade him good luck. Calum would need all he could get.

Elspeth was still hurling invectives at him, but he tried to block them out as he lifted her once more. After the brief rest on the horse, her energy had been restored and she fought him every step of the way as he carried her over the soft sand, onto the rocking deck of the boat and into the captain's quarters. The room had been stripped bare of anything that might be used as a weapon, reduced to little more than an empty chamber with a bunk covered by a thin blanket.

'Where are you taking me?' She demanded when he set her down. 'To Ireland?'

He rolled his shoulders back, grateful to not be fighting against her any more. 'It's a short journey,' he assured her.

The ferocity in her gaze wavered as she took in her surroundings, no doubt realising the hopelessness of her situation. She swallowed and regarded him with large green eyes from under her bright red hair. 'Can you at least untie me?' This was not ordered in the same haughty tone she had used previously, but in a small voice. One used when the person loathes requesting a favour. 'It's too tight about my arms and I want to push my hair away from my face.'

Though he knew better, he loosened the knot and slid the rope free, careful to bring it with him. After all, he had her knife now and there was naught she could use as a weapon within.

What more could she possibly do in a bid to escape?

Chapter Two

The tingling sensation of small pins and needles prickled up Elspeth's freed arms. Calum Campbell didn't wait to see what she might do once she had full use of her body again. Instead, the coward scurried from the room like the rat he was.

She glared after him, infusing the look with enough hatred to penetrate the sturdy door he locked behind himself. It had cost a piece of her pride to beg him to free her like that, submitting to his obvious attempts to overpower her. If she had known how to fight, she would have never been in this situation. An old angry frustration rose within her, one that extended through the course of her lifetime.

Yet again, she had been left to hide behind men, watching as they were slain before her eyes in their bid to see her protected. Her heart flinched as she recalled the face of the man who had died for her today. Not only him, but also the ones before. Although she'd been too young to remember what they'd looked like, she knew there had been four who'd died protecting her the night Alexander Campbell had attacked them so many years ago, before he was cast out of Scotland.

How many more would die and suffer because of her now?

She wished she had a weapon, something she could run Calum Campbell through with instead of being reduced to falling back on feminine meekness. It was pathetic.

But at least the ploy had delivered the results she'd hoped for. He had freed her arms.

She pushed her hair from her face and swept her cloak over her shoulder. If only he'd left her with her dagger then she could have possibly picked the lock as she'd seen a man do once before. Or hide behind the door to stab Calum through his heart.

If he had a heart.

Which he most likely did not.

What kind of man could order his men to attack nuns the way he had back at the abbey when he'd first attempted to abduct her? He was exactly as he was rumoured to be—cruel and without mercy.

She had heard much of him over the years. How he ate the hearts of his enemy, raw while they still throbbed in his bloodied palm. How he killed whole families at once as he laughed with joy. How he and his people lived in a palace in Ireland, the land worked by those who had been captured from Scotland.

Aye, he was the worst sort of man. And she would do everything in her power to kill him.

Her gaze darted around the room for something, anything, to use in an attack. Disappointment punched her in the gut.

The captain's quarters were completely stripped bare.

She crossed the room, her footsteps hollow thuds against the wooden floor. There had to be something left behind. Perhaps a quill that had been forgotten. Or even a shaving razor. Having such a weapon in her hand would surely give her the advantage.

But then she'd thought that of her dagger as well. It had offered little aid against Calum's attack, her wrist easily twisted into submission with the rest of her shortly following.

Frustration rose in her, ugly and painful where it caught in her throat like a hard knot. Though she hated Calum, she had to grudgingly admit he was far stronger than she had realised he would be. The weight of his body over hers had been impossible to fight and when she'd tried to crush his groin with her knee, his reflexes had been too quick, so her blow had landed ineffectively upon his solid abdomen instead.

Nothing.

There was nothing in this room she could use. Her fingers dragged along the wall in a bid to find a loose board. The circumstances she found herself in were desperate indeed. If she could not find a way to attack Calum, if she could not flee, what would become of her?

Would she be tortured? Thrown in the dungeon of that gilded palace in Ireland?

Would Calum force her to lie with him?

Disgust welled in the back of her throat, nearly gagging her. She would rather die by her own hand than allow him to touch her.

While Calum had not exactly acknowledged that they were indeed going to Ireland, it had to be their location. Where else would they take her?

Surely they weren't going to kill her. They wouldn't have bothered bringing her to the ship if they intended to kill her.

No, they would most likely use her for ransom or leverage her to get whatever they wanted from Ross. She was the family's weakest point. The helplessness of the situation burned in her chest like an ember, red-hot with its intensity.

She had no say in her future and was completely at their mercy. Not only Calum's, but also that of her brother—and even Leith. One of them would doubtlessly come for her, but at what expense? She didn't want them worrying after her, sacrificing themselves for her safety.

These thoughts assaulted her as she stood in the centre of the room, swaying slightly from side to side with the rocking of the ship. Hot tears filled her eyes, the only warm part on her otherwise freezing body. She swiped them away before they could slide down her cheeks.

Never had she been a simpering lass and she would not be one now. There had to be a way to escape or, at the very least, attack. Even on a ship.

If they were indeed going to Ireland and she did manage to escape, getting back to Scotland would be difficult.

But not impossible.

The chill in the room wormed its way down her back like icy fingers trailing the length of her spine. She shivered and wrapped her cloak more tightly around her. Not that it offered much warmth. The thing was soaked from the rain and leached away her heat rather than kept it in.

She caught sight of the blanket on the bed and buried herself under it. The mattress was lumpy, but though the blanket was thin, it was at least dry and soft, offering far more of a comfort than she had expected.

An idea came to her. She could use the blanket to her advantage, in an attack. There was hope yet.

She listened intently, learning the sounds of the ship.

While she had never been on one before, she was certain the bangs and clatters of docking would be different than those of sailing over the sea.

Between the warmth of the blanket and the gently rocking sea, Elspeth felt herself being lulled to sleep. Fortunately for her, the ship drawing to a stop was more apparent than she had expected, and it jarred her from slumber, immediately making her recall exactly where she was.

And exactly what she intended.

Wasting no time, she leapt from the bed with the blanket in hand and slunk against the shadowed wall where she could be hidden by the door when it opened. She pressed against the sturdy wall, heart pounding as she waited for Calum to enter the room so she could attack.

Ireland greeted Calum and his men with rough and rocky shores, a jagged welcome for a place that never ought to have been their home.

Hamish, a mountain of a man who had always been loyal to Calum, indicated the rope at his belt. 'Off to get your hellcat?'

'She's a delight to be sure,' Calum groused.

'Bram will be delighted his suggestion was so helpful.'

Calum glared at the other man. 'I forbid you from telling him.'

Hamish merely chuckled in response, revealing a broken front tooth beneath the weight of his russet beard. 'Is she at least bonnier than the rumours have suggested?'

In truth, it was difficult to discern how much weight the rumours held about Elspeth's appearance. The cloak was too voluminous, and her hair was like a living thing determined to hang against her face.

But it certainly did not offer a flattering promise for a woman said to be skinny as a twig with features too large for her bony face. Not that her appearance mattered. They need only acquire Ross's agreement that they could return to Scotland in return for her and they could have her back whether she was a troll or a beauty.

'I'll see to her if you like.' Hamish glanced towards the door to the captain's quarters. 'Lasses generally like me well enough. Even hellcats.' He offered a broad smile.

But Calum shook his head. Not that he was looking forward to tackling Elspeth MacMillan into submission again, but the idea of kidnapping her to ransom her for peace had been his idea. Only he would have his hands sullied by it.

'Best of luck to you then.' Hamish clapped him on the back and departed.

Calum hesitated by the door to the captain's quarters and once more regretted his decision to untie her. There was no doubt in his mind that she waited for him on the other side of the door, crouched low and ready to launch herself at him.

With a deep breath, he unlocked the metal latch and entered the chamber, his body tensed for a fight.

Except no one appeared to be in the shadowed room.

He stepped inside. 'Mistress Elspeth?' He asked the empty room.

No one responded.

His heart lurched into his throat. Had she managed to escape? But how when he'd nailed down all the shutters, when there was no way for her to leave. There had been no cries of a man overboard and Calum's constant vigilance on the door revealed it had not once opened.

She *had* to be in there.

He spun around as a red-headed wraith launched herself at him, a fluttering blue blanket gripped in her hands. He stepped back in confusion. What could she possibly do with that?

Before he could put the question at her bizarre motives into words, she whipped the blanket at him. It passed harmlessly over his body.

'Come now,' he said testily and went to grab for it. 'This is foolish.'

Only this time she parted the fabric as she brought it around him, trapping him in the bulk before she yanked with recovered strength. What had been a preposterous situation only moments before now lost its humour as he crashed hard to the ground in a tangle of thin cloth.

Her foot slammed onto the ground followed by another. Away from him. He threw off the blanket and lunged at her, swiping blindly with his hand. He touched the warmth of skin and closed his fingers around what appeared to be an ankle as he tugged.

A shriek emerged from her as she landed with a bang on the floor beside him. Immediately her skirts flapped as she tried desperately to get back to her feet.

'Be still, woman,' Calum said through gritted teeth. 'I don't want to fight you.'

'I will *never* stop fighting you.' She shoved up to a sitting position, her hair in a wild disarray around her face once more.

Calum swallowed down his weariness in dealing with so wilful a lass. Perhaps he ought to have let Hamish see to her after all.

She continued to rise, but Calum grasped her shoulders and pressed her down to the ground once more. 'Stop before you hurt yourself.'

'You mean before you hurt me?' She threw his hands from her and tried to scoot away, but he caught her by her skirts, pinning her in place as he pressed his body weight over her to keep her immobile.

She lay still suddenly. Too still.

He was reaching for his rope, but paused now, tensed to see what she intended with this new tactic.

Suddenly, she lurched forward and slammed her forehead against his. Pain erupted at the spot while white stars winked in Calum's vision.

The wretched MacMillan lass had headbutted him.

Chapter Three

The agony radiating through Elspeth's skull was so brilliant that it left her momentarily stunned. She blinked hard as she lay on the ground, but the dots of light did not clear from where they blossomed on the ceiling overhead.

Had she done it wrong?

Fear trickled like ice cold water down her spine.

She'd seen men headbutt others before, but they moved on afterward as though nothing had happened. Perhaps there was a certain way to do it, the force less than she had exerted. Her fingers crawled over her skin, seeking an abrasion or a dent that might indicate she'd cracked her skull wide open.

God, but the pain was exquisite.

She cradled her brow with her palms and waited for the churn of her brain to settle.

But surely she was not the only one suffering. After such a hit, Calum would be laid out on the ground, his head split open like a spoilt apple. She forced an eye open, peering around her hand to find he was not only still upright, but laughing.

His chuckle was rich, as though someone had just told the jest of the ages.

'Let me see your head,' he said, his tone cajoling.

Her ire rose. She would not be condescended to in such a manner.

'Come now,' he coaxed. 'I don't think you've ever slammed your head into anyone else's before. It's not something easily done and the pain of it will echo through your head for at least a day.'

At least a day?

Elspeth couldn't help the groan that escaped her.

'Can you sit up?' Calum reached a hand towards her, as though he intended to help her into a sitting position.

She tensed. Was this a trick? Something to lure her into a sense of complacency before he ripped her skirts up her legs? Did he mean to accost her here, with the door wide open?

The breath fled her lungs. She wanted to be braver, stronger, but she was so afraid, she could scarcely even think. Especially around the blasted pain ringing out in her skull.

When she did not take his hand, he carefully grasped her shoulders and helped her up. The captain's quarters whirled around her like a wooden top. She wobbled slightly, but strong hands rested on her shoulders, setting the world straight once more, the touch firm but gentle.

'I have you,' Calum said with a reassurance she did not want to feel. 'Let me look at your head, aye?'

With careful fingers, he brushed the hair from her face, smoothing it back. He gazed down at her with eyes that were a warm hazel, filled with concern and a hint of kindness that did not belong to the type of man who slew children while they slept in their cradles.

Her head spun, not only with the hurt of her injury but with confusion at her own thoughts. He was her enemy, a man who had abducted her to use as her brother's only vulnerable spot. And she was gazing into his eyes, thinking them fine?

But she was transfixed as his stare moved over her entire face, slow and with apparent interest. A low curse escaped his lips.

She sucked in a breath with terror. 'What is it?' she asked, hating the tinge of fear in her voice. 'Have I done irreparable damage?'

If she'd hurt herself too greatly, would escape even be possible?

'You're beautiful,' he said in a tone that seemed almost reverent.

'What did you say?' She blinked at him, sure she had heard him incorrectly. What did her appearance have to do with her injured head?

'You're probably the bonniest woman I've ever seen.' He continued to study her.

She ought to slap him for his forwardness, for regarding her so openly and for so long. But there was a light flutter in her lower stomach unlike any sensation she'd ever experienced before. While it was certainly foreign, it was not unpleasant.

'I mean, truly lovely,' he murmured.

His awe nipped at her. 'What did you expect?' she asked, unable to stop the note of offence from creeping into her tone.

'Not this.' He shook his head. 'The rumours—'

Elspeth stiffened at the mere mention of rumours. He must have noticed her reaction because he immediately went quiet. Perhaps he was not as stupid as she assumed.

She knew the rumours well, all sad truths about an awkward child who hadn't grown into her proportions yet. One whose arms and legs jutted awkwardly like sticks that weren't made to stack against one another. One whose large mouth and eyes were rivalled only by the size of her ears in her peaked face.

They weren't wrong. She had been homely. Even now, she preferred to keep her ears hidden from view beneath her mass of red waves whenever possible.

But he was not the only one to have heard rumours. And if there was any truth to hers, then logically there would be truth to his as well. After all, it was he who had attacked the abbey, causing nuns to run about in fear. And it was his father who had slain hers.

'Leave me be,' she said bitterly.

He shook his head. 'You know I can't.'

She pushed back from him, but the effort was in vain. The wall hit her back and the back of the door stood to her left. She was physically no match for him and they both knew it.

'You're on a ship that is docked in Ireland.' He pulled the rope free from his belt. 'Even if you escaped, there's nowhere for you to go.'

She scoffed. She was no fool. There were those she could go to for succour—people who would likely sail her back to Scotland where she could find Ross.

But he did not appear put off by her disbelief. His smile curled up with a confidence that squeezed her heart and a left her with a burgeoning sense of hopelessness in this strange new land where she was entirely alone.

She swallowed hard, as if doing so would keep the unexpected tears from filling her eyes. When that effort failed, she shifted her gaze away, letting her hair fall like a curtain over her face as he bound the coarse rope around her wrists.

Once she had wrested her emotions back under her control, she glared at him as he reached down to help her to her feet. Without her arms tied against her torso, she was able to push up on her own. She did so rather than accept his aid. She wanted nothing from this man but her freedom.

'Are you going to bind my legs as well?' she asked bitterly. 'I could always kick you if you leave them untethered.'

'Is that an invitation to remedy the oversight?' He lifted his brows.

Suddenly the warmth of those hazel eyes seemed to be mocking her. She wanted to grab a handful of his dark, mussed hair and slam his face to her knee the way she had seen warriors do. She wanted to grab the dagger from his belt, *her* dagger, and slit his throat. He was exploiting her, using her against her family.

And she would never again forget that he was her enemy.

Calum regarded Elspeth's scowling face. Even enraged she was beautiful. Creamy skin, eyes as green as summer grass, full lips that were red and ripe for kissing. Her skin had been like warm silk beneath his fingertips when he'd brushed back her hair.

He'd been expecting what he'd been told for years by his da who still had his spies in Scotland: a lass that was all knobby knees and elbows—sickly with a grey pallor and a face too small to fit all her features. Alexander Campbell hadn't expected her to survive childhood and laughed at how it would have been a mercy for God to take her young lest she grow into a homely woman.

God had not taken her, and Calum was thankful for

that. For Elspeth MacMillan had grown into her awkward body in the finest way any lass ever had.

But now was not the time to stand there gawking at her. There was never a time for that. She was his chance to reclaim his land without bloodshed, not for wanting.

He indicated the door as any courtier might, offering to let her to walk before him. She lifted her head with dignity and strode from the empty room with Calum close behind her.

The crew stopped their work as she paused at the railing, regarding them all below as a queen would do when addressing her people. It mattered not that her hands were bound before her, secured with rope. She stood in place, encouraging their perusal, her chin notched high, her shoulders squared as though challenging them to find her lacking.

And from what Calum could see, not one man did. The Campbells aboard the ship gaped up at her with awe. But it wasn't at what she represented as not all were in agreement with Calum on his plan for a peaceful resolution. There were several who didn't believe such an endeavour would be successful and had scant patience while they waited for the supposed failure to be realised. Nay, they stared at her for her incredible beauty.

Hamish approached with a grin and courteously indicated the waiting boatswain's chair. 'This way, Mistress Elspeth.'

She curled her lip at him as she spun on her heel and plunked down on the chair to be lowered to the vessel waiting below. It swayed and wobbled in a way that made her grip the chair on one side with her bound hands, but she refused to cry out. Two soldiers in the small vessel awaited her, easing her onto the boat where she was joined shortly by Calum and Hamish to be rowed to the shore where the horses were already waiting.

When they arrived, Calum guided her towards his own steed. 'You'll ride with me.'

Her eyes lingered on her own horse as one of the Campbell men mounted it. Rage flushed in her cheeks and left her with a flinty glare. 'On your horse with you? Face down or sitting?' she asked in a brittle tone.

'It's your decision. Will you try to escape again?'

Her jaw tensed. 'I'll sit,' she said at last and grudgingly allowed Bram and Calum to help her onto the horse.

Calum settled onto the saddle behind her and was immediately enveloped by a light, powdery perfume that seemed almost far too feminine a scent for the feisty lass. He'd caught a whiff of it briefly when they were in the captain's quarters, when he'd brushed aside her silky locks to reveal his first glimpse of her beauty.

As the horse set off, she swayed with the rhythm of its gait, in time with Calum's own body. It was far more sensual than he had anticipated and forced him to turn his thoughts to what needed to be done next rather than allow himself to end up with a cockstand.

Their settlement in Ireland was almost a day's journey from the shore. Normally, the trip could be made in one go of it, but with the sun sliding down in the sky, they were swiftly running out of light. There would be nothing for it but to make camp. Fortunately they had prepared in advance should they encounter such an issue and had brought tents along with them.

The vivid streaks of a sunset were already shifting to dusky violets by the time Calum found a clearing near a stream—an ideal location for pausing to camp. He drew his horse to a stop and the others followed suit behind him.

Elspeth stiffened. 'Why are we stopping?' Though she infused authority into her voice, the rapid rise and fall of her chest indicated her concern.

'To camp.' Calum leapt from the horse and held up his hands to help her down. She slid from the horse without his assistance and staggered slightly. He caught her by the waist to keep her upright. She was light in his arms, her shape slender inside the voluminous cloak that was still damp to the touch. 'We've several hours to reach our settlement and are making camp tonight before riding the rest of the way on the morrow.'

As he explained it to her, his retinue of men set to work erecting the small tents they'd brought to protect them from the incessant rain. Though they had wanted the precipitation for many months, its abundance now had done more harm than good as crops were washed away and the once dry earth had been dampened to the point of near flooding.

'Where am I to sleep?' Elspeth asked indignantly, her gaze fixed on the men as the tents began to take shape. 'With the men?'

'With me,' Calum replied.

Her head snapped to him, her cheeks bright with outrage. 'I would rather die.'

'I won't touch you.' He stepped back from her to put space between them, so his lack of intent was clear. 'I'm not that kind of man.'

Her eyes glittered with hatred in the near darkness. 'Rumours would suggest otherwise.'

'Not all rumours are true, are they?' he asked pointedly.

She fell quiet at that.

He regarded her in the dim light, taking in the way the

dusk cast her red hair in subtle hues of blue. Fire and ice. 'I'm not the man you think I am.'

'So you haven't abducted me?' She lifted her brows. 'You haven't tied me up and you aren't forcing me to sleep in a tent with you.'

He didn't respond. What could he say when she was right? He *had* done those things and would continue on with his plan until he could secure a meeting with Ross MacMillan to negotiate a truce.

Still, he hated the way Elspeth regarded him, her suspicion laced with contempt. She assigned his father's reputation to Calum, the same as everyone did, not realising how much he'd loathed his da and the man's violence.

Calum had been his mother's son, preferring a quiet life. His mum had been a woman of fairness, of kindness, willing to put herself at risk to save others. They had been close when he was a lad, when his father had permitted it. In the end, even her sweetness could not sway his father from allowing her to see Calum often.

It was her giving spirit which ultimately caused her demise as she weakened so others around her could eat. His da's spiral into his own cruel devices followed immediately after her death, when he did not have her pleas to temper his rage.

If anything, her loss had ignited it once more—a spark that had exploded into a conflagration that raged out of control more so than it had before when they were first kicked out of Scotland, one that threatened to consume the entire Campbell clan with his wrath.

An ache settled in Calum's chest, a familiar one that thundered to life whenever he thought of his mother, the unfairness of her death and at the denial of any semblance of love in his life once he had seen ten summers.

His father's death had not left such an impact on Calum. Rather, there had been relief. And guilt for his absence of grief.

Hamish nodded to indicate the tent was ready and Calum motioned for Elspeth to walk ahead of him. She didn't move.

A bone-weary exhaustion settled over him, tired of the constant battle with her. 'I don't want to have to use force.'

She remained where she stood. 'I won't walk like a lamb towards my own defilement.'

'I will not hurt you,' he said carefully. 'Nor defile you.'

She gave an unladylike snort.

His patience snapped then, its final thread worn to nothing through the day after several nights of poor sleep. He never did rest easy in Scotland and wouldn't until the land there belonged to him.

Instead of arguing further, he scooped her up into his arms and strode towards the tent, ignoring the way she writhed and squirmed in an effort to escape his hold. Only when they were inside did he set her down and tie the tent flaps closed.

'I won't touch you, but nor will I trust you not to run away,' he said with finality.

She could continue to assail him with her accusations and wrath and he would bear the brunt of it. While he wouldn't lay a hand on her, neither would he offer her the level of freedom she wanted.

Such a thing was a courtesy he could not afford to grant.

Chapter Four

Elspeth huddled in the corner of the tent. The thing was small enough that she could reach from one end to the other if she were to lay on the ground with her arms stretched wide. The area was lit with a single lamp, its diminutive flame sufficient for the limited space. Sharing such close quarters with a man of Calum's character was indeed disconcerting.

Even if it was at least dry.

His men hadn't stopped him as he'd carried her kicking and screaming into the tent. Doubtless they wouldn't stop him from doing anything else with her that he pleased.

A quick glance about the confined area reaffirmed that there was nothing she might use as a weapon. At least nothing that wasn't on his person.

There was no way around it—her situation was truly dire.

He stepped towards her and she did her best to keep from flinching. But rather than reach for her or try to attack her, he settled on to the ground beside her with enough space between them that she did not feel oppressed by his presence. He made a movement and she jerked away.

'Would you like me to untie your hands?' he asked in a quiet voice.

She thrust her bound wrists at him.

A smoky, peaty scent wafted from him mingled with a light scent of leather and something spicy she couldn't name. While it was not unpleasant, his presence was. Even if he was untying her at last.

The rope fell to the floor and Elspeth stretched her arms apart, appreciating the sensation and grateful to be free of the bindings. She could only hope he would leave them off for the remainder of the night.

He reached into the bag at his side and withdrew a loaf of bread, a square of cheese, some dried meat and a wineskin.

Saliva welled in her mouth. She'd had nothing to eat though the day, subsisting merely on the bursts of energy that shot through her veins as she tried to fend him off in her futile attempts to liberate herself.

'You must be hungry.' He broke the bread in half and extended it to her.

She wanted to decline. But the yeasty scent drifted towards her, crumbling her resistance as surely as the brittle crust disintegrated to dust onto the floor of the tent. Her stomach gave a savage growl of protest at her inclination and she was forced to accept the offering. Though she handled it lightly, the outside flaked away and her fingers sank into the soft insides. It was not stale as she had anticipated, but incredibly fresh. Most likely procured by one of the men who had ridden ahead.

'And thirsty.' He held out the wineskin.

She tried to swallow down a bite of bread, but her throat stuck together with the effort. Aye, she was thirsty. This time she didn't bother to hesitate and instead reached for the swollen vessel, popped free the cork and drank deeply.

The ale was cool against her parched throat, refreshing in a way that immediately revived her. She tore off a bit of the bread with trembling fingers and accepted the portion of cheese and meat he gave her. Though mindful to keep her ladylike appearances before the barbarian, she found his manners to be less deplorable than she had anticipated.

He ate slowly, chewing each piece carefully and drank from his own wineskin rather than forcing her to share. This was ideal considering she emptied hers completely as the meal concluded. Once her belly was full and her thirst slaked, exhaustion washed over her. Not that she would allow herself to relax enough to sleep.

Nay, she would wait for him to doze off first, then she would help herself to the weapons at his belt. Surely killing a man in his sleep would be easier than fighting with him in his full awareness. Perhaps then she would have more success.

Once she'd slain him, she could quietly slip out of the tent, walk her horse some distance away, then ride out to the nearest abbey. Surely they would offer her succour once she explained her circumstances.

She suppressed a shudder as she recalled what had happened at the last abbey she had turned to for sanctuary. Though by some miracle no one had been killed, the attack had been horrifying. Women screamed in terror and ran about in all directions as marauding men in Campbell colours brandished weapons and gave chase, their eyes maniacal with intent.

Calum had done that.

The food he'd given her soured in her stomach.

He set up a makeshift pallet on one side of the tent and then another on the opposite side. Not that doing so offered much space between them given the close quarters. The last thing Elspeth wanted to do was lay on the ground beside him, near enough to smell the interesting mix of his scent.

But she would have to at least pretend in order to maintain appearances to keep from arousing his suspicious of her intentions.

She lay upon the bedding. The clean scent of lavender that emanated from it was as surprising as it was welcome. But then, Calum appeared to care for himself. Though his dark hair was somewhat messy, it was in an intentional fashion, while his clothes, skin and trimmed nails were well-maintained and devoid of filth.

The discomfort of the day melted from her body as she lay upon the sweet-smelling bedding even as her mind churned with unease. Sleep teased at her, lapping languidly at the edges of her awareness the way the water of a loch did at the shore on a lazy summer day. A ping of metal broke through the silence of the tent as Calum unfastened his belt and pulled it from his waist.

Immediately, Elspeth snapped awake, alert, her attention focused on Calum and whatever purpose he had for removing his belt. But rather than approach her, he lifted his pillow and set the leather strap, along with his weapons, beneath it before laying down beside her.

'You didn't think I'd make it that easy, did you?' He smirked and then put out the light.

Darkness blanketed the space, leaving Elspeth momentarily without sight. The rustle of bedding told her Calum had settled back onto the ground. She waited for her eyes to adjust. As they did so, the warmth of the herb-infused bedding, the meal and ale resting heavy in her belly, all combined to dull her senses.

She startled awake again, unsure if she had dozed for only a few moments or a few hours. The darkness outside the walls of the white tent had not waned, so dawn had not begun to climb its way into the sky. Regardless of how long she had been asleep, there was still time.

Being as quiet as possible, she untied her cloak to avoid getting tangled in the fabric and slipped from her blanket. Regardless of how much time had lapsed, it was enough to have allowed her eyes to adjust completely. She could clearly make out Calum where he lay on the ground, his face turned towards her, relaxed in slumber.

The slight gleam of a hilt glinted under the edge of the pillow. She held her breath and carefully slid it free. The weight of it was familiar in her hand and she knew at once it was her own dagger. Surely such a coincidence was good fortune.

No sooner had the thought struck than a hand darted out like a striking snake and grasped her wrist, holding it in a firm grip. Her gaze flew to Calum's face and found that not only was he no longer sleeping. He was watching her with a level stare.

She had been caught.

Calum would have been a fool to believe Elspeth would not try to kill him. It was why he'd put his weapons beneath his pillow. He'd always been a light sleeper and the subtle shift of her breathing alone had pulled him from his dreams. Immediately he'd been vigilant.

Initially, he thought she would try to escape—at least, until she crept closer.

She was no mercenary, that was for certain. As she'd

pulled the dagger from beneath his pillow, the icy, damp hem of her kirtle had brushed against his arm. It would have woken him for certes had he not already been awake.

He held her in place now by her slender wrist, breathing in the feminine powdery scent of her. The dagger gleamed wickedly in her hand though her eyes were wide with surprise.

She'd taken off the cloak, revealing the fine shape of her body in a kirtle meant for showing off the feminine form. No doubt she was to be presented like a prize to the eldest son of the MacLachlan clan. A lass as bonny as her would entice any man, but especially so in that garment. Her waist was thin enough that he could easily span his hands around it, her breasts were generous and her hips so full and perfect that he wanted to grasp her to him, to fit flush against his pelvis.

His cock swelled in appreciation, but he tamped down his desire. Now was definitely not the time.

But then again, never would be the time. She was not his to want. She was a means to an end and nothing more.

Her match with MacLachlan was what had presented Calum with the opportunity to abduct her in the first place. If he meant to right the wrongs of his father, he certainly did not need to seduce the sister of the Mac-Millan Chieftain.

'Let me go.' She twisted against him, her eyes glittering with rage in the darkness.

Calum didn't release her. 'No.'

'I'll kill you.'

He met her gaze. 'You won't.'

'I will.' Her breathing came faster now. Nerves. She'd never killed anyone before. A warrior could tell.

She had no skill and the tremor in her hand said she realised the gravity of taking a life.

He released her hand and lifted his neck to bare it. 'Then do it.'

She leaned over him and moved the dagger, closer. The chill of the sharp blade rested against his throat.

The dagger shook against his neck, pulling slightly away as she prepared her body to shove forward and plunge the razored edge into his throat. In a single move, he swept the blade from his throat, grabbed her arm and twisted the dagger into his own grip as he rolled them both over so she was pinned beneath him.

He set the blade near her own throat, careful not to put the edge to her skin and fully aware he would never use it against her. Not that she needed to know that.

'I was going to do it,' she gritted out, her eyes sparking with malice.

He smirked. 'I know you were.'

The lass had more grit than he had given her credit for.

'You told me to do it.' She tried to shove his arm away, but his hold was too strong.

'I didn't think you would.'

'Then you have severely underestimated how much hate I have for you,' she said icily.

He studied her lovely face in the darkness. Her skin like smooth cream, her cheekbones high and elegant, mouth drawn tight in outrage. He wanted to kiss those lips until they softened and parted as she yielded to him.

'You never will beat me,' he said firmly, putting his thoughts to the moment and away from dangerous fantasies.

Her chin lifted with haughty arrogance as if she was not defeated and under threat of a blade. 'I could defeat you.'

'You don't know how to hold a dagger,' he said. 'You don't know how to fight.'

'Now you mean to insult me?' She gave a choked laugh.

'I mean to point out that you need training.'

Her furrowed forehead smoothed. 'Training?'

'Did the men in your family not teach you how to fight?'

She looked away. 'My uncle wouldn't allow it.' Her words were tight with buried anger.

He eased the blade back from where it lay against her throat. 'I can teach you.'

Her gaze flew back to him. 'What did you say?'

'I can teach you.'

She regarded him with renewed interest. 'Why would you do that?'

'I don't intend to keep you here for ever, lass. And every woman ought to know how to defend herself. Even a lady.'

Scepticism pulled at her brows. 'Are you not afraid I'll try to kill you with what I learn?'

'I've been training to fight since I was a wee lad. I'm not easily bested.'

'Of course you've been fighting that long,' she said vehemently. 'You're a Campbell.'

He couldn't argue with her there. The Campbells were a rough lot, especially in the time since they were banished from Scotland. He withdrew the dagger from her completely and remained where he hovered over the top of her.

'We're not all bad,' he kept his voice soft and hoped she would be able to discern the sincerity of his words.

The fierce expression on her face relaxed somewhat as she stared up at him, her lashes long and sable black against her fair skin. Unbidden, his eyes swept down to her full lips and he could not stop himself from wondering again what such a mouth must feel like against his own, what it must taste like when sampled with the tip of his tongue.

But she was not his.

The realisation pulled him from her lest he give into the enticement of wicked temptation that bade him stay there and lower himself on top of her.

'You should rest.' He indicated her makeshift bed. 'We leave at first light.'

Wordlessly, she pushed up to her feet and went back to her own pallet.

'If you think you can escape or try to kill me, know now you will not succeed.' He slid the dagger beneath his pillow once more and lay down. 'You're too important.'

Still she did not reply and when he looked over at her, he found her back facing him. A slight popping sound against the waxed linen of the tent told him it had begun to rain again. He stayed awake for a while, listening to it go from a light patter to a torrential downpour. It was easy to take comfort in the soothing sounds of a storm when one was dry and warm inside.

Or at least mostly warm.

The night air crept into the tent with a vengeance that had chilled his bones to the marrow. It was a welcome chill by comparison to the heat that shot through his body when he'd stared down at Elspeth, when he was repeatedly tempted to kiss her.

He glanced to where she lay and found her shivering beneath her thin blanket. Her garments were still damp, and no doubt were trapping in the cold. She would have to wait until their arrival at the village to find different clothing. But for the time being, he scooted closer to her, slow and careful so as to avoid frightening her and slid his blanket from himself onto her.

She rolled towards him in her sleep and nestled close against the heat of his body as a soft hum of contentment sounded from her throat. He should return to the opposite side of the tent, he knew, but there was so little space between them when he was there, it hardly made a difference. Especially if he might keep her warm.

And so he stayed, breathing in the alluring scent of her, trying to ignore the way her soft exhales brushed against his chest and how badly he wanted to curl her into his arms.

He waited until she stopped shivering before finally letting sleep claim him, knowing he had to wake before she did the following day, lest she mistake his intention.

Chapter Five

Every part of Elspeth was stiff when she finally woke the next morning. Her dress and cloak were still damp and the ground was hard beneath her. Beige oilcloth filled her vision and she froze, caught in the grip of confusion.

All at once, it rushed back to her. The abduction, the awful time trapped in the captain's quarters and how she had failed so miserably at trying to kill Calum and break free.

She stiffened at the thought of him, that he was there with her while she had been sleeping and vulnerable. With great apprehension, she peered over her shoulder, expecting to find him there. Only his empty palette lay on the floor of the tent, absent its blanket. It was then she noticed she had not one blanket upon her, but two.

Most likely one had belonged to him.

But why would he give her his blanket? Especially on such a cold, wet night. And after she had tried to kill him, no less.

Perhaps from guilt. For what he'd done in abducting her to use against her family.

She pushed up from the bed and her skin prickled with

the chill as the blankets fell away. Her hair must look a fright. She glanced down at her wrinkled kirtle and the stained cloak. Everything about her must look a fright.

And though she should not care, she could not help the self-consciousness creeping over her. She would be facing the whole Campbell clan later that day and despised representing the MacMillans in such a dishevelled state.

The ties to the tent were secured to keep the flap from opening. But did it mean there was someone nearby? If there was not, she might well be able to make her escape.

She did what she could to set her appearance to rights. Any attempts to run her fingers through her hair were curtailed by the numerous snarls and tangles. Failing that, she did what she could to smooth her tresses and tugged at her kirtle to remove what she could of the wrinkles as she strained to listen to outside noises to indicate if anyone might be around or not.

Beyond the thin walls of the tent there was only silence.

Her heart slammed in her chest as she approached the tent flaps and tentatively slid one tie free. She froze, expecting someone to reprimand her for trying to leave.

Hope shot through her with enough force to leave her fingers trembling as she pulled the second one free, then the third and fourth until finally she could push the tent flap open to icy morning air. And potentially her freedom.

The sun was brilliant and left her momentarily dazzled. She shielded her face from its rays as something thudded into the grass at her feet. Her gaze shot to the ground where a dagger jutted from the soft earth.

Her dagger.

She snapped her attention back up as Calum approached, appearing far more refreshed than she felt.

'Was that meant to be a warning to keep me from escaping?' she asked.

'It was meant to give it back to you while the men pack up camp so I can teach you to use it.'

Her stare drifted to the dagger again. 'Aren't you afraid I'll try to kill you with it?'

He smirked. 'I'm sure you will, which is why you will only get it back for the lesson.' He nodded to the blade. 'Go on, pick it up.'

Still, she hesitated and scanned the surrounding men as they broke down the simple tents. They paid her no mind, but even then, she could not stop the unease creeping over the back of her neck.

Surely Calum was not actually giving her a weapon.

Was this some sort of cruel trick?

Tentatively, she bent down and retrieved the blade. The hilt was cold against her palm, but she appreciated its familiar weight in her hand.

A weapon.

She could throw it at him.

Her pulse kicked up.

She'd seen men do it a thousand times before where the weapon sailed effortlessly through the air and stuck fast in their target. Another glance towards the other Campbell men confirmed they were not paying any mind to the side of camp where Elspeth and Calum were.

When she turned her attention back to him, his brows were lifted with thinly veiled amusement. 'I know what you're going to do.' He put his hands on his hips, squaring his chest towards her. 'You want to throw it at me. Do it.'

She didn't pause this time and hurled the dagger towards him with all the strength she had. It spun wildly through the air and landed somewhere halfway between them, falling flat and harmless onto the thick grass.

Heat flooded her cheeks. She had missed. Even if she had thrown it far enough to reach him, it would have landed an arm's length to his right.

'I know you don't believe me.' He strode to the dagger and lifted it from the ground before walking towards her with it extended, hilt first. 'But I don't want to hurt you. And if teaching you to defend yourself is the best way to make my sincerity clear, so be it.'

She took the dagger, its hilt now wet from the previous night's rain which still clung to the grass. 'Why do you care what I think of you?'

'Because I'm not my father.' He searched her gaze with his hazel eyes. They were soft in the morning light, flecked with gold and bits of green. A dark fringe of long lashes gave him a sensitive appearance and pulled at her inclination to give him a chance to explain himself, to truly listen.

She looked away, breaking the unwelcome connection.

'I don't trust you.' She said it quietly, realising after the fact that she had done so more for her own benefit than his.

He was her enemy, not someone to be trusted, no matter how tenderly he regarded her.

But if he was going to teach her to use a weapon, she would learn as much as was possible. And when the time came, she would use it against him to save herself and save her family.

Of course, trust could not be so easily established. Calum was well aware of the difficulty he faced, and yet it didn't stop him from craving her confidence.

'When you hold the dagger, you do so by the blade, not the hilt.' He pulled his own weapon from its sheath and demonstrated, lightly pinching the edge.

Her lashes lowered as she studied his hands and then mimicked his hold with her own weapon. She had slender hands, her fingers long and tapered. In that flash of a moment, he could understand why her uncle forbade her from fighting. She had the delicate hands of a lady, not ones that had been callused and roughened by survival.

It was a shame to think of something so lovely being marred by a need to fight.

But then, those ladylike hands didn't match the spirit of the fire-haired lass in front of him.

'You hold it loosely,' he instructed. 'As though it may slip from your fingers.'

It dropped from her grip and he chuckled. 'Perhaps a wee tighter, aye?'

She scooped it up and immediately copied the way he held his blade again, her face set with determination.

'When you throw it, let the weight of it pull away from you and keep your fingers pointing where you want it to go even after it leaves your hand.' He released his dagger in the manner which he had just described.

It sank into a tree trunk, exactly where he was aiming.

She released her blade, but it tumbled clumsily through the air before the hilt bounced over the ground. He glanced at her, but she didn't seem at all put off by her miss. Nay, a flash of resolve shone in her eyes as she strode towards her blade, swiped it up and repeated the action.

'You said I was important last night.' She aimed the dagger once more. 'How am I important to you? What do you intend to do with me?'

'I'm hoping for a peaceful resolution,' he replied. 'I don't want to fight. I want our land in Scotland back so we can return to what is rightfully ours.'

She scoffed and threw a hard look at him over her shoulder. 'You expect me to believe you don't want to fight? I imagine that's part of your ploy, to lull us to a false sense of security and then strike. 'Tis exactly the kind of thing your da would do.'

She was right. It was.

Calum approached the tree and dislodged his own dagger. 'I told you before, I'm not like him.'

'You've incited not only the MacMillans by taking me, but also the MacLachlans,' she replied in a casual tone and tossed the dagger. 'I was on my way to wed Leith MacLachlan. My abduction will not be taken lightly.' The weapon flopped uselessly onto the grass again.

Calum was aware she had been travelling to Castle Lachlan for a union with the Laird's eldest son. 'I'm sure you'll be returned to your love soon.'

She pressed her lips together and scooped up the dagger. This time she didn't wait with a long set up like the previous occasions and instead loosed the dagger from where she stood. It sank into the centre of the tree as though she'd spent a lifetime honing the skill.

'You do love him, don't you?' The question slipped from Calum before he could stop himself. 'Or is this one of those arranged marriages for alliances?'

It was a foolish question to ask when he didn't even know what love was. The only love he'd ever known was the innocent kind between a mother and son, one abruptly cut short when he'd turned ten and his father had declared too much contact with his mother would make him soft. There had been no love in his life since.

She looked up at him, studying him. The morning sun caressed her face, casting her skin in golden light and the green in her eyes shone as clear as sea glass. Her beauty struck him anew and once more he was seized with the temptation to pull her against him, to breathe in the sweet powdery scent of her and let his lips graze over the length of her elegant neck.

'It doesn't matter,' she said as if he were daft.

He blinked, a man woken from a spell which had left him transfixed. 'What doesn't matter?'

'Love,' she replied. 'It doesn't matter when it comes to marriage.' She spoke the words with conviction, as if she was reciting a lesson rather than speaking from her soul. 'We weren't even properly betrothed. There wasn't enough time. You and your father attacked and my brothers and I were to be married off for alliances. I want to keep my people protected rather than throw them haplessly into war. That is why I agreed to wed him. Because of you.'

The malice in her glare told him it was one more slight for which she held him accountable.

'And I'm doing this to save mine,' Calum replied firmly.

Before he could explain how he had tried to keep his father from the attacks, Hamish approached and regarded Elspeth with a casual grin. 'We're ready.'

She glared back.

At least Calum was not the only one subjected to her spite.

He nodded at Hamish, conveying his gratitude for the other man breaking up camp while he had this time to speak with Elspeth in an effort to try to earn her trust. He only hoped he had made some progress. Having her be compliant would make keeping her for leverage a much less distasteful situation for all involved.

'I'll let you keep your wrists unbound while we break our fast and while we travel.' Calum strode to the tree and pulled her dagger from its trunk.

Her stare followed his hands as he returned her dagger to a sheath at his belt.

'I wouldn't try to escape if I were you,' he said as he led her towards the small fire where the men were breaking their fast with bread and ale.

She tilted her head slightly in question.

'Aye, you could find a nearby castle and seek their help, but chances are likely they'll hold you for ransom,' he replied.

'Like you?' she demanded.

'Nay, not like me.' He didn't elaborate. She would most likely not be treated with the deference he'd shown her and knew she would be held for a considerable amount of coin. Even without his explanation, it was enough to make her gaze grow wary as she glanced around the surrounding area.

Elspeth said nothing more as they broke their fast by the fire with the other men and then mounted Calum's large horse. Soon they would arrive at the miserable existence they'd carved out for themselves on the ragged outskirts of Ballymena where the land did not farm well. Soon she would understand, when she saw it for herself.

Chapter Six

Emotions warred within Elspeth, churning between a tentative desire to believe Calum and a torrent of fear that this was all some great ruse. His men had brutally slain many of her brother's soldiers and the Campbell clan had attacked the convent. She could see in her mind's eye the dark coloured gambesons and the insignia of the boar's head those men had worn as they'd terrorised the peaceful women of the abbey. It was also Campbell men who'd threatened her in the castle when she was too young to fight for herself, forced to rely on MacMillan men to keep her safe.

Then there was her own da, a man who had been brave and honourable, who'd ruled his land with a fairness that made the people love him. He had been cut down by Alexander Campbell, slain without thought or mercy. It had been the final offence committed that forced the King to expel the Campbells from Scotland.

Calum said he was not like his da. And what if he was not?

What would that make him? Was he not still her enemy?

She didn't know how long the journey took, only that

her thoughts flipped back and forth through the duration. Rain began to pour down on them after a spell, drenching her already damp clothing. It mattered not when she hadn't been dry to start with.

But even as the storm began in earnest, a cloth hovered over Elspeth's head as Calum held a length of plaid over them both, protecting her from the elements. It was a kind consideration. One which made her musings that much more convoluted.

The smoky scent of peat filled the air and a haze appeared in the distance. Most likely the settlement where Calum and his clansmen had taken up residence in Ireland. The rain pooled into wide puddles as they approached, but the horses sloshed through them with little effort.

Now she would finally see it, the palace where Alexander and Calum were rumoured to have hoarded all the treasure they'd stolen from the Scottish clans over the years. It was said they'd taken women as slaves and kept them scantily clad to serve them. Ice prickled in her veins. Would she be such a woman?

Suddenly any inclination towards trusting him shifted direction and swung the opposite way, filling her with distrust once again. Though she didn't want to admit it, there was also fear. It left an undeniably metallic taste in her mouth and made her pulse race.

She remained stiffly in front of Calum and hoped she'd sufficiently masked the emotions overpowering her.

At last the village came into view. Numerous huts were packed tightly together with people gathering in the alleyways, no doubt eager to lay eyes on her.

She was being paraded before them like a spoil of war.

'You need not keep the rain from me,' she said to Calum and lifted her head haughtily. 'I'm not going to melt.'

He hesitated, but then lowered his arm. The rain spattered over her face and hair, drenching her immediately. Still, she kept her chin elevated and her back straight. If she was to be subject to their scrutiny, she would not have them find her deficient in any way.

However, as she was paraded through the village, she could not help but notice the state of Calum's people. Skinny children in filthy clothes who watched her pass with wide eyes. Their parents were dressed in similar rags, as though they did not care enough for themselves to mind their appearances.

Anger sizzled through her.

Calum lived in a palace of great wealth while his people wore rags.

His people were neglected. Horribly so.

He was waging war and stealing her from her home while his people wore threadbare clothing in the chilly climate and their homes suffered from disrepair. Several huts were sagging to one side, others were missing chunks of thatch, still others had collapsed entirely on themselves.

The more she saw, the more the outrage burned in her veins that they suffered with such a louse of a leader.

On the opposite end of the village was a large wooden structure, one of the old wooden castles that were no longer being built as they were slowly being replaced by stone.

Surely this was not the palace of splendour…

It was to this large building where Calum guided their horse to a shabby courtyard that consisted of uneven, muddy ground rather than cobbled stone.

He leapt from the steed's back and offered Elspeth his hand. She did not take it, opting instead to make her own way down. He said nothing and handed the reins to the stable lad.

Elspeth's gaze shifted to the castle, taking it all in. Its condition was as poor as the huts. The entire thing seemed to lean somewhat to the right and several logs were missing from the surrounding walls, making them appear like a gap-toothed grin.

In truth, it was a miserable building that scarcely looked able to withstand a strong wind. Mayhap inside was opulent with riches?

Her heartbeat thundered in her ears to think about being inside, where she would be held captive. Who knew what sort of things might happen to her within, where there were locked doors and few witnesses. The uncertainty sent her thoughts skittering in a thousand different directions. 'Now what will you do with me?'

'Keep you here until your brother responds saying he'll be willing to exchange my lands for your safety.' Calum indicated she should walk ahead of him.

She did not. Her breath came quickly, yet somehow she felt as though she could not draw enough air. 'And if he does not?'

'He has to. He has the King's ear and can use that influence to ensure our lands are restored.'

They passed through the large doors of the keep into the shadowed interior where several servants stopped to regard her with the same wide-eyed curiosity as the villagers had. But there were no gilt-edged tapestries or heaps of gold and gemstones lying about.

There were no tapestries at all, or scarcely any furnishings for that matter and the floors were absent of rushes. But there had been so many rumours, so many tales alluding to the wealth kept in Ireland. Where was it all?

If this was what the castle looked like, she could only imagine the state of the dungeon. A place where she might well end up to ensure she did not escape.

It was on the tip of her tongue to ask if that was Calum's intent, but part of her did not want to know and the other part of her did not want him to see her fear. For truly she was afraid of the idea of being locked in a dungeon, the cell damp and cold and filthy. A shiver rattled down her spine.

They reached the end of a long hall and she stopped, uncertain if she ought to go right or left up the stairs.

'We need to get you warm.' Calum guided her up the stairs.

Where they would be alone. Once there, no one would be around to stop him from whatever he meant to do to her. She was no fool. She knew how often maidens were sent home after being abducted, debauched and spoiled, their innocence lost.

Leith would not want her. No man would.

As if reading her thoughts, Calum shook his head and put even more space between them. 'You don't have anything to worry about. I'm taking you to a room where you will stay alone. But your kirtle has been drenched since yesterday. You need dry clothes and a warm bath, aye?'

A warm bath?

She tried to keep the longing from her face. A warm bath would be truly heaven.

Her legs moved of their own volition, taking her up the stairs towards the promise of sinking into a luxurious bath and washing the grime of travel from her skin. And to be warm again!

He stopped before a door and opened it, indicating she ought to go in first. She did as he silently bade, taking in the empty room. A bed was set to one side with a narrow trunk at the foot while a simple table and chairs sat before the empty hearth.

'I'll have someone sent immediately to set a fire for you,' Calum said. 'I know you've been cold as your clothes have not had a chance to fully dry.'

She gazed up at him, wary but still warmed by his consideration. 'Thank you.' Her voice was loud in the quiet chamber.

He regarded for a long moment and again she was struck by the tenderness in his hazel eyes. They said nothing as they studied one another, entirely alone and incredibly intimate.

She ought to be repelled, she knew, but there was something about him that drew her curiosity. Her interest.

Their situation was not threatening. He had not tied her up or chained her to the bed or insisted she don inappropriate attire.

Elspeth found she enjoyed the way he looked at her, the way he allowed her to gaze openly at him in return, as though learning about each other through searching one another's eyes. What she found within his appeared to be earnest and kind.

The walls around her heart began to crumble somewhat.

His lashes lowered as he considered her mouth and for less than a second, she thought he might kiss her. Unbidden, her attention went to his own lips, full and pink against the dark shadow of his unshaven jaw. They looked soft and she found herself wondering if they were, surprising herself with the realisation that though she should not want his kiss, she truly did.

Something in Calum's chest loosened as his eyes locked with Elspeth's. Whatever fear had plagued her when they first strode into the castle depths had melted away, leaving her lovely face softened. She now appeared serene. Sensual.

His blood went hot as it quickened through his veins and throbbed in his loins. He ought to speak, to offer an excuse to take his leave. But he wanted to close the scant distance between them, to gently run his hand down her cheek to see if her skin was as silky soft as he remembered, to lower his lips to hers and taste what he knew would be sweet.

He refrained from giving in to his desires, but nor did he find himself able to comply with what he ought to do. As a minute dragged into two, her breathing came faster and her gaze dipped to his mouth, as though she were thinking the same as he. As if she wanted it all as badly.

Except that she was his prisoner, his only means to bargain with his enemy and seeing his people saved, to prove he was not the same tyrant as his father.

And she was promised in marriage to another man.

He would not kiss another man's woman, no matter how informal their arrangement might have been. No matter that she did not love Leith MacLachlan.

Kissing a woman, dishonouring her commitments, was something his father would do.

It was that thought which finally swayed him.

'I must go.' Calum's voice was gravely deep, almost

unrecognisable even to himself. 'Alison will see to anything you need.'

Elspeth tucked her full lower lip into her mouth and nodded. How he longed to put his thumb to her chin and pop it free, to bend forward to suckle it into his mouth before parting her lips and stroking his tongue against hers.

He stepped back and turned abruptly to leave the room lest he fall prey to his desire.

What was amiss with him? Usually, he was more in control of his thoughts than this.

He closed the door and locked it, sliding the key into his pocket. Only his chatelaine, Alison, had the other key. There would be no escape for Elspeth.

Even her name in his mind sent a fresh wave of desire sweeping through him.

No woman had ever rattled him as much as Mistress Elspeth MacMillan. No woman had ever made his blood simmer in such a way. He glanced about the empty corridor before adjusting his swollen cock to a place of less discomfort, grateful the tunic and gambeson he wore most likely hid his state of arousal.

Especially from Elspeth. He didn't want to frighten her off with his sudden longing. Not when she was just beginning to warm to him, and able to gaze upon him without loathing.

All at once a sobering realisation withered any lust lingering in his mind.

This was the first time he had returned to Ireland without his father. Calum was now Laird of the clan. It was his responsibility to assume leadership among his dying people in a land that did not want them, and against an enemy who had not been given the option to see reason before the onset of battle.

Calum went first to the small kirk near the castle, where his father had already been buried beside his mother. But even as Calum stood before the freshly turned earth, still damp from the rain which had blessedly abated, he could not summon grief. For his mother whose grave was dotted with grass from the months since her death, his heart crushed in on itself with pain at her loss—for the love she had bestowed upon him when he was a boy and for the distance his father had forced him to keep later. But for Alexander…

Calum turned abruptly and made his way to the castle once more, towards the solar where he had much business to conduct in light of his father's recent death and Elspeth's capture. He'd seen how his people had regarded his returning retinue from Scotland, the hope that lit their eyes when they saw Mistress Elspeth. While his idea wasn't unanimously popular, he knew the people were still willing to give him a chance. And he could not let them down.

Hamish was in the small space when Calum arrived, standing beside the hearth.

He looked up as Calum entered the room and lifted his brows. 'The rumours about the lass's looks are wrong, it would appear.' He let out a low whistle and traced the shape of Elspeth's body with his hands in the air, paying special care to emphasise her backside. 'Did you see the curve of her arse when she took off her cloak?'

Ire rose in Calum, sharp and fast. 'Enough,' he said in a gruff tone. 'We've much to discuss that doesn't pertain to the prisoner. She's been locked in her room and will be tended to until we hear from Ross MacMillan.'

Hamish shrugged indifferently and approached. 'Do you think he'll trade your land for his sister after all the blood we've spilled?'

'I'm not my father,' Calum said firmly.

'He doesn't know that, and Alexander committed more than his share of violence upon the MacMillans.'

Calum sighed. 'It's worth the chance at least. Already too many husbands, fathers and sons have been killed. On both sides.'

'People will think those lives have been lost in vain.' Though Hamish said it without malice, the truth behind his words stung.

'Aye, but what happens when we have no more men left to fight?' Calum demanded. 'Or if we do finally get the land back and another war starts, there won't be enough men left to defend the women and children who will settle on our lands once more. This is the only way.'

Hamish nodded with understanding, but the look of concern crinkled at his brow. 'I'll always support you, you know that. As will Bram. But I worry that not everyone will.'

'I fully expected as much.' Calum pulled the heavy chair from the desk and sank onto the hard surface. 'But I have their support now as we wait. Let's hope it doesn't take too long.'

'I have faith in you.' Hamish settled a hand on Calum's shoulder before departing the room.

Calum sat back at the desk and regarded its aged, scarred surface. The desk had been his father's. As had the room and the castle.

It had been a difficult time for all the Campbell clansmen, cast from their home and shoved about by the Irish until they were finally forced to settle on land no one else wanted. Through it all, Alexander had wanted his wife and son to have a place to be protected so he had insisted the castle be constructed immediately.

Of course, if Calum's father had truly wanted them to be protected, he wouldn't have been so aggressive in his need to grow his territory in Scotland. If he had remained happy with what they'd had, they would never have been banished from their home in the first place.

A familiar rage burned in Calum's chest. His father's answer to everything was violence. Even when it came to Calum himself.

Those violent tenancies were what had put the Campbells in the situation they were in now.

Alexander Campbell had died on the very battlefield he'd insisted on creating several days prior, slain in single combat by Fergus MacMillan. His body was brought back while Calum had sought Elspeth before she could be married off to the MacLachlan lad. Yet rather than grief for the loss of his father, Calum was overwhelmed with a profound sense of relief. There had been too many years where Alexander's malice had needled through Calum's tender skin, never fully succeeding in toughening it. There had been too many moments of physical outbursts where fists and kicks had found him, rattling and knocking Calum about in an effort to make him a man. He had always been a disappointment to his father right up to the very end when he'd vehemently protested Alexander's attacks.

There was no one to force Calum's hand now.

The Campbells were his to see to and his approach would be done with more finesse and with measured tactics rather than brute force. He would put the needs of his people before his own pride and prayed that would be enough to see them all saved.

Calum opened a drawer to his right where a stack of accounts lay in a haphazard pile. A swift glance through them confirmed what he already knew, there was little coin, little food and even less optimism for a positive future.

Staying inside the solar would do no good. What Calum needed was to be out among his people, another hand in the rain-drenched fields or offering assistance in repairing the small huts which were slowly collapsing into ruin.

His efforts would create a better life for his people as long as his plan didn't fail. Which it very well might given Ross MacMillan's hatred for the Campbells.

And that raised the question that if Ross refused to comply and give the Campbell land back, what was Calum to do with Elspeth MacMillan?

Chapter Seven

The assumption that Elspeth would be scantily clad to serve Calum had been a wild assumption, clearly as much of a false rumour as the grandeur of the castle, which was nearer to being a pile of sticks than it was to a palace. However, Elspeth was genuinely concerned about her impending death.

From sheer boredom.

The room was so small that Elspeth could cross it in fifteen paces. Or in seven long strides. Or thirty heel-to-toe steps. She'd done it all, including leaps and jumps and everything in between.

It had been all she could do to keep from going mad as the seconds dragged into minutes to create an eternity every day.

The warm bath had been a luxury she had received on the first night of her arrival and had not been repeated in the last sennight, leaving her with only the pitcher and basin to tend to her daily ablutions.

She had hoped at some point that Calum would return to offer her some more lessons on throwing the dagger. While she hadn't been especially good, it had been a relief to finally begin to learn. And of anyone she'd ever known, he was the only one willing to teach her. Her uncle had not allowed it, her brothers were always too busy, and Leith had laughed at her when she'd asked.

A familiar, gentle knock sounded at the door and Elspeth had to refrain from running to the door to greet Alison.

The older woman entered with the same quiet ease as she always did. The small ring of keys rattled from the belt at her waist. Elspeth could not stop her eyes from straying to them. Strung along that metal ring lay her freedom.

But even if Elspeth could bring herself to overpower the kind, old woman, escaping the castle would be impossible. And if she truly did succeed in that, there was nowhere for Elspeth to go. She was trapped alone in a foreign land with no allies or friends.

'Good morrow, Mistress Elspeth,' Alison said in her compassionate voice. 'I trust you slept well?'

'Aye, thank you.' In truth, Elspeth had not slept well. She never did. The bed was comfortable enough, but it was at night that memories of Calum crept back into her thoughts. The way he had looked at her before he'd left her in this room, how her breath had caught when she'd thought he might kiss her.

But while she tried to push her mind from such ideas, her dreams freely roamed with their own desires. All with wicked delights.

In her dreams, he pulled her to him and tilted her face to kiss her mouth. His hands moved over her body and allowed hers to do the same as they both sought the intimate places burning with foreign and delicious lust.

She often awoke at dawn each day with a pulse of longing throbbing between her legs and an ache she had never before known.

Her days were filled with nothing. Truly nothing. There were no books within the castle, and she was not to leave her room. And so, she counted her steps from one wall to the other and she brushed her hair with five hundred strokes. Perhaps the first time she'd ever done so in her life. Her mother would have been delighted in that at least, for never had Elspeth's tresses shimmered as they did now under such fastidious care.

The worst of it all was that during the day, Elspeth was left to her thoughts and recollections of those sensual dreams.

Alison carried a tray of food to the small table by the hearth. The embers had long since turned to ash. The meager pile of logs was never sufficient to keep the fire going through the night.

In truth, there was never enough of anything in the castle.

Elspeth's stomach gave a savage growl of hunger, echoing her sentiment. Nothing, of course, except time.

'Is there perhaps any mending I might help with?' she asked.

Alison straightened and put a hand to her lower back, gently massaging an unseen ache. 'You're a lady and ladies don't do the mending.'

'There must be something for me to do,' Elspeth protested. Angry frustration tightened the back of her neck. 'I cannot stay locked in this room for the rest of my life with nothing to do.'

Alison regarded her with her soft blue eyes and guilt

nipped at Elspeth for having been cross with the kind woman.

'I'll speak with the Laird on the matter,' Alison promised. 'Until then, mind you eat your food before it cools, aye?'

Elspeth thanked the woman and obediently sat down to the pottage and bit of bread. It was a quarter of the portion she would eat normally and did little to take the edge off her hunger by the time she was done.

She ran her finger around the clay bowl to catch whatever remained and sucked it from her finger, wishing there was more bread. Or perhaps a bit of cheese. Possibly another mug of ale. Even a bit of kidney pie and she *loathed* kidney pie.

If there was any bit of extra food lying about, she would gladly take it.

A knock sounded at her door, absent the familiarity of Alison's quiet rap.

Elspeth stiffened at the intrusion by a stranger. 'Who is it?' she asked.

'Calum,' the masculine voice replied. 'Alison said you wished to speak with me.'

Calum.

Heat rushed through Elspeth as the dreams she tried not to think upon flew forefront to her mind. Her hand went to her hair, unbidden, suddenly grateful she'd had the opportunity to brush it with such care. If only she was wearing a finer kirtle than the simple blue one Alison had found for her.

'Aye,' Elspeth answered in a voice that did not feel as confident as she wished it to. 'You may enter.'

The key rattled in the lock and the door swung open. He strode into the room, his dark hair mussed as always, his brows pulled down in the way that made him appear senti-mental and his extraordinary eyes warm with concern. 'Is something amiss?' he asked as he shut the door behind him.

'Aye.' Elspeth got to her feet and found her knees had gone rather weak.

He strode towards her and carried with him the scent of peat and leather. Her throat went dry.

She fixed her eyes on his to avoid looking at his mouth, or at the line of muscle showing just beneath the neckline of his maroon tunic.

'What is it?' he asked in a low voice that sounded in-timate in her addled mind.

What was it?

Oh, there were so many ways to answer such a question.

It was that he haunted her dreams. It was that he was her enemy, but she couldn't stop remembering his benev-olence. It was that she wanted to know more about him, why his eyes were so sad, how so sincere a man could be the child of a man who'd been so cruel.

What it felt like to have his lips on hers.

With such truths roiling in her mind, she struggled with something she could say aloud. 'I…' she faltered. 'I'm bored.'

His brows raised. 'Bored?'

She nodded. 'There isn't anything for me to do. There are no books, no needlepoint.' Though truly, she despised needlepoint. 'There is no herb garden to tend or anyone to play games with. There is nothing. There's not even enough food.'

He looked to her bowl and a muscle worked in his jaw. A wild urge to brush her fingers over his sharp jaw to feel the flicker of movement as that little muscle moved under his skin nearly overtook her.

She clenched her hands into fists to refrain from doing so.

'There isn't enough food for anyone,' he said slowly. 'We've given you as much as we can afford to spare, which happens to be more than most in the castle have to eat.' His hazel eyes found hers and his wounded expression cut her to the quick.

Elspeth covered her mouth with her hands, as if she could pull back the harsh complaint. 'I didn't realise that.' The guilt of his criticism burned in her chest.

'We live a hard life in Ireland,' he continued. 'We've been relegated to land no one else wanted, have little we can sell for coin as a result and not enough food. It's why we want our land in Scotland back.' His brows flinched downward in a pained expression. 'It's why I was forced to abduct you from your family. It was the only thing I could think to do that would keep any more men from dying.'

'My guards died,' she said softly, remembering the younger man who had been so kind to her in the forest.

'Only the one,' Calum clarified. 'After I left to chase you, the remaining guards were captured, tied up and left where they would be found by searching guards from Castle Lachlan who would come to see where you were.'

The air rushed in and out of her lungs, but still she was plagued with light-headedness.

'I don't want to hurt any more MacMillans or Mac-Whinnies, MacDonnells or MacLachlans. I want peace. And taking you…' He sighed, regret clear in his voice. 'Taking you seemed the most peaceful way to obtain that.'

'For your people,' she said through lips she could not feel.

He nodded. 'What would you do for your people? To save them?'

She swallowed, refusing to answer. She was ready to marry a man she didn't love for her people, to ensure their safety. A man who she would still be expected to marry upon her return, as agreed.

Suddenly that expectation weighed more heavily on her than it had previously. For never had Leith ignited Elspeth's body the way Calum Campbell did. And no matter how much she tried to put that from her mind, it remained stubbornly in place.

It had been Calum's intention to avoid going to Elspeth's chamber until Ross MacMillan agreed for her to be returned to him in Scotland in exchange for peace between their clans. That way he need only see her the one time. That way he would not be tempted by the Mac-Millan lass.

Calum ought to have stuck with his original plan.

Except that he had thought of her constantly over the last sennight. As he'd helped his people repair their homes and toiled in the unproductive fields alongside them. No longer did he have to bear the brunt of his father's scorn for giving aid to their people, something that Alexander had always seen as beneath him and his son. Nay, now Calum was completely free to offer them his help in any way he could.

Through it all, Elspeth had remained in his mind. He wondered what she did in the room all day and couldn't stop from wondering if she thought of him as often as he thought of her. Not that it mattered when she would hopefully soon be returning to Scotland. And especially not when she was to be wedded to the MacLachlan lad.

She was to be a means to an end and nothing more.

Now that he was standing before her, his heart thundered in his chest and every inch of him was highly aware of her. The way she smelled of that sweet, feminine powdery perfume, how her red hair fell in soft waves around her fair face, the glint in her lovely green eyes and how her mouth seemed to soften when she looked at his lips. As if she too wanted to sample a kiss.

He hadn't meant to divulge the state of his people to her, but did want her reassured that they weren't intentionally trying to starve her. And there was no way to say that without confessing how badly off his clan truly was.

Sympathy lit her eyes now and ebbed the discomfort of his admission.

'Can I help?' she asked.

'Your being here is helpful.' He smirked. 'As long as you don't run away.'

Colour warmed her cheeks and heightened her beauty. 'There were many women and children when we entered the village. Is there nothing I can do to offer them aid? I often helped back at my brothers' castles. Perhaps I can prepare simple herbs for healing or assist with mending.'

'You truly must be without purpose up here,' he said with intentional sarcasm. As he looked around the room, he caught sight of how empty it was. No doubt she was indeed being honest about her boredom.

Still, her offer was kind and had been entirely unexpected.

'It would be a better thing to know I am helping others rather than sitting here with nothing to do,' she said. 'And I would feel better knowing I am earning my share of the food I am given.'

Again she flushed, and he recognised the reaction

now as an expression of guilt. As haughty and difficult as she had been when he'd taken her, her walls were beginning to crumble.

Of course, it might be a trap.

He'd be a fool not to at least consider the possibility.

'If I agree to let you help, you'll be under constant watch,' he cautioned.

She nodded. 'I assumed as much.'

'And if you try to escape, I'll have no choice but to put you back in this room without the hope of leaving again until I hear from your brother.' He didn't specify that he'd heard nothing as yet from Ross MacMillan. In truth, he had expected to receive a reply by now. The delay was worrisome.

'Please take me out of this room.' She pleaded with such sincerity, he finally nodded, acquiescing.

'I had plans to go to the village after speaking with you,' he said. 'You can join me for the day. We'll see how it goes before I agree to the morrow.'

Then again, she might not want to go back the following day either after she saw how much work there was to be done.

But her face brightened. 'Aye, that would be perfect.'

'If you're ready...' He raised a brow.

'I am.'

He glanced at her unbound wrists and prayed to God he was not making a terrible mistake. Before he could change his mind, he opened the door and led her from the room. Part of him had expected her to bolt down the hall, running with a frenzy, but she did not. She remained at his side, truly appearing eager to do anything but stay locked in that room.

Not that he could blame her. He had never been one for inactivity himself.

They threaded through the narrow corridors of the small castle and exited the keep into the village. He had seen it through her eyes when they'd first arrived. The huts wilting on their structures, missing thatch, the skinny inhabitants all underfed, overworked by the hostile land and exhausted by their efforts.

'My father was so focused on preparing for war that he didn't pay any mind to the needs of his people,' Calum said by way of explanation.

It was a flimsy justification. In truth, there wasn't enough money and there wasn't enough food. His father's intent on preparing to attack Scotland didn't help when matters were already so dire.

'Calum,' a little voice cried out.

A small blond boy in a long dingy shirt raced up to him. 'Will you be fixing our house next? Mum said she hoped you were as she don't have another pot to catch all the rain leaking in.'

Calum considered the wee lad, recalling his name from memory, though it'd been at least two months since he'd seen him. 'Lead the way, Jamie.'

The boy beamed up at him and waved for them to follow.

Elspeth turned a questioning look on Calum.

His cheeks warmed as he offered a light shrug. 'While we're waiting to hear from your brother, my men and I have been doing what we can to repair some of the homes.'

'And you've given up fighting altogether?'

Jamie stopped impatiently and waved at them to join him. Calum quickened his pace, remembering clearly what it was like to be a child with far too much energy when around dawdling adults.

'Nay,' Calum replied. 'We cannot completely forego all fighting in case your brother won't comply. War is still an option, though it is not what we want.' He hefted his small bag of tools and cast an assessing glance at the ruined thatch where a chunk was missing before turning his attention to Elspeth once more. 'I'm tired of fighting and am saddened by how many homes are without husbands and brothers and sons. We cannot continue to stay here. The pestilence killed off many of our people and the already difficult land has been made nearly impossible to farm with the constant rain. If we stay here, we will all die.'

She studied him for a quiet moment.

'This way.' The lad dipped into the hut.

Calum allowed Elspeth to enter first and stepped in behind her. The inside of the single room home was dark and smelled of wet earth, redolent of smoke from a hearth fire recently extinguished. The shutters were open, allowing a cool breeze to freshen the air.

A woman in a homespun kirtle looked up at their arrival. 'Ach, Jamie, you didn't have to do that.' She put her hand to the top of the boy's head affectionately and regarded Calum. 'Forgive me, Laird, the lad acts on his own mind more times than not.' Her dark hair was pulled back in a loose braid and fatigue shadowed her eyes.

She was far too slender. Given her son's healthy glow and full cheeks, it was obvious where the woman's food went.

'We were coming this way anyway,' Calum said and snuck a wink at Jamie who grinned up at him, revealing a missing front tooth.

'I've brought Mistress Elspeth to aid you with mending if you need it.' He indicated Elspeth at his side.

Jamie's mother furrowed her brow with uncertainty.

Elspeth stepped forward. 'I want to help in any way I can.'

At that moment, a baby let out a cry and the woman's gaze darted to a cradle tucked in a corner.

'Jamie, will you show me where the mending is?' Elspeth asked the lad.

His face lit up. 'Aye, we've got quite a bit of it as my mum has been so busy with the new bairn.' He held out his hand, which Elspeth took as he pulled her over towards a basket.

She chatted a moment with the lad as he told her which clothing belonged to whom. The smile on Elspeth's face appeared genuine as she listened while shifting through the clothing—rags really—and never showed judgement. If Calum had thought she was beautiful before, the kind-heartedness she exhibited now made her positively radiant.

Not that it mattered.

She would soon be returning to Scotland, Calum reminded himself.

She was not his to have.

It was a reminder he would need to keep forefront in his mind, for when he returned her to her brother, surely Leith MacLachlan would make good on his promise and wed her. What man would not?

Envy was an emotion Calum had pushed away most of his life. His mother had always said there was no sense to the feeling, and he had always agreed. Until now, when he truly wanted something that could never be his.

Someone.

For the first time in Calum's life, he felt himself truly coveting what would someday belong to someone else.

Chapter Eight

Being in the company of young Jamie and his mother, Sorcha, gave Elspeth an appreciation for how the Campbell clan lived that she could never have gleaned from her room in the castle. They had offered to share their meagre portion of bread and ale with her, but she had refused, saying she was not at all hungry though of course she was famished. Their generosity and appreciation were so genuine, it touched Elspeth's heart and left her with an understanding she had lacked before concerning the dire situation the Campbell clan faced.

She spent the day with the family, helping Sorcha by mending clothes while the steady rustle and bang of thatch being repaired on the roof came from above. And when Calum had finished, there had been another family to help and then yet another. Elspeth was glad Alison had not finished mending the fine green gown she'd worn upon arrival, a task the chatelaine had refused to allow Elspeth to do. The simple, homespun dress Elspeth now wore made her more well-received by the Campbell women, who all wore kirtles of similar fabric and fashion.

What's more, the garment was far more comfortable.

The looseness of the sleeves and back tailored more towards function than fashion.

Despite the circumstances that had brought Elspeth to the remote village in Ireland, she had enjoyed the opportunity to meet the people who lived here.

She noted that each family greeted Calum warmly with a regard that could not be feigned. In each smiling face and excited child, Elspeth could see that Calum was not at all the man she had assumed him to be. He did not slay children before their mothers, he gave them rides upon his back. He did not burn homes but repaired them, and ensured the family within was safe and comfortable. He did not take women at will, but instead gave them hope when they had nothing left.

He could not have been further from Elspeth's expectations if he had tried.

When at last their day came to an end, Elspeth was weary with the kind of bone-deep exhaustion that comes from good, honest, hard work. And she was glad for it.

She exited the hut of a woman with twin daughters who were a delightful handful and looked up at the roof to find Calum's form set against the brilliant setting sun as he continued to work. 'It's time for supper,' Elspeth called to him.

'I'm nearly done.' There was a bit more rustling about as he adjusted a layer of thatch.

Elspeth put the flat of her hand to her brow to shield the sun as she gazed upward to see what he was doing. Her breath caught at the sight.

Whatever his hands were occupied with was entirely lost on her. There was no seeing past the broad, naked back, browned by the sun and slick with sweat, revealing every ripple of muscle as he moved. Her mouth went dry.

She'd seen men without their shirts when the soldiers trained, but none were as glorious as Calum Campbell. After a quick glance about to ensure no one saw her watching him, she curved around the hut in an effort to catch sight of the front of him.

'A moment longer,' he said, completely oblivious.

''Tis fine,' Elspeth called cheerfully. 'Take your time.'

She stood on tiptoe and craned her neck to see around the powerful arm he'd braced himself with. Hard lines of a carved abdomen were just barely visible. She bit her lip and leaned to the right, nearly teetering over.

'A man like that is worth falling over for.'

Elspeth jerked upright at the sound, her cheeks on fire.

Sorcha gave a good-natured chuckle. 'You could do far worse than the likes of Calum Campbell, mistress.'

'I wasn't…' Elspeth's cheeks scorched with heat. 'I mean, I was, it's just…'

'Your secret is safe with me.' Sorcha winked and disappeared back inside her own hut.

Still on the neighbour's roof, Calum pulled his linen shirt on and gathered up his tools before hopping down to the ground. His face was flushed, his hair even more dishevelled than usual and the sleeves of his leine were pushed up to his elbows, revealing his strong forearms lined with muscles and dotted with dark hair.

He gave her a boyish grin. 'I didn't mean to take so long.'

She shook her head. 'It wasn't at all an issue.'

Her gaze slipped to his exposed skin, unable to stop herself from wondering what his arms might feel like around her. She recalled how those strong, capable hands of his had so gently brushed the hair from her face when he'd checked her forehead after she'd headbutted him.

What would his touch feel like on the rest of her body? What would those rippling muscles be like under her fingertips? She tipped head over heels into a quiet fantasy of running her palms over his gloriously strong back as she and Calum walked silently back to the castle.

'Thank you for your help today,' Calum's rich voice interrupted the imaginary play of her hands over him.

'It was entirely my pleasure,' she replied earnestly. Not only for seeing him in such a way, but for truly making a difference to people in need. 'I plan to help every day if you'll allow it.'

'Aye, of course. I'll be glad to have your help for a few days.'

A few days. A reminder at how limited her time with his clan would be.

'Have you heard from my brother?' she asked.

Calum hesitated, his mouth drawing tight.

She rubbed at a sore spot on the pad of her thumb which had reddened from so many passes with a needle. 'Ross can be somewhat stubborn. I take it you've not heard from him then.'

Calum shook his head. 'I expected to receive a reply from him several days ago.'

'I can send a letter to my brother as well,' Elspeth offered.

Calum's brows pinched together. 'You would do that?'

'Aye, if you think it would encourage a prompt reply.' She reached for his hand, not realising the intimacy of the action until after his large fingers were held in her grip. 'I want to help, Calum. I didn't understand before.'

'You cannot understand the situation unless you see it.' He glanced down at their hands as though realising the same thing. But he did not pull away and instead nodded. 'Aye, having you write a letter to Ross would help. At least he would know you're not injured.'

Elspeth flushed and withdrew her hand from Calum's as the idea of her brother worrying after her safety gripped her heart. Had she not known Calum to be the man he was, she would have been gravely concerned for anyone left to his mercy based on her previous knowledge.

Her fingers tingled where she had touched Calum's and she rubbed her fingertips together, savouring the sensation. 'It will ease my mind for him to know I'm well.'

They crossed into the courtyard of the keep. Within minutes, he would be leading her back to her chamber. Would he lock her in as before? Would he trust her, certain she couldn't bring herself to leave, especially now that she was aware of the life she would condemn his people to when they were already in such a sorry state?

'As I mentioned earlier, I am still training the men.' Calum slowed his pace, so they took longer to arrive at the keep. 'I know you mentioned wanting to learn to fight.'

Elspeth sucked in a breath. 'I do.'

'You may join us if it pleases you to do so,' he said, sliding her a glance.

'Aye, it very much would.' She beamed at him. The sudden urge to throw her arms around his neck and kiss him tugged at her, but before she could even close the distance between them, Alison's voice drifted over to her.

'Mistress, I've been wondering when you'd be back.' Alison came and took her arm, offering a slight incline of her head respectfully towards Calum. 'Come, the evening meal has just been prepared. You settle in your room while I fetch you a trencher.'

'Have her ready by dawn tomorrow, Alison,' Calum said, not looking at the chatelaine, but at Elspeth. 'She'll be learning to fight with the men.'

Alison nodded. 'Aye, Laird.'

With that, she hastened Elspeth back to the bedchamber. But this time, Elspeth did not regard it with the same displeasure as before. Now, she knew she would be outside once more the following day, and that her time in Ireland would be productive.

What's more, she would learn how to fight. Ironically, after all these years, the one man willing to train her with swords and daggers had for years been her family's mortal enemy.

If Calum had known what joy helping his clan would have brought Elspeth, he would have offered some time ago. And if he'd known how her lovely face would have lit with such excitement, he'd have had her on the training field from the first day of her arrival.

He waited for her the next morning with more anticipation than he ought to allow himself. She was a woman who belonged to another man and the daughter of a rival clan, one who his father had wronged tremendously for decades. A few conciliations could not remove the stain of hate she must surely still feel for him.

The soldiers were already in mock combat when she arrived. He'd sensed her nearby, above the sharp ring of metal on metal and the grunting efforts of his warriors. Her hair was bound back in a thick red braid that bounced off her bottom as she crossed the courtyard to him.

Colour flushed her cheeks and wisps of hair that had come loose danced around her bonny face as she grinned up at him. 'I'm ready to become a warrior.'

He offered her the dagger he'd taken from her when she was first abducted. Rather than accept it, her gaze slid behind him to where several practice swords were propped against the back wall. He lifted a brow in silent question.

'I thought...' She exaggerated the effort of looking around him to the weapons. 'I thought I'd be learning to use one of those.'

'Perhaps in time, when you're stronger.'

'I'm plenty strong.' Her eyes flashed with the challenge.

He held his hand out in invitation. 'Pick one up.'

She strode over to the swords with all the confidence of a knight about to do battle, gripped the hilt and scraped the tip across the ground. She flicked a nervous glance in his direction, as if confirming that he had indeed seen her struggle, then yanked it upright.

A victorious smile spread over her lips.

Her triumph was short lived, however, when the heavy blade wobbled and tipped back to the ground.

'It's heavy,' he confirmed.

'Not so very heavy.' She stubbornly hefted it up once more. Sweat breaking out on her brow.

''Tis a bit obvious, don't you think?' He strode around her slowly, an instructor assessing the work of his pupil. Though perhaps an instructor shouldn't appreciate the view so much.

'Obvious?' Her arm shook with the effort to keep the weapon aloft.

'A woman racing at someone with a sword she can scarce carry.' He stopped in front of her. 'Your enemy will know you're coming.' He almost flinched at his own use of the word 'enemy.' In past years, that had been him and his clansmen.

'It's the best weapon to kill with,' she ground out with the great effort of holding it steady. 'For protection.'

'I disagree.' He rushed forward with the dagger, gentle when he held her shoulder and gentler still when he put the blade near her chest, careful not to touch her with its razor point.

The sword fell from her hands and she gasped in surprise.

He met her clear green eyes and his heart stuttered off beat. God, but she was so very beautiful.

Focus.

'No one suspects a hidden dagger,' he said, putting himself back on task. 'Surprise is always the best tactic. A lass with a sword doesn't offer much of a surprise, at least not by the time you get to your opponent.' The point of the dagger was still beneath her breasts which rose and fell with her quickened breath. He pulled away quickly and fixed his attention on her face.

'I see.' She lifted her head to gaze victoriously at him. 'Then I suppose I've the mindset of a warrior already as I've used surprise to my advantage before.'

'Aye, indeed you have. How *is* your head now?' He brushed his thumb over her brow with a chuckle.

She scowled playfully at him, but laughed in spite of herself.

'You've got a warrior's heart, lass.' He picked up the claymore. 'And that will take you farther than a sword meant for a man to carry with two hands.'

Her mouth fell open. 'Two hands?'

'You didn't ask how to hold it.' He offered her the dagger and this time she took it. 'Now throw it like you did before.' He gestured to the target set up several paces away.

She turned towards it, her eyes narrowed with determination and flung the blade. The weapon skittered onto the ground.

Last time had been a brisk instruction. This time would allow him to be more thorough. He reclaimed her dagger and brought it back to her.

'Stand directly before the target with your hips straight.' He put his hands on her kirtle where her slender waist flared to her generous hips in an effort to guide her into place. Only when his palms rested on the swell of her curves did he realise the inappropriateness of his touch. But though her cheeks reddened, she simply nodded, her focus set on her task.

'Keep your hold on the blade loose, as I told you before.' This time he put his hands over hers where she held the dagger, ensuring it was not too tight. Her fingers were delicate and soft beneath his touch, making him long to curl his fingers against her smooth palms.

'Aye, like that,' he said against her ear.

She pulled in a soft breath and slid a searing gaze up at him.

'Focus on the target,' he encouraged. It was a reminder to them both why they were here.

She had a wedding to attend upon her return and he had the wellbeing of his people to see to without the distraction of an unattainable woman.

The instructions were ones he had given in the past to warriors who were just beginning their training. But never before had the process seemed so sensual.

Their proximity left her powdery scent intoxicating him like the finest ambrosia. He found himself wanting to touch her hands, her waist, her hips, whenever possible, to tease himself further with want of her. But he would not be that man.

He restrained himself as much as possible, even when he could tell that his proximity made her nipples go taut against the homespun kirtle she wore, even when she bit her lower lip and looked at him with unmistakable desire.

Their focused efforts were not in vain. By the end of the practice, she was sinking the dagger into the target on every throw.

'Thank you for taking the time to teach me.' Elspeth handed him her dagger and let her fingers linger against his palm.

It was Calum's pleasure to do so, but he refused to say as much. Instead, he withdrew his hand from hers. 'On the morrow, I'll show you how to fight with a dagger. I know you don't think it as fine as a sword, but the dagger's ability to be concealed makes it a handy and lethal weapon.'

'I look forward to it,' she said, her eyes sparkling.

He walked with her into the keep where the thick wood blocked out the sun and cooled the sweat on the back of his neck from his exertions. 'Thank you for the letter you wrote to your brother on our behalf.'

He'd been loath to mention it before, to break her concentration from her task, or to interrupt their quiet intimacy with the reminder that she had been abducted forcefully for the purpose of exploitation. That they were, in their blood, enemies.

She nodded, her body tensing. 'I hope it helps.'

'I'm sure it will.' He'd read the missive she'd written to her brother, though he'd hated doing so. Unfolding the letter had felt like an invasion of privacy. And yet, he could not risk the lives of his people to trust her so implicitly.

There had been nothing amiss that he could see. Rather, she had been complimentary of his treatment of her as she implored her brother to consider a truce on behalf of the widows and children of the Campbell clan.

As they entered the Great Hall, Alison came into view, prepared to escort Elspeth back to her room.

'Tonight there is to be a feast,' Calum said before she could walk away to the chatelaine. 'To announce me as the official Laird of the clan. I... That is, if it pleases you to do so... Perhaps you would...'

The invitation bumbled from him in a stilted garble that made him want to slap his palm to his brow to knock the right words free.

Instead, Elspeth merely smiled. 'I'd love to.' Her eyes held his for longer than they should have before she swept away to join Alison.

Though her response had been casually given, it stayed with Calum through the remainder of the day. He should not have asked her. Not only because she was their prisoner, but also because soon she would have to return home. Away from him.

To another man.

One she didn't love.

The reminder crept into his thoughts, unbidden and yet still welcome. Aye, he should not be so eager to see her join him that night at the feast, and yet he could not help being grateful she had agreed.

Chapter Nine

Calum spent far too long preparing for the feast, wanting to be as well put together as was possible. Not only was it his formal presentation as Laird for his people, but also with the keen awareness that Elspeth would be there.

No matter how much he tried not to think of the feisty lass, his mind continually drifted towards her, wondering what she might wear, if she might dance with him, what they might discuss…

The feast was nearly ready to begin, the meagre food stores opened up, albeit with an eye towards prudence, for the occasion. There was freshly baked bread, several deer poached from lands that did not belong to them, vegetables dug up from their small harvest.

People were seated along the trestle tables, and mugs were filled with wine and ale as the servants distributed a veritable feast of food. All was in order.

Except that Elspeth was not in attendance.

A flicker of disappointment passed through Calum. For whatever reason, it appeared she had changed her mind. Perhaps too tired from their training earlier.

He should not have worked her so hard.

Or…

He had not ordered Alison to lock Elspeth's door, giving her the freedom to come and go as she pleased. Fear glided down his spine. Perhaps she had escaped.

Surely after what she had seen the day before with his people, after having written such a heartfelt letter to her brother and with their shared time spent on the training ground that day—surely with all of that, she would not have left?

And yet, it was certainly something to consider.

It wasn't until his hands began to ache that he realised he was clutching the arms of his chair. He pushed to standing, intent on summoning Alison to his side to question Elspeth's whereabouts when the doors to the Great Hall flung open and Elspeth stepped through them like a goddess.

She wore the same green kirtle she'd had on when he'd taken her, but now it was free of wrinkles and freshly laundered. The fine attire was a far better fit to her shape than was the loose homespun kirtle she'd been wearing the last few days. He could not stop his stare from outlining her curves as she gracefully sauntered towards him.

Her hair was unbound, as usual, the wavy locks gleaming in the light like silken fire. A simple gold necklace sparkled at her throat and a cloth of gold belt encircled her narrow waist before trailing gracefully down the front of her skirt to her hem.

The hall went quiet as she strode towards the dais, her head held high, her gaze fixed straight ahead. As if she were the mistress of the castle and had every right to be there.

By her late arrival, she made it known to all that she was in their presence, that she was a beacon of hope.

While she could not silence all the doubts that still lingered among his people, the act would doubtless quiet more than one wagging tongue.

When she reached the dais, one of the servants pulled out the chair at Calum's right to welcome her to sit in a seat of honour. She lowered herself gracefully and glanced towards him. It was then he noticed the gold chain at her throat had been one of his mother's, the only one he had been unwilling to part with to pay for food and other supplies.

A small sunburst charm winked up at him from the hollow of her throat, a ruby set at its centre. To him, it was a memory of the life they'd had before they were cast out of Scotland, the promise that it could be that way again someday. Alison knew what that necklace meant to him.

And yet she had deemed Elspeth worthy of wearing it about her throat, indicating that the chatelaine thought highly of the MacMillan lass, as did he.

'You look bonny,' he said.

'So do you.' She closed her eyes in a moment of instant regret and shook her head. 'I mean, you look handsome.' Colour ignited across her cheeks.

Heat touched his own face at her compliment. He'd taken care with his appearance and wore a gold brocade tunic his mother had stitched with her own hand the prior year.

Elspeth reached for her goblet of wine. 'I'm pleased you are Laird now.'

He reached for his own drink, eager to smooth the sudden shyness between them and the unspoken words about who the previous Laird had been and what had transpired under his rule.

'Forgive me,' he said in a low voice for only her to hear.

She turned her wide green eyes on him, studying him.

'For taking you from your home,' he continued. 'For having to use you in such a fashion. If I could have come up with another solution, if there was another—'

She shook her head slightly and he fell silent.

'What you did was wrong, but it was done for good reason.' Her gaze shifted away, blocking him from being able to gauge her reaction as she spoke. 'We all do things we don't wish to do for the sake of our people.'

Though he could not bear witness to how she felt as she spoke those words, he understood them.

Leith MacLachlan.

The man she did not love.

Calum didn't speak for a moment as he cut a choice piece of venison and eased it onto her plate. She glanced at it and though she nodded her thanks, she did not begin eating immediately. 'Why did you agree to join your father to attack our people?'

'My father threatened to throw me in the dungeon if I refused.' Calum sighed at the memory. Alexander's face had gone purple with rage at Calum's initial refusal. 'I'd hoped that in joining him, I might suggest ways we could resolve things peacefully. It was a small likelihood, but a stronger one than if I was sitting in the dungeon.'

'And the abbey?' she pressed. 'Was that you or your father?'

He shook his head, frowning. She'd mentioned the abbey before, but he had no memory of his father suggesting they attack it.

'It wasn't me,' he replied. 'My father didn't say anything about it either, but that doesn't mean he didn't do it.' He hesitated, his stomach clenching at his next question. 'Were many injured?'

'None, thanks be to God.' Elspeth took a bite of the meat and chewed thoughtfully. 'Do you know why I want so badly to learn how to fight?'

He couldn't help his involuntary flinch. 'Does it have to do with me and my father?'

'The castle was attacked before your people were cast out of Scotland.' Elspeth studied the food in front of her. 'I was given to a nurse to hide while my father's men made a diversion to keep me safe. It was the first of many times men have died for me over the years. It's unfair that they should die because I am to live, that lives must continue to be placed at risk. But I will never forget what any of them have sacrificed for me.'

'I'm sorry.' They were small words for the enormity of emotion blazing through him in that moment—the regret, the concern, the rage at his father.

She looked at him, her distant gaze focusing. 'You are the first person to help me learn how to defend myself. You are not at all what I expected.' She ducked her head. 'There are many rumours about you.'

'People believe what they want to.' Calum cut another slice of meat for his own plate and sipped his wine. The velvety richness of it slid down his throat and warmed him from the inside out. 'I think I've already mentioned we're learning rumours have no bearing here.'

'Some are true.' She wrinkled her nose and drank from her goblet.

He lifted his brow in question.

'I was a homely lass when I was young.' She gave a self-deprecating laugh and studied the plate in front of her. 'I was far too thin and hadn't grown into my features or limbs.'

'You're bonny now.' Calum resisted the urge to touch her hand under the table.

'I still haven't grown into all my features.' She turned to him, bit her lip and pushed her hair back behind her ears.

They were slightly larger than normal and stuck out a fair deal, but they did nothing to detract from her beauty. 'You're not convincing me that you're not entirely lovely.'

'If you don't think they're too big, you're the only one.' She laughed and let her red locks fall back over her ears like a curtain shielding them from the scrutiny of others. 'I was always picked on about them.'

'You're bonny no matter the size of your ears,' Calum said insistently.

Elspeth shook her head as though in disagreement, but a pleased smile spread over her lips. 'Baubles such as this take the attention from them.' She fingered the necklace.

'You don't need such tricks, though the necklace is lovely on you.' He regarded it thoughtfully. 'It was my mother's.'

Elspeth's mouth fell open. 'I don't have to wear it. I didn't know.' She reached to the back of her neck for the clasp.

He stopped her. 'She wore it when we lived in Scotland. When our lives were prosperous. She took it off when we were sent to Ireland. I think for her, it became a symbol of everything we lost. But I see it as everything we have to gain.' The small red stone winked where it sat in the hollow of her throat. 'I can think of no one worthier of wearing it than you.'

'I'm sorry life here is so difficult.' Elspeth lowered her hands. 'Will you tell me about your mother?'

The subject of his mother was not something he spoke

of often. But then, who would he speak of her to? His father whose disposition grew vengeful with grief whenever he heard her name? Bram who was focused only on strategy and battle plans?

There had been no opportunity to speak of her, until now. With Elspeth who understood the loss of a mother as she had lost hers early as well.

And so, as they ate, they spoke of their mothers. How his own had raised him with gentle kindness and how the roughness of this land had finally overwhelmed her frail body. They also spoke of Elspeth's mum, who had succumbed to the pestilence that had raged through the land over ten summers ago.

As they were finishing the last of their food, music began to fill the Great Hall as people shifted the trestle tables away to create a dance floor. Already couples were coming together in the open space, moving in time to a jaunty tune.

Elspeth's foot tapped on the ground in time with the drum's beat.

'Would you like to dance?' Calum asked.

'I would love to.' Elspeth lifted her hand to allow him to pull her to her feet.

He rose, then took her hand, helping her up, then led her to the makeshift dance floor. The wine he'd consumed was a rare treat in Ireland as they could scarcely afford much. The richness of it left his thoughts soft and hazy.

Elspeth's eyes sparkled and her cheeks and lips were rosy from the drink. She laughed as they came together on the dance floor and kicked their legs out in time to the music before leaping as one. They looked at one another and laughed again, their shared joy making Calum feel light with a happiness that he could not recall having experienced in years.

They danced thus on through the night until finally the Great Hall began to empty, and the music drew to a close.

'I think 'tis finally time for the feast to come to an end.' Calum spun her around one last time.

Her hair fanned out brilliant red around her before she came to a stop in front of him. 'I don't want it to end. This has all been so enjoyable.'

'Indeed it has,' Calum agreed.

He wished the night truly could last for ever. Because for the span of an evening, neither of them had to think about the war between their clans or the possibility of her leaving soon or even who awaited her when she returned and what that meant.

But the servants were already hard at work cleaning the large room and feasts were enough of a tremendous task without revellers lingering behind.

'Come, I'll walk you to your bedchamber.' He offered her his arm, which she took without hesitation.

They chatted as they made their way up the wooden stairs—not about their families or the dire situation both faced, but of one another, of the shared amusement that night. All too soon, they arrived at her bedchamber door and their steps and conversation dwindled to a stop.

He ought to have bid her good evening with a slight bow and taken his leave, except he was rooted to the spot, held in place by the way she gazed up at him, her expression affectionate. Expectant.

Her hand remained on his arm as if she were loath to let him go. Indeed, he did not wish to lose her light touch. He wished it would travel up his arm to his chest, then to his jaw as she guided him down to her lips.

He leaned towards her without realising what he was doing, eager to brush his lips against hers.

She was not his, he knew, but he could not stop himself from trying to steal just a single kiss.

All night, Elspeth had wondered what it would be like to kiss Calum Campbell. She had truly enjoyed their time together, cherishing his company, in the dancing skills he exhibited and the chivalrous way he led her to her bedchamber after.

Now, he leaned towards her, his eyes closing as his face lowered to hers. Her heart thundered in her chest like the drums of the musicians in the Great Hall. She wanted this, to tilt her head back and allow his mouth to descend on hers.

Would it be delicate and simple? A whisper of their lips against one another?

Or would he be bold in his affection as she heard some men were, stroking his tongue against hers?

She had never been kissed and the appeal of both were more than she could bear.

A delicious chill of anticipation tingled over her skin.

He stopped just before their mouths touched and his breath swept over her chin, spicy and alluring. Her body was alight with awareness, desperate for his touch.

But her mind was at war with her longing, reminding her of her obligations.

There had been no formal betrothal to Leith, it was true. There hadn't been time. But he had wanted to wed her since they were children, often telling her that if there was no one else that she would wed him when they were grown.

While she had never agreed to it, Ross's letter to the

MacLachlans to secure a union between herself and her childhood friend had been met with a ready agreement by the other clan. She had an obligation to Leith, no matter where her heart or her body wished to lead her.

Calum's hand came up to her face, his touch light where it caressed her cheek.

She closed her eyes, hating her responsibilities, hating to put an end to this otherwise magical moment that she wanted to yield to. 'We cannot do this.'

Part of her hoped he would ignore her words, that he would pull her against the strength of his lean body and claim her lips with a passion that would ignite them both.

When a moment passed without his mouth on hers, she blinked her eyes open and found him standing a respectful distance away, his hands behind his back.

'Forgive me,' he said. 'For a moment I forgot myself.'

''Tis Leith...' she stammered. 'I...'

He shook his head. 'You need not explain, lass.'

She wanted to explain, to tell him about the dreams she had of him every night and how she wished to experience them when she was awake. With him. How she longed to feel the strength of his arms around her and be enveloped by his tantalising, masculine scent, to lose herself in their shared lust.

But by telling him these things, she knew she would be betraying Leith.

Her letter would convince Ross of her safety. She knew her brother well. The time she would be in Ireland with Calum would be short lived. When she returned to Scotland, Leith would be waiting for her and she would make good on her obligation.

She would not do so sullied and have Calum blamed for the act.

Aye, Calum and his people would no longer be a threat, but there would always be other clan battles. Having the MacLachlans united with the MacMillans would always ensure their survival.

So, aye, she wanted to tell Calum all those things, but knew she could not.

'I'm sorry,' she said softly.

'The fault is mine.' Calum bowed respectfully to her, took her hand and offered a gentle kiss upon the back before straightening and taking his leave.

He had not made sure she went into her bedchamber. Which meant he would not be there to lock the door after her.

He trusted her.

Alison had left her door unlocked earlier that day as well, but she had led her into the room. This was the first time Elspeth had been left to enter of her own volition.

She was no longer a prisoner, but a guest. In truth, she'd felt that way since the day before when she had assisted the people with their daily tasks and when she'd trained that morning with Calum and his warriors.

Though she'd been there only a short time, she already felt as though she belonged with the Campbells. More so than with her own people. She wasn't needed by the MacMillans, aside from the ability to create another alliance. Outside of that, she was expendable. None of their castles needed a mistress now that her brothers were wed and their wives had assumed the task of overseeing their households. There were no children who needed looking after yet and when they did appear, there would be nursemaids to see to them. The villagers were well f and cared for.

She was not necessary in their lives.

But with the Campbell clan, she could do good for the people. They needed her. And a part of her, something empty and unfulfilled, needed them as well.

Ross would doubtless disown her for even contemplating such a thing. After all, Alexander Campbell had killed their father.

It was an offence easily forgotten when she was with Calum, but that did not make the transgression go away.

She slipped quietly into her bedchamber as her heart wrestled with her mind. Her father had been a good man, just and loving. His death had devastated the family, especially once their uncle had assumed his place and ruled in a manner that demanded immediate obedience.

Elspeth and her brothers had always mourned their father's loss.

And now she found herself drawn to the son of the man who had killed him. Nay, not only drawn to him, but respecting him.

Ross would see it as the ultimate betrayal.

For it truly was a betrayal to her clan, was it not?

Yet when she closed her eyes and leaned her poor, tormented head against the door, it was Calum's face that rose in her mind. It was the tease of his lips near hers that stole her breath. And she could not help but think what might have happened if she had let him kiss her.

It was those thoughts she held onto as she readied for bed and sank beneath the sheets. For now, at least while she was in Ireland, she resolved to indulge the fantasies in her mind. Her obligations would come when she returned to Scotland and she knew that time would come far sooner than she was ready to face.

Chapter Ten

The following morning, Elspeth woke to find Alison in her room with a fresh ewer of water for her morning ablutions.

'If you'd like to break your fast in the Great Hall, you may,' Alison said when she saw Elspeth had roused. 'I'm glad the Laird has finally seen your good heart for what it is. Your stay here will be far more pleasant now that you have the freedom to move about.'

Elspeth smiled gratefully at the older woman as she was helped into a fresh kirtle and her hair brushed smooth.

'You had a late night,' Alison said. 'I didn't expect you to be awake for some time.'

Elspeth recalled the night before with a wash of heat over her face. There was a part of her that wished the night had been later still, even if such thoughts were terribly wicked. Even if she knew deep down that she could not allow herself such liberties.

When she was ready, she and Alison made their way to the Great Hall where small baskets of bread sat along the length of the table. The portions were meagre as usual, and the clan respectfully each only took a small serving to ensure there was enough to go around.

Elspeth could not stop the ache in her chest to see such consideration among the clan. At her side, Alison stiffened.

Elspeth turned to her with concern. 'What is it?'

'Bram has returned.' The older woman nodded towards a dark-haired man crossing the room, one Elspeth briefly recalled from the shore before she'd been tossed into the boat headed for Ireland.

Bram.

Calum's right-hand man gave her a dashing smile and winked at her as he passed. He was the kind of man who knew how to look at a woman, whose apparent confidence said he had the exact right words to say—the type Elspeth had never been drawn to.

But it was not his demeanour which soured her stomach to the idea of eating, but his very presence. For if he was in Ireland, that meant Ross had issued a reply.

'My brother has responded,' Elspeth said softly to Alison.

'Thanks be to God.' Alison glanced heavenward.

A restless energy charged through Elspeth. 'I should go to Calum.'

Alison waved for Elspeth to follow. 'Right this way.'

In all the time Elspeth had been in Ireland, she had not spent much of it wandering through the castle. The floors creaked and there were almost no furnishings through the halls. Evidence of the clan's limited means was apparent at every turn.

'He's in the solar where he usually is each morning,' Alison said. 'I'll announce you.'

'That's not necessary.' Elspeth stepped towards the door to keep Alison from entering before her. 'Thank you.'

Elspeth wasn't sure why she did it. Propriety dictated that they not be alone, but really did it even matter any more? Her pulse ticked faster as she pushed through the door and into the small room. The shutters had been opened, letting in a crisp morning chill as well as copious amounts of sunlight that spilled into the room in splashes of bright gold.

Calum sat at his desk, a letter pinched in his fingers. He looked up and the missive slipped from his grasp, floating to the desk. 'Elspeth.' Quickly, he got to his feet.

'Calum.'

Their eyes met and all the breath sucked out of Elspeth's lungs. In that instant, she recalled the night before as they'd stopped outside her bedchamber. He'd meant to kiss her. And she had wanted him to.

God, how she had wanted him to.

'Forgive me for last night,' he started.

She shook her head, not wanting his apology. Not wanting his regret.

He fell silent, but the concern on his brow did not smooth away.

Her attention went to the letter on his desk. 'Bram has returned. I take it you've received a reply from Ross?'

Calum nodded slowly. 'It's not what I was hoping for, but what I was expecting.'

Elspeth frowned and approached the desk. He handed her the parchment with Ross's familiar slanted writing scrawled over it.

While I believe you have Elspeth, I expect she was coerced into writing what she did. If you truly want to talk about peace, come to Scotland and discuss it like a man.

'Discuss it like a man?' She lowered the letter. 'What does he mean by that?'

Calum took Ross's response from her and set it on the desk. 'I don't believe there will be much talking.'

Elspeth's stomach clenched in a flash of fear. Her eldest brother would kill Calum for having abducted her. Ross was a fair and just man, like their da, but it did not mean he would not seek vengeance.

'You can't go,' Elspeth said.

'I can and I will,' Calum said gravely. 'Alone.'

She gasped. 'Nay. Let me come with you, let him see that you meant me no harm. Let me speak with him.'

'It's far too dangerous, Elspeth.' Calum shook his head. 'I forbid it.'

'You forbid it?' She lifted her brows, challenging his order and fully determined to win.

'I mean the danger is far too great and you might get accidentally injured.' Calum approached her and her heartbeat thundered in her chest. 'You're too dear to me.'

She swallowed.

Too dear to me.

She wanted to close her eyes and beg him to continue speaking such words of affection, to vow to stay in Ireland where nothing could harm her. But such things were not the reality of their situation. Leith would be her future.

'I can't let you go alone,' she said with finality. 'I know Ross and how to speak to him. He'll listen to me. If you go alone, he'll kill you.'

Calum shook his head.

'He will,' Elspeth said before he could protest. 'I know my brother. You've stolen me away. With the rumours about you and your father, he'll assume the worst. If I'm there to prove that I'm hale and hearty, that I've been safe and well cared for all this time, he will believe me. I know he will.' She put her hand to Calum's chest. 'If you are killed, who will look after your people?'

She should have withdrawn her touch from him, but left her fingers where they lay on Calum's tunic. His body was firm and warm beneath the linen, his heart tapping a frantic rhythm against her fingertips.

Rather than pull away from her, he covered her hand with his large one. 'If I allow you to join me, I want to ensure you're properly trained before our departure, aye?'

Elspeth nodded.

'You must promise me that if the situation seems dire, you won't intervene,' he said. 'If I'm attacked, I don't want you struck by accident. Battle can be confusing and when a blade is swinging about, its path is not easily stopped.'

'Aye, if I sense there is danger, I will not stay.' But as she spoke those words, she knew they were not true. If Calum was attacked, she would do everything possible to keep him safe and ensure Ross listened to her about what she'd learned of the Campbell clan. Even if doing so might come at the cost of her own life.

Ross had demanded Calum arrive in three days' time at Castle Sween. That did not give Calum much time to work with Elspeth. The training wasn't because he anticipated Ross would harm Elspeth, but more than that, he feared what might happen to her later in her life. Clans were often at war and he had come to care for her— far more than he should. No matter where she went, he wanted to ensure she could protect herself, especially after his own people had instilled such fear in her for so many years.

Still, he wished she had not insisted on going, that he could keep her in Ireland where she would not be involved. Especially if Ross got hold of Elspeth once more, then Calum would lose his bargaining power and would have no choice but for his people to fight.

But she was right. If anyone could convince Ross that Calum meant peace, it was her. Especially when her letter had already had more success than his.

Regardless of the outcome, after their arrival in Scotland, Calum would doubtless never see Elspeth again. It was a realisation that rendered him bereft.

If nothing else, he wanted to leave her with the gift of knowing how to defend herself. A skill it did not sound like anyone else had ever had any interest in teaching her and one that was vital for a woman to know. Especially one in a position of power, like Elspeth.

The first of the two days flew by in a series of repeated dagger throws until she once more sank the blade into the target on every try. Calum tried to keep his distance, touching her as little as possible, doing all he could to avoid temptation. But she was a flame and he was but a simple moth, drawn to her brilliance, her magnificence, wanting nothing more than to be enraptured by her.

The second day was even more of a struggle with close combat as the two of them worked in the shade, lunging and jabbing with blunted weapons as he taught her how best to evade and attack. The time was bittersweet and poignant with the realisation that this would be their last opportunity to train together.

'I want you to reconsider coming to Scotland,' Calum said during a brief pause from their training while they both caught their breath. 'I'd prefer you remain here on the morrow.'

Elspeth shook her head, her brow glistening with a light sheen of sweat despite the cold day. 'Nay.'

Her hair had been bound back in a braid that had been carefully plaited to still cover her ears. The small note of self-consciousness endeared him to her all the more.

'I was afraid you were going to say that,' he said.

'Don't try to distract me.' She crouched low, her face set with a determination he had come to know well. It made him admire her for her efforts, for her inability to ever accept defeat.

He couldn't stop the grin from spreading over his lips. 'One last sparring and then we must prepare for supper, aye?'

She nodded and tucked her dagger close to her body to prevent it from being seen, exactly as he had instructed her. There was so much more he still wished he could teach her, so much more time he longed to spend in her company, but the days passed too quickly.

If nothing else, the amount they had been able to train would give her a bit of knowledge in defending herself if she practised, which he knew she would. Between that and her tenacity, she would do better than most noblewomen in her position for certes.

And perhaps it was best for her to be out of his sight. As he spent more and more time with her, she lodged herself more firmly in his thoughts.

She charged at him suddenly and smoothly swept the dagger from where she had it hidden against her waist. As the weapon came towards him, he blocked her with his forearm and ducked. She immediately withdrew in preparation for a second attack—exactly as he had shown her.

Before he could fully straighten, she was whipping the blade at him once more. He arched back to avoid the dull edge. However, as he did so, she hooked her leg behind his and tugged so it fell from beneath him. He pitched backwards, falling hard into the soft grass.

She appeared above him with a triumphant grin. 'I win.'

'You've improved.' He pushed to his feet. 'Though these are only a few basic moves, aye?'

'It's better than any I've learned elsewhere.' She shrugged. 'At least I have a chance of somewhat protecting myself in the future.' She pursed her lips. 'Thank you for this gift. You didn't have to do it. I know you took time away from your people to help me with something I've always wanted.'

'I want to ensure you'll always be safe,' Calum said. 'Perhaps it's selfish.' He shouldn't have confessed as much, but there was no drawing it back once it had been said. Especially not with a lass like Elspeth.

She lifted her brows. 'How so?'

He looked up at the sky where the afternoon sun was beginning to lower. 'Perhaps I want something for you to remember me by.'

When she didn't reply, he turned to her and found the playful look on her face had become more serious. 'I won't ever forget you. What you've done for your people. What you've done for me.' She smiled softly at him. 'You're a good man, Calum Campbell.'

'I didn't think I'd ever hear those words from a Mac-Millan.'

She smiled in reply. 'A fortnight ago, I didn't think I'd ever have said them. I'm glad things have changed.' She pursed her lips. 'I wish...'

She glanced away.

'Aye?' He nodded for her to continue.

She shook her head as tears welled in her eyes, turning the pale green to a brilliant emerald. 'I don't want Ross to hurt you.'

He took her hand in his. There was a slight blister against her palm, one he hadn't noticed and one she had never complained of.

'I promise to be careful,' he soothed.

'I wish things were different between our clans.' She searched his gaze with her own.

There was more in her eyes than she was saying. It was those unspoken words that he longed most to hear.

'After this, they will be,' he insisted.

Though he felt as sceptical as she looked at such a declaration. They would never see one another again. She would wed Leith MacLachlan and he would live his life with only these memories to sustain him.

'This is our last time together alone,' she said softly.

An ache filled his chest and he gave a solemn nod.

'When I didn't let you kiss me after the feast,' she rushed. 'It wasn't because I didn't want to. While there was no formal betrothal to Leith, I felt an obligation to him.'

Calum gently squeezed her hand. 'You don't have to explain.'

'I want to.' She stepped closer and her breath quickened. 'I wanted to kiss you then. To see what it was like to have your lips on mine and your hands...' Her cheeks went red with a ferocious blush. 'I don't want you to think I didn't want it. That I don't want you.'

He swallowed, but it did little to alleviate his dry throat.

Her admission left his mind reeling. He'd worried he had been too forward or that she might still be afraid of him.

But now…now he knew that she wanted him as badly. A stronger man would have walked away. He *should* walk away.

She put her free hand to his chest, leaving the other holding his as she moved closer. That tantalising powdery scent of her teased at his senses as her skirt brushed against his shins. His heart slammed with unnatural force within the confines of his chest.

'What are you doing?' he asked.

'Making sure I don't regret never having done this.' She pushed up onto her toes and pressed her mouth to his.

She was sweeter than he had imagined, a honeyed taste flavoured her innocent kiss, and her lips were as soft as rose petals warmed by the sun. He wanted to pull her to him and continue to kiss her thus, to relish what he had just sampled and deepen it to taste more.

But she drew away and he did not reach for her to pull her back. What she had given him was a gift, one she was comfortable giving in light of their circumstances and one he would cherish for ever.

For after tomorrow, they would never see one another again.

Chapter Eleven

Grey skies greeted Elspeth the following morning. Moisture hung thick in the air as she mounted her steed and rain drizzled upon them as they started a journey that would take several hours to meet the ship that would carry them back to Scotland.

The Campbell land in Ireland might be inhospitable, but Elspeth had found the people to be kind and with a giving spirit that enabled them to rise above their hardships. Among them, she had felt welcome, with a comradery she had not known for far too long.

She and Calum had greeted one another with silent nods that morning as they'd mounted their horses. After all, what more was there to say to one another in public that had not yet been said when they were alone?

Or rather what was there left that *could* be said.

She had confessed enough to a man whose affection she could not accept in a land where she could not belong. In a day's time, she would be back in Scotland, fulfilling her obligations for the sake of her family and her clan.

A woman's duty.

It's what she was always meant to do, even if it left

her with a sensation that the life was being choked out of her, leaving her suffocating under the responsibility.

An icy wind cut across the Irish landscape as rain pelted down at them from swollen clouds. Alison had washed and readied Elspeth's green kirtle for the journey, the attire befitting a noblewoman, but Elspeth immediately missed the comfort of the homespun cloth. The chatelaine had tried to convince Elspeth to take the sunburst necklace, but she had refused. Not only as it had belonged to Calum's mother, but for what it meant to him—hope for a better future. She would not take that away from him.

Elspeth had her memories from her time with the Campbell clan—with Calum—she needed nothing more. Indeed, physical reminders of such emotional joy might be too painful in her new life.

The hours in the saddle riding towards the coast left Elspeth stiff and freezing despite having pulled her cloak tightly about her. While the waxed linen kept out most of the rain, there was little one could do to stave off the savage gusts shoving at them in repeated assaults.

At long last, the sea came into view, an angry black-grey beneath the darkened sky, the large ship docked as close as possible. A small boat with a handful of oars waited on the shore with several crew members lingering around it. Elspeth's stomach fluttered with nervousness.

This was it.

The chance to save the Campbell clan, her opportunity to convince Ross of Calum's sincerity. And she could not fail.

The sky was nearly black as night behind the wide canvas sails of the ship and the sea rippled with white-capped waves. Though Elspeth was no sailor, she was aware this would not be an easy journey.

Her assumption was echoed in Calum's frown as he stared hard at the sea.

'We don't have the time to wait for this to pass,' Elspeth said. 'Especially not with how great the rains have been recently. We might well be waiting here for a sennight.'

'Aye, that appears to be the way of it.' He ran a hand through his dark hair, leaving it even more mussed than normal.

They boarded the small boat, which bucked and rocked as it was pushed into the water. Elspeth's stomach roiled with the motion, but she did not speak up. If her memory served correctly, the journey would only take a few hours.

Surely she could endure such discomfort for a few hours.

As the men rowed the wooden vessel towards the ship, water swelled up around them and washed over the edge, bathing them all in frigid sea water. Elspeth kept her toes propped on the bench and off the bottom of the boat to keep her hem from sitting in a pool of water.

By the time they approached the ship, her head spun with the incessant rocking and the contents of her stomach had long since curdled.

'The ship is larger,' Calum said over roar of rain pouring down into the sea. 'You won't be able to feel the waves as much.'

Elspeth gave a miserable nod. When they finally reached the ship, she eagerly climbed the ladder to the wide deck. However, the relief she had anticipated did not come. She closed her eyes as she was rocked back and forth, but it made the sensation worse. Sweat prickled at her palms and brow despite the bitter cold. She opened her eyes and tried to find a place on the deck to lock her gaze in the hope it might help.

Calum's brows pinched with concern as he regarded her. Suddenly self-conscious of her appearance, even in such a miserable state, Elspeth smoothed her hair back.

'Perhaps I ought to rest,' she suggested weakly, unsure if she could even be heard over the storm.

'I'll show you to the captain's quarters, though you probably know the way yourself.' He winked at her in a bid to be playful, but her lips could scarcely lift to smile in return.

A particularly nasty wave slammed into the ship, knocking her off balance. Calum reached out, fast as lightning and steadied her. 'If you continue to feel unwell, come out to the deck. The fresh air might help, aye?'

She nodded and hastened into the captain's quarters, relieved to find that it had been outfitted once more with essentials for a more comfortable journey. She hung her cloak on a hook and collapsed onto the bed, nestling her head against a thick pillow as she pulled several blankets over her cold, wet clothing.

But as she lay there, the rocking seemed to grow worse. Rather than be lulled to sleep, her stomach fought every jolt, every sway.

She squeezed her eyes shut, willing the sensation to go away. Time had passed, though she knew not how much. She could bear the misery no longer. She pushed up from the bed, nearly falling as the entire room tilted to the right.

Staggering on the slanting floor, her body went immediately hot and her mouth filled with saliva. She was going to be ill.

Men were shouting on the other side of the door, but she paid them little mind as she pushed outside. Rain slapped her in the face, stinging and choking her all at once. The violence of it was so instantaneous that for a slip of a moment, her need to purge had somewhat abated.

The relief did not last long, and she managed to make it to the rail in time to heave the contents of her stomach overboard.

'Elspeth.' Her name sounded behind her, nearly a whisper against the cacophony of the powerful storm and roiling waves.

And they were indeed roiling. The sea rose and fell around them in great extremes, going higher than the bound sails and sinking down in massive valleys that the bow fell into with a shuddering crash.

She gripped the rail as the entire vessel pitched first upward and then slammed down. The impact was such that her fingers were wrenched from their hold on the sodden wood and she was flung backwards.

Strong arms caught her and turned her about. Calum was there, holding her in his strong embrace, her rock amid a wild storm. His hair was plastered to his head and his clothes were completely drenched.

'You cannot be out here,' he shouted to be heard about the storm. 'It's not safe.'

'I'm so very ill,' Elspeth said. Or tried to say. The wind snatched her words away, carrying them off into the churning sea.

'Go back to the captain's quarters.' Even as he said it, he guided her towards the stairs leading to the stuffy room from which she had just escaped. His hands continued to hold onto her, firm and careful, keeping her upright on the slippery deck.

An indistinguishable shout came from overhead and the boat tilted hard to the right. Calum braced himself and wrapped his arms around her.

'Hold on,' he cried.

A massive wave rose over their ship, higher than the masts, like a great beast emerging from the depths. It hovered over them for a heart-stopping moment before collapsing down upon them.

The force of it was tremendous, like a sack of grain dropping on Elspeth's head. The pain of it mingled with the shock of the icy waves and in that instant, her brain churned with confusion, not knowing which way was up or down, left or right.

Water swirled around her, every which way, its suction like a giant trying to rip her limbs from her torso. It pulled at her skirts, her hair, so they were suddenly yanked sideways and she was dragged away from Calum's solid grip.

Salt water clouded her vision but not enough that she couldn't make out the edge of the ship rushing towards her and the ominous sea churning beyond, waiting to swallow her whole.

She was gone. Calum groped in the swirling water as the wave withdrew back towards the vast sea. Nothing.

Elspeth had been pulled from his arms.

His heart caught in his throat.

Lightning flashed overhead and revealed a brilliant streak of red amid the water that poured towards the starboard side of the boat. She was going to be swept overboard.

Calum launched himself from where he stood so he was as much a part of the wave as Elspeth as he stretched desperately for her. His hand brushed something. He closed his fingers around it and held on with every ounce of strength he had as he braced his legs for the impact against the side of the boat.

The wave drained away in a massive rush as his feet slammed against the hard wooden edge. With everything he had left in him, he jerked his hand back, flinging Elspeth behind him.

She landed with a hard slap onto the deck and remained where she lay. Motionless.

Calum scrambled to his feet and rushed to her. She was a pile of dark cloth and wet, red hair.

'Elspeth?' He swept her into his arms and rushed her to the captain's quarters where he could see properly without the driving rain battering against his eyes.

He slammed the door behind them as if doing so would keep out the wrath of the storm. Her face was pale, even in the dim light of the cabin and she was not breathing. He turned her onto her back and slapped a hand between her shoulder blades.

She coughed abruptly as water splashed onto the floor, immediately followed by a harsh and ragged inhale.

He patted her several times more on the back for good measure and let her catch her breath before turning her slowly to face him. She blinked in shock, her eyes widening with the realisation of what had almost happened to her.

Calum's own heart caught with that same fear.

He had nearly lost her. Had she gone into the waves, there would have been nothing he could have done to save her. Not in such a violent sea.

Emotion swelled in the back of his throat. He knew his concern should be about what her loss would have meant to his clan, but in that moment all he could think of was what her loss would have meant to him.

He cared for Elspeth—aye, he knew that. But he hadn't realised to what extent. Not until he had very nearly lost her.

'Calum?' she asked in a raspy voice.

'You're safe now.' Or at least safe from being washed away. The men who handled the ship were sailors, men who knew well how to avoid the draw of the sea after such a wave. Thus far there had not been any announcements of a man overboard and Calum didn't expect there would be one.

'You saved me,' she breathed.

He nearly hadn't. He had actually let her go. The force of the wave had jerked her from his grasp. Because he hadn't held on tight enough. And it had nearly been her demise.

'I was being sucked into the sea,' she said hoarsely. 'It almost had me, Calum.'

'But I have you now,' he said firmly. 'Not the sea.'

Tears sparkled in her eyes and her chin, which she so often lifted in defiance, began to tremble as emotion overpowered even her stubbornness.

He drew her against him, embracing her. Her arms came around him and clung to him as though she expected the wave to come at her once more. She gave a strangled sob.

'You're safe, lass.' He stroked her slender back, his fingers tangling in her hair.

Her shoulders shook and she began to sob in earnest.

In all the time he had known her, never had he seen her cry. She was a fighter, a woman who didn't give up no matter the cost. Seeing her break down now showed him a vulnerable side of her. One that tore at his heart and left her presence permanently embedded there.

The ship continued to pitch and roll as he held her as her tears fell and warmed the chill of sea water at his shoulder. After several moments, she pushed away, swiping at her eyes.

'Forgive me, I'm not one to cry often.' She shook her head and gave a sheepish, embarrassed smile.

'Don't worry.' He ran a hand over her damp cheek. 'I know you're tough as a warrior. Remember, I'm the one you headbutted.'

'The wave was just so sudden,' she said starkly. 'And the realisation that I could've been…' Her words tapered off and her mouth pinched together in a thin line.

'You're safe now,' he repeated and resisted the urge to draw her towards him once more.

She trusted him enough to cry in front of him. He was grateful for it and glad he could offer her comfort.

But that had to be all there was between them. No matter how much it pulled at his heart to let it be.

Outside, the waves had begun to calm, though the ship still swayed. As the sun eventually peeked through the clouds, it revealed a green pallor to Elspeth's skin. Her hair was in a tangled red mass over her shoulders and slung about her back. The care Alison had put into the kirtle was now wasted as it had become a sodden, wrinkled mess.

'We're almost to Scotland now,' Calum said, hopeful that what he said was true.

'I don't want to go to Scotland.' Elspeth regarded Calum with a miserable expression. 'I would rather endure this journey a thousand times over than marry Leith.

I know as a woman, it is my duty to the clan, but I don't want to.'

It was exactly what Calum had wanted to hear, yet he also hated it. For they could not recast their lot in life.

'I would rather it was you,' Elspeth reached for him.

Calum could resist no longer and drew her into his arms. 'I would rather it was me as well.'

He shouldn't have said it. He had his own obligation to his clan, and it did not include wedding Elspeth. Not when she was so integral to their peace.

She pulled in a soft breath as she gazed up at him with such longing, it nearly tore his heart from his chest.

He wanted to kiss her then. God, how he wanted to kiss her. The longing for it made his soul ache and his palms tense with the need to skim them over her curves. He wanted nothing more than to capture her lips, to brand her as his.

He recalled the sweetness of her mouth when she had pressed the chaste kiss to his lips the night after their practice with the dagger. Recollections of it had followed him into sleep that night, had roused him in the morning and was a comfortable companion as they crossed the sodden Irish landscape to the ship they now sailed upon.

Elspeth wet her lips by pressing her tongue between them, leaving them tantalisingly moist with temptation. Her gaze searched his, as though weighing something. She began to reach for him, then stopped partway and a pained expression pulled at her brows. 'But we know our duty.'

Calum swallowed down his disappointment and forced gratitude into its place. Aye, they did know their duty. She would return to the life she was expected to fulfil and he would do all he could to win his people's land back without violence.

Except now it wasn't enough. Now he also wanted her.

He nodded and shifted away from her, putting space between them before the lure of temptation was too great. Reminding himself once more, she was not his to love.

And it was nearly time that both of them would see that understanding realised.

Chapter Twelve

Elspeth had never been more miserable in her entire life. Even though her stomach was empty, it continued to remain unsettled, rolling with the ocean swells. The storm had ebbed away, thanks be to God, or she may not have survived at all.

But it was more than her nausea, or her freezing, wet clothing or even the way the salt water had left her wet hair in a sticky gnarled mess. Her greatest affliction was the breath-stealing pain in her chest every time she thought of Calum.

She didn't want to marry Leith. Being with him had never woken any semblance of passion within her. No matter how much he cared for her, she knew in her heart that she would never love him. Yet she knew with the equal certainty that she could not bring herself to betray him.

Even if this might be the only time in her life she would ever have the opportunity to taste passion, even if the possibility of love was standing before her now, it didn't matter. She would have to turn her back on Calum and what was growing between them.

The clatter of an anchor rattled through the hull and Elspeth cringed at what she knew that meant. The door opened and Calum entered, returned from having seen to the sailors to ensure all was well. She wanted to run into his arms, to be held in his powerful embrace once more.

She got to her feet and his eyes widened. 'Your skirt, Elspeth.'

She dropped her head and down at her kirtle. A massive rip showed down the length of her skirt, most likely from where he had grabbed her and tugged her back from the pull of the ocean that had threatened to wash her away.

She gasped in horror and picked at the ruined fabric to inspect the damage. The tear went from her waist all the way down to the hem. Her chemise was visible through the damaged skirt, nearly transparent with seawater.

She hadn't noticed it earlier in her distress with the folds of her gown bundled in her lap.

Her hands went to her hair, touching the damp, tangled mass. Any attempts to finger comb it would be futile. Not when it was so tacky with sea water. Despite the icy chill of her hands and feet, her face was still hot from having sobbed earlier and her eyes were gritty from her tears.

She had wanted to meet with Ross so he would be convinced that she had been well cared for. Now she was going to him looking as though she'd been thoroughly ravished.

She nearly spoke her concern aloud, but stopped herself at the last minute. Calum would grasp any excuse to keep her from the meeting with Ross. It had been mentioned enough times that she suspected Calum had a bad feeling about it. She would do nothing to perpetuate his unease.

Regardless, she knew her discussion with her brother might be the only thing to actually convince Ross, even with her looking so dishevelled.

'My skirt is torn.' Elspeth tried her best to pinch the fabric together.

Calum's eyes narrowed. 'Elspeth...'

'It's fine,' she said. 'Please, let us remove ourselves from this ship.'

He nodded, his stare fixed still on the ripped kirtle. No doubt he was thinking the same things she had.

In truth, it didn't matter what she looked like, only what she said to her brother. She quit the room, grateful to suck in mouthfuls of the damp, salty air and endured the small boat ride to the shore where they waited for their poor horses to be retrieved from their stalls below. Never had she been happier to have solid ground under her feet. But even as she stood upon the firm surface, it seemed to roll and sway beneath her.

She leaned to offset the sensation, nearly staggering.

Calum reached for her and helped steady her. 'The sensation will abate in a while.'

And it did. Though not soon enough that Elspeth would ever be convinced to board another ship again.

Once the horses were unloaded and fully recovered from the rough voyage they'd all endured, Elspeth, Calum and Bram mounted their steeds and made their way to the outlying area of Castle Sween where Ross would meet them.

The wind whipped at Elspeth as she rode and helped to dry her tresses somewhat, though the stickiness in her hair kept her from being able to tame it into anything respectable. There was nothing for it but to appear as she was.

They were nearly to the meeting point when two horses appeared in the distance, heading towards them, one with a cart being drawn behind it. As they rode closer, it was impossible not to recognise them. Elspeth's heart caught in her throat.

Ross.

And Leith.

Within seconds, they were face to face, their steeds drawing up short. Ross looked to Elspeth and roared in outrage. 'What have you done to my sister?'

He leapt from his horse, his blade giving a menacing hiss as he pulled it free from the sheath.

'Nay, Ross,' Elsbeth cried out. 'He's seen me well cared for.'

Ross's face went uncharacteristically red. 'That is not what your appearance suggests.'

Leith guided his horse closer to her, the cart behind it clattering. 'Elspeth, come with me.'

'Nay.' She backed her steed from the man to whom she had grudgingly stayed honourable. 'We were caught in a fierce storm on the sea and I was nearly washed overboard. Calum saved me.'

'He saved you?' Leith asked wryly, the bitter sarcasm on his face robbing him of his handsomeness.

'You wouldn't need to be saved if you hadn't been taken from us in the first place.' Ross fixed his gaze beyond Elspeth to Calum. 'Get off your horse and come fight me like a man, Campbell.'

'He wants peace.' Elspeth edged her horse closer to Ross. 'His people don't have enough food in Ireland. The land is practically barren and they are starving. What I wrote to you in my letter was voluntary and by my own hand. Everything I said is true. He only took me as a desperate means of finding a peaceful resolution between our clans. He wants to return to Scotland so that his clan can have fertile land to farm once more. It was his father who wanted to fight, not him.'

'Is that so?' Ross asked, disbelief lacing his words. 'Is it his father who continues to attack our men in the colours of the Campbells? Is it his father who has razed several villages, leaving many innocent souls slain? If so, pray tell me how the man can accomplish such a feat when he is dead?'

She didn't dare look at Calum. Doing so would only make her appear to doubt him.

And she did not.

Did she?

She leapt from her horse. 'Ross, please listen.'

His gaze went to her torn kirtle and wild rage blazed in his eyes. 'Be gone from this discussion,' his voice trembled as he clearly tried to maintain his control. 'Campbell, fight me like a bloody man.'

Angry tears filled her eyes. Before she could protest further, Leith was there, pulling her back, away from Ross as Calum leapt from his horse. Calum ran towards her, but Ross cut him off with a thrust of his blade.

'Nay,' she cried, too stunned to move. Had her thoughts not been caught in an unexpected maelstrom of turmoil, she might have immediately fought Leith off. But as it was, she did not fully recover herself until they were already several paces away.

'Stop.' She twisted in Leith's grasp. 'Release me at once.'

This man was the one she had held forefront in her mind while in Ireland, granting him a loyalty he did not deserve. All to be manhandled into submission like an errant child.

'I'll not let you back with him,' Leith said in her ear as he continued to draw her away from Calum and Ross as their swords clashed in a sharp ring of metal on metal. Bram had also leapt from his horse as though he meant to help, but stood back as several soldiers approached and restrained him. MacMillan men.

Her brother was fighting with the man she cared greatly for. And she wanted neither of them to be harmed.

'Cease this at once,' Elspeth demanded.

Leith's hold tightened on her. 'He's clearly had you, but I'll still wed you, Elspeth. You needn't worry about the state of your virtue with me.'

She stopped fighting long enough to cast a look of horrified indignation up at Leith, who used that moment to toss her into the crude cart being pulled behind his horse. The bottom was covered in thick hay, which she floundered in while he secured a thick canvas over the top.

Elspeth struggled to her knees and pushed at the canvas. It held fast, tied deftly from the outside.

She gave an angry cry of indignation and pushed at it, but the canvas did not budge. The cart lurched forward and she was knocked hard to the right, bounced around as Leith took off at a fast clip with the cart rattling behind him.

And all the while, Calum was getting further and further behind her, left to the mercy of a very angry Ross.

'I don't want to fight you.' Yet even as Calum spoke, he lifted his sword to block an attack.

'What did you do to her?' Ross asked in a cold, low voice.

Calum stepped back, putting space between them. 'I held her in Ireland for a spell while I waited to hear from you.' He wanted to look behind him, to ensure Elspeth was a safe distance away, but he didn't trust the man standing in front of him not to use the opportunity to attack.

'Elspeth was well treated,' he insisted. 'I would never do anything to hurt her.'

'Elspeth?' Ross's eyes narrowed. 'You're using her Christian name now?'

'I would never hurt her,' Calum repeated vehemently.

Ross uttered a curse under his breath and the tip of his sword dipped to the ground. 'She cares for you.' Red suffused his face. 'And you for her.'

'She is to marry Leith MacLachlan.' But even as Calum tried to deny his affection for Elspeth, his protest emerged without conviction.

'Aye, she is.' Ross stepped closer and lifted his weapon with intent once more. 'And you'd best not even entertain the idea of wedding her yourself.'

Calum had not actually had such a thought. At least, not until that very moment when the suggestion planted a seed that immediately blossomed into an idea of what such a life could be. Their clans united in peace. Elspeth holding a bairn in her arms at his side and clansmen who were well-fed, happy and safe.

'You're thinking it now,' Ross accused as he lunged, weapon drawn.

Calum jerked back from the Chieftain of the MacMillan clan, refusing to battle Elspeth's brother. Alexander Campbell had already done the MacMillan clan an egregious offence when he'd killed Elspeth's da and uncle.

Calum would not now repeat the same mistake with her eldest brother.

Wherever Leith had taken Elspeth, they would doubtless be quite a distance away by now. Calum needed to get free of Ross, to go to her. The urgency of it pressed upon him.

Ross charged at Calum once more, swinging his blade with lethal accuracy. Calum blocked the blow, though the effort behind the strike was enough to make his bones rattle. Ross scarcely gave him a chance to recover before arcing his blade towards Calum again.

'I don't want to fight you,' Calum said through gritted teeth.

'I'll die before I let you take Elspeth again,' Ross said with all the protectiveness of an older brother.

Bram was held by two of Ross's guards off to the side. He met Calum's eye and nodded.

Immediately Bram pulled his blade free and attacked the two men. Calum could not see what transpired between them with his own battle with Ross, but the ring of metal colliding from his sword mingled with that of Bram's.

There was a reason Calum always kept Bram at his side. The man not only offered excellent advice, but he was also the most accomplished warrior Calum had ever seen. Calum did not worry about his righthand man.

'I don't want to fight,' Calum said again. 'Please, let us cease this before any more have to die. Let's call a truce.'

Ross did not bother to reply as he swung again.

The constant clang of striking weapons coming from Bram's location was not as rapid now, which meant only one guard likely remained.

Calum continued to block Ross's blows without fighting back, wanting nothing more than to go after Leith.

Suddenly, the sound of battle where Bram was went silent.

Ross and Calum looked at each other once then simultaneously gazed to where the MacMillan guards lay dead.

'I told you I don't want to fight,' Calum said softly.

Ross kept his blade swinging, his face calm with a resolve that sent a shiver down Calum's spine. Calum whipped his own weapon before him, protecting himself from a strike that would likely have cut him in half.

Ross pulled his blade back, preparing to strike again. In only that blink of an instant, Bram was there, assuming the fight for Calum, freeing him to go after Elspeth.

'Don't kill him,' he told Bram. 'And don't die.'

Bram gave him an exasperated look of incredulity, but Calum didn't stay long enough to offer a supportive smirk. He dashed to his own horse and tore off in the direction of the cart.

The wooden wheels did not travel well through the soggy earth. Certainly, it could not go at the speed Calum could on his fastest horse, the one he'd specifically chosen for this meeting. While Elspeth had faith in her brother's willingness to listen when it involved the Campbells, Calum did not.

It appeared he had been correct and now he was glad to have brought his fastest horses.

He raced over the countryside, following the twin grooves that cut deep into the earth, revealing the rich soil like an open wound beneath. His horse thundered over the ground as if seeking Elspeth with the same desperation as Calum.

It was as if they were on the ship again and the waves

were dragging her from his grasp, leaving him with not only the possibility of losing a peaceful existence for his people but also Elspeth herself.

He had to give her up at some point, he knew that. But not now. Not like this. Not before he'd fully confessed his feelings towards her.

For he wanted at least that chance before she slipped away from his life for ever.

Chapter Thirteen

The dagger.

The thought came immediately to Elspeth. However, the cart rattled with such violence as it sped over the rough Scottish terrain that she could scarcely grab the weapon from her belt. Finally, she clasped the hilt in her palm and raised it to punch through the canvas.

But before she could, there was a great bang followed by a sharp drop that jarred Elspeth, pitching her to the side so she was forced to catch herself to keep from being thrown to the opposite end. The impact was so violent that the hilt slipped from her grip, for when she straightened, the blade was no longer in her hand.

Desperation seized her as she began frantically patting through the hay in search of her weapon. For what seemed an eternity, she continued to sift through until at last her palm met cold metal.

She snatched up the dagger and shoved it through the canvas overhead. Frigid air washed over her as she rent the hole large enough to thrust her body through. The cart was travelling fast, jostling and bumping over the countryside.

Leith looked over his shoulder at her. 'Elspeth, nay— get back down.'

'Stop the cart,' she cried.

'I'm getting you to safety.' He alternated between glancing back at her and returning his focus to the path in front of them.

'I don't need to be saved.' She stood up in the cart, braced by the torn canvas on either side of her. 'If you don't stop this cart, I'll jump out.'

He pulled on the reins and the horse finally drew to a stop. The creaking rattle that had been so deafening moments before now went completely silent with only the wind rustling through the dry grass.

'He's not the man you think he is,' Elspeth said, her voice ringing out in the quiet. 'He's not like his da. The reason he took me was to try to negotiate with Ross, to come to a resolution where his clan can return to their land without more fighting.'

And now he might be killed for his efforts to obtain peace. A frantic need spurred through her once more. She had to get back to Ross, to try to convince him.

Leith leapt down from his horse and approached her. 'Calum Campbell lied to you, Elspeth. His men have been attacking villages for the entire time you've been in Ireland.'

She shook her head. 'That cannot be true. He would never do that.'

'It is, Elle,' he said, falling back on her childhood name.

'He's not a violent man,' Elspeth insisted. 'He's kind and giving, he is loyal to his people and is burdened by how many have died.'

'You speak as though he didn't hurt you.' Leith's gaze slid down her kirtle to where her skirt was torn. 'Did he?'

Though Leith claimed to not care about the state of her maidenhead, the weight of his assessment fell over her as he clearly gauged if she had been ravished by Calum or not.

Now she wished she had.

'He saved me from being washed overboard,' she said in a brittle tone. 'It's why I look the way I do. He was as good to me as he is to his people. Come, please, Leith— we cannot let Ross kill him.'

Indeed, it might already be too late. Elspeth's heart kicked against her ribs at such a thought.

'All that matters is that you're home and we can keep you safe.' Leith smiled up at her. He was a handsome man when he smiled like that, with deep blue eyes and a dimple that showed in his right cheek. His sandy-coloured hair had gold running through it from the sun and his body was strong from his training with a sword. He was the kind of man women followed with their eyes when he strode by.

But he was also the type who noticed their attention and preened for it.

'Leith…' She shook her head, unsure what to tell him.

'I'm pleased to see you again.' He held up a hand to help her from the cart. 'I worried something might have happened to you.' His pleasant expression faltered. 'I brought the cart in case you couldn't walk.'

She looked back from the direction they had travelled. Calum was battling Ross there. Her heart couldn't bear it for either one of them to be hurt. Or worse…

She accepted Leith's hand and jumped down.

'We must go back.' She moved swiftly towards the horse, meaning to untether it from the cumbersome cart. 'We have to stop them from fighting.'

Leith grabbed her arm and tugged her towards him. She shoved away. 'Stop. We must go back.'

A wounded look touched Leith's face at her immediate rejection. 'What are you doing?'

But rather than leave her to go the horse, he recovered and reached for her again, this time drawing her to him with a firm grip that pinched her skin.

'You're hurting me.' She twisted to free herself, but he only held on more tightly.

The sound of thunder rumbled in the distance. Nay. Not thunder. Hooves pounding against the earth.

Elspeth's attention snapped back to the trail as Calum came into view, racing towards them on his mount.

'He won't take you back to Ireland,' Leith growled in her ear. 'Not this time. Not while I'm here.'

Calum came to an abrupt stop before them and dismounted, his sword in his hand. Without blood upon the blade. Elspeth exhaled a relieved sigh.

Still, her heart clenched, for Ross would not have let him go without a fight. 'My brother?' she gasped.

'Bram is fighting him,' Calum said. 'I've told him not to kill him.'

Which meant Bram might well die. A sob choked from Elspeth.

'You'll not get her again,' Leith stepped backwards, dragging Elspeth with him. As he did so, he gripped her arm with such malice that she cried out in pain.

Calum's eyes flashed with outrage. In the blink of an eye, he charged at Leith and swung his fist. Elspeth turned her face to the side to ensure she was not struck as well as the thwack of Calum's knuckles connected with Leith's jaw.

The brutal hold on Elspeth's arm relaxed. She twisted from Leith's grip as he staggered back.

'You'll pay for that, you filthy Campbell,' Leith growled as he tugged his blade free of its scabbard.

'Nay,' Elspeth shouted.

'He hurt you,' Calum said vehemently.

'I'm not injured...' Neither were paying her any mind as they circled one another, intent on fighting.

In that swift instant, she knew there was only one man she cared for. And only one thing to do.

'Leith, I cannot wed you,' she said forcefully.

He turned to her in shocked offence. 'Because he took you? You said he didn't touch you—'

'Nay, he didn't...' She drew a deep breath, steeling herself to speak the truth after all this time. Her words would wound Leith, she knew, but they had to be said. 'I cannot marry you because I don't love you.'

Leith blinked, his expression one of incredulity. 'What did you say?'

Her heart slammed in her chest, but she stood her ground. This needed to be said and he needed to understand. 'I cannot marry you because I don't love you.'

Leith shot an angry glare at Calum. 'Is it him?'

Suddenly she was breathless.

Aye. It was Calum. He had shown her how she could burn with desire and how her nights could smoulder with longing simply by thinking of him.

What's more, he was a man she truly admired. A man who cared more for his people than he did of his appearance or his effect on the opposite sex, like Leith.

Aye, the way she felt had everything to do with Calum.

His gaze weighted on her and it was all she could do to keep from looking his way. Instead, she met Leith's blue eyes. 'It's you, Leith,' she said truthfully. 'I've never wanted to wed you.'

He pulled at his collar, appearing to suffer some level of discomfort. He flicked a glance towards Calum, as humiliation reddened his cheeks. 'We've talked about it since we were bairns.'

Ire rushed through her. Had he not listened to her at all in the years they had known one another?

But she already knew the answer. He had not. It was so typical of him that she ought to have expected it. He only ever thought of what he was going to say rather than listen to her.

'Nay,' she said with finality. 'You talked about it. You asked me to promise I'd wed you, but I never agreed to it.'

'We're betrothed now,' he protested, anger edging into his voice.

'It was never formally announced in a church.' She folded her arms over her chest. 'It was never signed by Ross. I never agreed to it.'

'You don't have to agree to it,' Leith said irritably. 'You're a woman.'

She gritted her teeth. 'I don't love you.'

'You will, over time,' Leith said quietly.

Elspeth bit her lip, hating the sympathy welling inside her. 'I don't think so. I've always regarded you as a brother. It couldn't ever be anything more.'

'Elspeth,' Leith stepped closer, reaching for her.

She stepped back and all the confidence drained from his stance.

'What of our clans?' Leith asked.

Elsbeth managed to keep herself from flinching. She was beholden to the MacMillan clan first and foremost.

'By convincing Ross that Calum is an honourable

man, there will be no need for such clan alliances as there would be no threat of war.' Or at least she hoped.

Leith scoffed bitterly, the coldness of his demeanour creeping back. 'Ross would rather die than be on peaceful terms with a Campbell. Do you not remember your own da who suffered at his father's hands?' His lip curled in disgust. 'I release you from your obligation to wed me. For I would never marry a woman who was a traitor.'

The words were a dagger meant to strike her in the heart and they hit their mark. She staggered at the impact of his vitriol.

'Elspeth,' Calum called.

He stood beside Leith's horse where it had been unhitched from the cart and waved for her to join him. Elspeth did not hesitate.

'Forgive me if I've hurt you,' she said to Leith quietly and ran from him, unable to take the fiery glint of hurt in his eyes a moment longer.

She swiftly mounted Leith's horse as Calum climbed up on his and together they were off. Though to where or for how long, Elspeth knew not.

All she knew was that she had just gambled everything and hoped she did not lose.

Calum looked over his shoulder to ensure no one followed behind them.

Of course no one was. Leith would be able to do nothing with a horseless cart but wait for one of his men or one of the MacMillan men to retrieve him from the empty hills.

'Where are we going?' Elspeth asked. The wind tore at her hair, making it stream behind her like ribbons of fire.

Her cheeks were flushed from the brisk wind. She looked fiercely alive and more beautiful than he'd ever seen her.

Calum regarded her, awed by the incredible woman that she was, and the depth of her trust in him. She had sacrificed much in the last few hours.

For him.

And now she was free. Not just from the risk of being taken back by Ross, but from the bonds that had tied her to Lieth.

'There's a cave not far from here,' Calum replied. 'Bram will meet us there at daybreak on the morrow.'

'Daybreak?'

'He won't kill Ross, nor will he allow himself to be slain,' Calum reassured her and explained. 'Bram is not only a skilled warrior, he is also very clever. If anyone can find their way out of a battle, it's him. However, once escaped, he prefers to remain hidden on his own through the night to ensure he's not being followed.'

Elspeth nodded in understanding.

There was so much Calum wanted to say to her as they made their way to the cave set off to the side of the beach. Yet the darkening of clouds overhead told them there would soon be another storm upon them. They needed to make haste to their shelter.

Before the sun could begin to set, they arrived on the edge of the shore where a deep cave had provided Calum and his men shelter over the last few months. First while they were scouting out the land, and then later when the attacks were underway.

Calum shuddered at the memory. He hated the ugliness of battle, how unnecessary it all was. But his decision to join his father in an effort to sway him from war had been in vain.

The wind picked up along the coastline, tugging at their clothes and hair. A flash of lightning in the distance warned of the approaching storm. They were running out of time.

'Bring your horse inside,' Calum instructed as he led his own into the cave.

It would keep them hidden well out of sight and protect their mounts from yet another downpour. The light was fading quickly, especially inside the cave. Calum set to work getting a fire lit in the small stone pit his men had created on one of their first nights staying in the cave.

No sooner had the flames crackled to life than a soft roar outside indicated the rain was coming down with force. Elspeth stared into the small blaze, her distant gaze indicative of tumultuous thoughts. And how could she not have them, when she no doubt feared for her brother's life?

In truth, Calum did as well. And for Bram's.

Ross was a formidable opponent and if Bram couldn't find a way to easily escape...

Nay, he couldn't think of it.

Calum sat beside Elspeth. Startled from her thoughts, she looked up at him, her expression soft with affection. 'I thought I would never see you again after today,' she said quietly.

He swallowed down the rise of emotion as the memory of his own palpable fear swelled within him. 'I thought I would never see you again either.' He longed to pull her against him and savour the feel of her body against his, the reminder that she had indeed lived. Instead, he reached for her hands, taking them within his own.

The air between them nearly crackled with their need for one another.

Elspeth looked away suddenly. 'I have to find a way to gain an audience with Ross without him taking me back to Castle Sween.' She shook her head, her irritation apparent. 'There has to be a way.'

'I don't think there will be.' Calum withdrew his hands from hers, knowing she was putting off his affection—and rightly so. This was where their focus needed to be—on tactics, on saving his people. 'The guards around him will be heavy until they are sure we've returned to Ireland.'

'Perhaps I can try speaking to Fergus,' Elspeth said. 'He's the more reasonable of my two brothers.'

'He doesn't have the power Ross does.'

'But he could speak with Ross.' Elspeth sat up straighter. 'I'll go to Fergus. He will need convincing, of course, but I think I can do it. And if they take me and keep me at Castle Barron, I will find a way to escape if they won't listen to me.'

Calum frowned. 'It's too dangerous.'

She gave a mirthless laugh. 'He is my brother. He won't harm me.'

'And if Ross disowns you?' Calum asked.

She drew in a hard breath that told him everything he needed to know. 'He wouldn't do that.'

A knot formed in Calum's gut, an immediate understanding that if she did indeed go to Castle Barron, he would likely never see her again. And if she was disowned, the burden of such a loss for his sake would stand between them for ever.

Like the stain of her father's blood on Campbell hands.

Firelight played off her face and glinted in her brilliant red hair. Just when he thought he might not have to bid her farewell, he once more understood this very well might be the last time he saw her.

He wanted to draw her to him, to press his mouth to hers and once more sample the sweetness of her lips. This time there would be no barrier of Leith MacLachlan standing between them. Only the very stark realisation that she was a far better woman than Calum would ever deserve.

Calum knew well there was an attraction between them, but with her family at war with him and the future stretching before her, nothing could ever come of it. How could she ever fully accept him when their families had been killing one another for decades?

'He wouldn't disown me,' Elspeth repeated. 'But I think when Ross finds out I'm at Castle Barron, he will ensure I cannot leave. And he will most likely insist that I marry as he and Fergus had to do.'

Pain squeezed at Calum's chest. 'Leith.'

Elspeth nodded.

Aye, Leith had said he would never marry a traitor, but Calum had not missed the way the man looked at her. He would take her as his wife in an instant, no matter that she had blatantly rejected him.

And doubtless he'd make her suffer for her disloyalty.

'But if marrying Leith meant Ross felt secure enough with his alliances to at least listen to you, and even helped ensure your people's freedom...' She regarded him with unguarded hope. 'You would have a peaceful resolution and the restoration of your lands for proper crops so your people would no longer starve. You would have everything you needed.'

Not everything.

For in such a scenario, he wouldn't have her.

Chapter Fourteen

Unease settled in Elspeth's chest despite her bravado. She wanted the Campbells to have their land back and certainly she wished for it to happen without a clan war that would only lead to more death.

But she did not relish the way in which it all happened.

In her heart, she could not believe that Ross would disown her. Not when the three siblings had become so close after first their mother's death and then their father's.

But she knew without a doubt her eldest brother would insist on her marriage to Leith. Ross was a chieftain and his job was to secure alliances. It was a sacrifice Fergus had made and one Ross himself had made. It would be Elspeth's turn and she had no right to refuse.

Leith's anger would no doubt show itself in their marriage. She should never have told him she did not wish to wed him. Except that in that moment, when she'd felt forced to watch the two men fight, it was all she could think to do to still their blades. In that instant, she had chosen one over the other and could not stop herself from siding with Calum.

'Don't go to Castle Barron either,' Calum said abruptly. 'There has to be another way.'

Elspeth studied him in the firelight. His hazel eyes appeared golden, and shadows played over his high cheekbones. He was the most handsome man she had ever seen. One whose intentions were selfless and good, a man she would choose for herself should she have the opportunity to select her own husband.

But she did not.

She was, as Leith has so starkly pointed out, a woman. Her future was not hers to plan. She would be sold to the highest bidder, the greatest alliance, like chattel to be bartered with in an agreement.

That would be her fate. If she'd had the opportunity to think thoroughly earlier, she would have understood that. There was no escape.

But her mind had been so muddled, whipped into a frenzy with fear.

For Calum.

'There is no other way,' she said in a soft voice.

Her pulse quickened as a realisation came to her. She was no longer promised to Leith. She had broken whatever agreement had been made between her brother and Leith's father. There would not be another until Ross had her back at Castle Sween. Or until there was peace between the Campbells and the MacMillans.

Right now, she had no obligations to Leith. She could at least make love to the man she did want.

It had been difficult to turn away from him earlier when they'd first entered the cave. But it had become such a habit to fight her desires when it came to Calum that she had resisted his allure. The more she had to put him off, the more she yearned for him.

Now she did not need to fight her attraction to him any longer. At least, not for this one night while she was free.

She leaned closer to Calum, so her knees brushed his. 'I'm not promised to Leith any more.' Her heart pounded harder as she held his gaze. 'And I will not be until Ross makes another arrangement.'

A muscle worked in Calum's jaw. 'What are you saying?'

Heat swept through her body and set her pulse echoing between her legs. What she was about to suggest made her body hum to life with desire.

'I want to experience passion,' she said quietly. 'With someone I long for, not someone I'm forced to wed.'

'He may not wed you if he suspects…' Calum swallowed.

'Then that would make me happier still.' She adjusted her position so she sat on her knees and took his hand in hers.

Calum regarded their joined hands. 'And if you decide later you can love him?' He shook his head. 'I don't want you to regret this.'

'I will never love him,' Elspeth replied with certainty. 'And I won't ever regret this. I'll never regret you.'

She rose higher on her knees and ran her hand down his face. The shadowed growth of hair on his jaw prickled against her fingertips. She brushed her thumb over his lips, a soft, warm contrast to the sharpness of his whiskers. And one she intended to explore.

'Elspeth,' he said in a warning tone. 'This cannot be undone.'

'I know.' Then she pressed her mouth to his, for she had never been more sure of anything in her life.

She had always done everything that was asked of her, been the person she was expected to be. Never had she tried to do anything for herself—not until this very moment. She would not allow herself to be plagued with guilt or regret and pull away.

Nay, she would live every moment of this, savour it, so that she could spend the rest of her lifetime reliving it in vivid detail.

She knelt slightly over him, his face in her hands as their mouths touched. She kissed him once, twice, three times before he finally responded, as though waiting to be entirely confident this was what she wanted.

He pulled away and shifted to his knees as his fingers threaded through her hair. Their shadows danced across the walls of the cave, illuminated by the flickering firelight.

His fingertips touched the underside of her chin, guiding her face up to his. When his mouth claimed hers, the kiss was firmer than hers. Determined.

He was skilled in his affections, as evidenced by the way his tongue brushed her lips as if he knew she would gasp in delight. With her lips parted, his tongue swept against hers, a light grazing first and then a sensual stroking that left soft moans humming at the back of her throat.

Never had she realised kissing could be so seductive. For the more their mouths and tongues connected, the hotter she burned, like the centre of a fire where the embers glowed with pulsing red intensity.

Calum growled and drew her body against his. Evidence of his desire strained at her lower stomach and made her breath catch with wondrous surprise. His hands moved over the swell of her hips to her slender waist while their bodies undulated together with a lustful, natural rhythm. She explored his torso as his palms grazed over her, first tracing the strength of his chest, then his flat stomach and the power of his broad shoulders. Though cloth separated her from his skin, she enjoyed the way the evidence of his muscles moved and shifted beneath her touch.

He deepened the kiss so their mouths slanted over one another's. Elspeth arched towards him, desperate to have his thick, hard column fit more tightly against her. He caught her bottom with one hand, encouraging her movements as he pushed her towards him with each mock thrust.

His mouth trailed lower down her throat and sent a fresh wave of delicious chills dancing over her skin while his free hand brushed against her breast. She panted with pleasure, wanting more. Needing more. Needing him.

Heat throbbed between her legs with an infuriating insistence she couldn't ignore. One she was eager to finally see sated.

His hand closed over her breast and his fingertips found the bud of her nipple, teasing over it until she cried out. He pulled at the ties of her kirtle and she did not move to stop him, eager for him to remove the damaged garment and her chemise—all barriers between his touch and her bare skin.

She wanted to be naked against him, their bodies yielding to the passion they had fought for far too long.

The chill of the cave washed over her exposed bosom for only a brief moment before the warmth of Calum's hands covered her once more. He lowered his head and parted his lips and suddenly the caress of his hands was followed by the heat of his mouth as he suckled the bud.

Pleasure needled through her as she clasped his head, holding him to where he loved her breasts. Her cries echoed off the stone walls around them, accompanying the crackle of the fire warming her backside.

He pulled free her cloak and let it fall to the right of them both before unlacing the remainder of the ties from her kirtle so it gaped open. Her heartbeat thundered in her ears and echoed between her thighs as he got to his feet and pulled her with him.

Aye, this was exactly what she wanted.

Him. Her. Together.

It didn't matter what she had to face in the future, so long as she could have this one moment to relive for the rest of her existence. While he finished unlacing the ties of her kirtle, she pulled at the sleeves, tugging the damp fabric from her shoulders and letting the torn garment crumple to the ground at her feet, careful of the fire.

Calum stared at her in only her chemise, no doubt the damp, thin fabric was made transparent, especially with the fire light behind her. She lifted it over her head and let it fall to the ground, so she stood before him entirely naked.

As a girl, she had been hopelessly insecure about her appearance. Never had she thought she'd grow into a woman who would have a man look at her as Calum did now.

The blatant appreciation in his gaze quelled any self-conscious unease.

'You're beautiful,' he whispered, his tone awed as his eyes travelled down her body.

She reached for his gambeson and carefully unfastened it so the padded armour parted down the centre, revealing his damp tunic beneath. They both had been drenched through when he'd saved her and their clothes had not had a chance to dry in the damp air of the cave.

He pulled off his tunic and the linen shirt he wore came off with it. Firelight danced over his naked torso and teased tempting shadows over his lean muscle.

Elspeth swallowed. Her fingertips brushed over his skin, soft and warm with firm, powerful strength beneath.

'You're beautiful too,' she said softly.

He gave a somewhat shy smile at the unusual praise, the same as he'd done when she'd called him beautiful at the feast. But he truly was beautiful in the way ancient art was beautiful—a loveliness for the eyes to appreciate.

'And handsome,' she teased.

But there was little playfulness in his expression when he looked at her with such longing. Her heartbeat caught.

She touched her hand to his face and lifted up onto her toes to kiss him. As she did so, their naked bodies touched, all of her crackling with awareness as they touched, skin to skin.

This night, she would take what she wanted and would enjoy every blissful moment.

Desire roared through Calum's veins as her naked form stretched over him, her arms threading behind his neck. The built-up yearning from the last fortnight had crowded into his thoughts throughout the days and consumed his dreams every night. For so long he had put off his longing to hold her, touch her, kiss her.

And now…

He groaned as he gazed down at her nudity, unable to stop stealing appreciative glimpses. Her breasts were firm and creamy, tipped with tight pink nipples he intended to sample at least several more times before dawn put an end to their play. She had a flat stomach with a small, indented navel and her hips flared out in a way that made him want to hold her while she rode him while driving up inside her. Her hair spilled down her shoulders like wildfire and her eyes flashed with the same lust coursing through his veins.

She too had fought off her own attraction for him.

It had been between them, humming with the same vibrancy as the onset of an unexpected storm prickles the air before unleashing its power. That force was in Calum now, building with barely restrained control.

He wanted to lose himself in their kisses, to grab her full hips in his hands and plunge into her so they joined in a desperate, panting rutting.

But he stayed his actions, no matter how tremulous it left him. Though it was unsaid, he was aware of the likelihood that she was a maiden and while he had never deflowered a lass before, he knew he would need to take great care.

But that wasn't the only knowledge to hold him back. It was also that this would be their one and only time to enjoy one another. After this shared night, she would have to go to her brother, who would doubtless ensure Calum never had the opportunity to be near her again.

And though she had sought a reprieve from her obligation to wed Leith, he knew she could never be totally free and would likely have to marry him.

Emotion drew tight in Calum's chest.

He would not think of losing her now. Nay, he would make love to her as she'd asked him to, so that she might always have this moment to cherish.

As would he.

He swept his hand down her lovely face and lowered his mouth to hers. She parted her lips as she lifted her chin upward, her tongue stroking his with the same eagerness that burned within him.

He caught her round bottom with both hands, and gently pulled her to him so their hips fit together. Though he still wore his trews, his powerful erection pressed against her sex. She gasped and arched against him.

His hand eased down her body, pausing to caress her firm breasts, to graze the buds of her nipples before trailing lower past her slender waist to the thatch of red hair between her thighs. He drew away slightly as his fingers slid between her thighs, watching her expression as he gently swept his touch over the seam of her sex.

Her eyes widened and she sucked in a hard breath.

His fingertips came away slick with her desire. A groan of lust rasped up from his throat. She was so wet.

So damn ready.

But not yet.

He traced his fingers over her again before finding the little bud of her sex. She whimpered and clung to him. With the pad of his thumb, he rubbed against the sensitive nub while he gently probed inside of her with his middle finger. With great care, he lightly stretched her core as he pleasured her.

Elspeth's panted breath blended with her moans as his touch moved over her, the whisper of her breath against him was warm and sweet where it rushed across his skin. His cock was about to burst with each sound emitted from her, evidence of her incredible enjoyment.

Before her body could release, he pulled his hand away and lowered her so she lay atop her cloak, rather than the sandy ground. She gazed up at him with brilliantly green eyes, her breath gasping from her as she rubbed her thighs together in innocent frustration.

'That was incredible,' she breathed.

He leaned over the top of her, but she sat up, meeting him halfway, her gaze locked on him as she reached for the ties of his trews.

'Elspeth,' he said raggedly.

But he was too late. She tugged one, then another and his ready cock sprang free. Her eyes widened as she gazed down at him, erect and swollen with a lust greater than any he'd ever known. She reached for him, her actions hesitant as her fingers wrapped around him.

He gave another groan that seemed to emerge from somewhere deep inside his soul.

'It's so hard,' she breathed.

That wasn't anything he didn't already know. But he couldn't form the words to say as much. Not when the breath was hissing from between his teeth as she began to stroke her hand over him from base to tip and back again. His thighs tightened at her careful ministrations.

'Nay.' He put his hand over hers, stilling the motion. 'Lay down, lass.'

She bit her lip as she released him and sank to the ground, her eyes locked on him. He got to his knees and crawled over her. She parted her thighs to cradle his weight against her as they met one another with light kisses that rapidly ignited into ones of passion that slanted against one another. His hand found her naked breast once more, this time her nipples were taut against his fingertips as he caressed them.

He kissed down her neck and pulled one of the pink-tipped buds into his mouth, flicking his tongue against it. Her cries rang out on the cave walls, hoarse with pleasure. She began writhing beneath him again, arching up with anticipation.

Still delivering passionate kisses over her body, he continued lower, down to her navel and further still.

Before she could ask what he was doing, he settled himself between her legs. Her breath caught and she froze. He caressed her inner thighs with his fingertips, gently parting her further as he craned his neck forward, his eyes locked on her face to bear witness to her pleasure, and he dragged his tongue over her sex.

Chapter Fifteen

Elspeth sucked in an inhale of astonishment as Calum's tongue ran over her, not once but repeatedly. Before she could even truly register the shock of it, came the understanding of pleasure at such an intimate kiss.

Her body was alight with lust, each stroke of his tongue against her most private place was like fire crackling over dry tinder. She gripped the cloak beneath her with both hands, clutching not only the damp fabric in her fists, but also clumps of sand beneath.

His finger probed at her again, gently nudging against her. Inside her. All the while, his tongue circled and flicked and teasingly sucked at her.

Suddenly the intensity of it was far too great. Her head spun and her body tensed.

Rather than draw away from her, Calum caught her hips with his hand and the maddening thrust of his finger and the flick of his tongue grew bolder, faster, until the world around Elspeth splintered apart. She cried out in euphoria as it washed over her with the same lapping waves as Calum's wicked tongue.

Only when she began to slowly blink her eyes open

once more did Calum straighten over her, a lazy, proud grin on his face.

She wanted to say something profound, to let him know how incredibly wondrous his loving was to her senses, but all that emerged from her throat was a whimper of desperation.

She wanted more.

Reaching for him, she drew him up towards her.

She wanted *him*.

He stretched his body over her, the light sprinkling of hair tickling her skin where they touched. The heaviness of his arousal rested against her thigh, near her sex.

A shiver of anticipation rippled down her back and left delicious chills racing through her.

She knew what came next from castle gossip amongst the servants. Oftentimes their tongues were loose when they thought no one was around. Except the intimate acts were never anything she had considered wanting to do herself. Certainly not with Leith.

But Calum...

She moaned as he leaned over her and kissed first her collarbone, moving down her throat, the lobe of her ear and then her lips. With one arm bracing his form over her, he took hold of his arousal with the other hand and gently nudged the blunt edge against her entrance.

Elspeth widened her legs to better accommodate him, eager to feel him filling her, for their bodies to be completely joined. He glided the swollen head against her, dampening himself with her juices.

The sensation was the greatest tease of all and left her moaning with the need to be sated.

'You're sure?' he asked in a ragged voice.

She blinked up at him. 'Aye, please don't stop now.' She held his gaze. 'I want this. I want you.'

And she meant every word.

In a life where she would sacrifice everything she wanted for what everyone else needed, she longed to at least have this one experience to cherish.

Already, the sensations were wonderfully overwhelming. The familiar peat and leather scent of him surrounding her in a way that left her feeling heady, the rasp of his chin against her delicate skin as his mouth pressed hot kisses to her body, the lines of his warrior's body and how those powerful hands could be so gentle. So sensual.

He set his jaw and nudged his arousal against her once more. The tip of him fit against her.

Her breath came in excited pants, eager for him to continue.

He was breathing hard too as he flexed his body forward, every muscle in his body practically shaking with the effort as he pushed into her. There was an unfamiliar sting between her thighs, but she clenched the cloak beneath her and ignored it.

Calum, however, did not. His brow furrowed with worry. 'Did I hurt you?'

She shook her head, wanting nothing more than for him to continue, for their coupling to begin to feel good as she knew it eventually would.

He gently eased out before nudging inside her once more, this time slightly deeper. The slight discomfort returned, but rather than allow herself to concentrate on it, she looked up at him. She focused on his face, memorising his sharp jaw and high cheekbones, both accentuated by the shadow of raspy whiskers. His heavy, expressive brows set atop long-lashed hazel eyes that regarded her as if she were the only woman in the world. As if he cared for her more than any other.

That thought made her heart squeeze with yearning. For more than just the physical connection. For the emotional as well.

For what she could never have.

And yet, she wanted to be lodged within his chest the way he was within hers.

'Elspeth,' he whispered her name with such tenderness, it was as though he had heard her wish and shared her sentiments.

He lowered his mouth to hers and kissed her as their bodies joined together once more. Elspeth arched up to him in the same rhythm he carefully thrust into her, now fully buried to the hilt.

Warm pleasure radiated from where their bodies connected and left a tantalising tingling sensation racing over her skin. She gasped with delight.

Calum groaned at her response and his thrusts became deeper, firmer. A moan rose up in Elspeth and she wrapped her arms around him to secure them more closely together.

Whatever discomfort or foreign sensation had existed now disappeared beneath the decadent friction building between them. Calum gave a soft grunt in her ear with every solid thrust into her, the sound as sensual and primitive as the act they shared together.

He shifted his position over her and suddenly with each subtle movement, his body rubbed at the sensitive bud of her sex. Elspeth groaned in surprise as each flex of his hips sent glorious prickles of pleasure rushing through her.

Her body tightened in the familiar way it had when

he had loved her with his mouth. This time, she did not wonder at what it meant but instead opened herself up to the experience and let it wash over her.

When her crises overtook her, her cries rang out on the cave walls around them. Calum's hips jerked into her, burying deep within her sex. He climaxed with a roar that blended with the sounds of her pleasure as his seed spilled into her.

It was exactly as she had wanted.

She had hoped he would release into her, where a child might take root. For a bairn would be all the better to remember him and this incredible night when he'd pleasured her in a way she wanted from no one but him.

They remained clasped in one another's arms, holding each other tightly and Elspeth wished for the moment to last for ever.

Even though she knew it would all be ending far too soon.

Calum didn't want to let Elspeth go.

Not only at that moment, but in all the ones that would follow. He had never shared a connection with anyone the way he did with her. For the whole of his life, he had never belonged.

When he'd been a boy in Ireland, his father had told him he was above those around him. The son of a laird. While Calum never believed it himself, others did. He was not invited to play with other lads his age and they all seemed to harbour a resentment towards him for the wrongs his father committed that had banished them to Ireland.

As Calum grew into a man, he never truly felt accepted by his people.

Even now, he was their leader and had to assume a confidence in their situation that he did not feel. If he let them down, his people would die.

But the cost…

Calum rested his forehead on Elspeth's. Their breath was still ragged from their rigorous coupling and his heart still raced.

'I have to do this,' she whispered.

He tensed. She meant she had to go to her brother, to likely sacrifice her future for the sake of his clan.

If it even worked.

He withdrew from her and laid beside her. 'There has to be another way. Something that will be guaranteed. Something that will keep you from having to go to your brothers.'

'You've tried meeting with Ross,' Elspeth protested. 'And you saw how well that went. We still don't know about Bram…'

She pressed her lips together, not saying more.

Ross was a strong warrior. While Calum knew Bram would comply with his Laird's demand not to kill him, Ross was under no such orders.

It was Bram Calum worried most for.

'Bram will be fine,' Calum said with an assurance he was trying to convince himself to feel. 'He always is. And I know he would not have hurt your brother.'

'And what of your people?' She asked.

'There has to be another way,' Calum insisted. 'We can return to Ireland on the morrow, try for another opportunity to convince Ross with letters.'

'He'll never give you a chance while he assumes your men are attacking our people still.' Elspeth frowned. 'Why would he think that?'

Calum's stomach sank, the same as it did when Ross first mentioned the attacks. There hadn't been time to discuss it with Elspeth when they were escaping and then the intimacy between them had consumed them completely in the most wonderful way.

Nay, it was not something that could be brought up until now.

The truth of it was that the men attacking the villages could very well be Campbells—those who had supported his father's intent to take back the land by force.

Calum thought he had addressed all the remaining Campbell warriors, quelling their protests with promises for a better life for them and their families. They had all agreed to allow him the chance before resorting once more to violence.

But with the Campbell army divided between he and his father for so long, it was impossible to know which men had been killed in battle and which had remained in Scotland, still loyal to the former Laird's ideals even after his death.

Perhaps Calum had not been as thorough as he thought.

This might well be all his fault. The realisation hardened like a ball of ice in his stomach.

'What is it?' Elspeth asked.

'They might be Campbells,' he answered slowly.

She jerked back from him as though he'd struck her. 'You said your people wanted peace.'

He winced at the betrayal in her words. At the thought that he might have just damaged the trust he'd worked so hard to establish.

'The last of my da's supporters,' he explained. 'They still want war. They want to make your family and all the other clans suffer as they did. I need to catch them in the act and stop them. Then we can return to Ireland where we will wait to hear from Ross again, once the attacks have ceased.'

She chewed her lip and said nothing, a clear indication the plan did not sit well with her.

'Then you don't have to go to your brother alone,' he said. 'You won't have to be sent off into marriage.'

He reached for her and she slowly eased back towards him. But though she did return to him, he could sense a shift in her—a slight wariness. There were too few people in Calum's life that he felt comfortable opening up to. Really, only her and Bram, who had been Calum's most trusted warrior first, and then friend later.

The idea of losing her twisted like a poisonous vine inside him.

He wrapped her in his arms, as if he could hold tight to her faith in him, to keep it from slipping away.

Her skin was like fine silk beneath his touch, and he could not stop his fingertips from stroking over her flat stomach. A soft sigh of pleasure escaped her.

He nuzzled the delicate curve where her shoulder met her neck, and she leaned her head back with a moan as her bottom pushed against him.

She would trust him again, in time. For he would do whatever was necessary to earn it back. So long as he had time.

For now, they could enjoy the intimacy between them, making up for what they had been forced to deny themselves.

They explored one another through the night while they left their clothing propped before the fire to dry. Calum didn't know how long they enjoyed one another, but at last, they finally sank into slumber, curled up together beneath the blankets of the bedroll, exhausted and thoroughly sated.

Never had Calum experienced anything more exquisite than Elspeth cradled against him, her sensual curves warm where their bodies fit perfectly against one another.

Years of discipline had Calum rousing before dawn, before Bram was set to arrive, so he could wake Elspeth and they could dress. But their garments were stiff with dried seawater and the skirt of Elspeth's kirtle was still ripped. If nothing else, they were warm and dry.

No sooner had they donned their clothing than a familiar voice sounded at the cave, calling Calum's name.

Bram was back.

Relief flooded Calum, leaving him with a final hope that his most trusted warrior had obeyed the orders to refrain from killing Ross, or Elspeth's wavering trust would be the least of his concerns.

Chapter Sixteen

Elspeth's heart gave a leap at the sound of Bram's voice echoing into the cave.

Ross.

Her brother's welfare shoved to the forefront in her mind, she raced towards Calum's lead warrior for news.

There was a slash in Bram's arm, the sleeve dark with dried blood and his right eye was shadowed with a deep purple bruise. But he was alive.

Calum met Bram and clasped arms with him, the relief on his face at his friend's survival apparent.

'My brother?' she gasped.

Bram squinted at her. 'Aye, the bastard is still alive and in better shape than me. I only just managed to escape and had to hide in the nearby brush to avoid his blade.' He scoffed. 'Your brother may be a chieftain, but he fights with the skill of a mercenary.'

Elspeth couldn't still the swell of pride in her chest, buoyed further by the confirmation that Ross was indeed alive. Thanks be to God.

'Come, let me look at your arm.' She waved Bram towards her, though questioned her offer as soon as it was made. After all, she had nothing to bandage it with, let alone stitch the wound with if the skin was gashed open.

He shook his head. 'I already saw a healer. She gave me this for you as well.' He reached into his bag and withdrew a simple brown homespun kirtle.

Elspeth breathed a sigh of relief. 'Please let me know who she is so I can repay her kindness.'

Bram gave a cocky grin. 'Don't worry, I already did that for you.'

Elspeth took the kirtle and lifted her brows, earning her a laugh from Bram who knew she understood exactly what he meant.

'Well, the plan to appeal to the Chieftain of the Mac-Millan clan didn't work.' Bram lifted his shoulder as if being left behind to try to survive a difficult battle was of little consequence. 'What are we considering next.'

Elspeth put her attention to the kirtle, not wanting to discuss the new plan or what it meant.

'We need to find the men who are attacking the villages,' Calum replied.

She didn't have to look up to know Bram was watching her. His gaze was a tangible thing where it rested against her awareness.

'She already knows that it might be some of our clansmen,' Calum added.

Her pulse quickened. Aye, she did know about how the Campbells might still be responsible for attacking her people. For mercilessly slaying innocent lives. And she hated how it rattled her confidence in him.

It should have been something he told her earlier, before she had trusted him so implicitly. Before, she had stood up for him in front of Ross, turning her back on her own family, her own obligations to her clan.

All the while he'd suspected that his clansmen were still killing hers when she had been led to assume they all wanted peace.

She had been a fool to hand over her faith so fully and without question. She knew that now and would be far more cautious going forward. The starving people and children in Ireland could not be feigned and she truly did want to help them. But if Calum's kin were indeed attacking innocent villagers—*her* people—he should have seen to that before ever asking for the possibility for a truce.

Or perhaps he had known and simply hoped it would not come to light. His ready explanation the night before certainly made the latter seem like a possibility.

'Elspeth, are you well?' Calum's voice was low and intimate beside her.

It awoke in her a fresh yearning that heightened her awareness as she recalled all the ways they had pleasured one another the night before. Aye, even after he had confessed his father's supporters might indeed be behind the attacks.

She had thought to put distance between them after his admission the night before, but as soon as his lips grazed over her throat, as soon as his touch teased a sizzling path down her stomach, all thoughts had fled and were replaced with undeniable desire. Now her cheeks scalded with humiliation at how weak she had been.

And for all the pleasure they'd taken from one another, she was wary now of trusting him as fully as she had done only hours before.

She tried to smile at him. 'Aye, I'm fine.'

'Bram is freshening up.' He indicated a rear portion of the cave that curved around at the back, offering the other man some privacy.

And them as well.

'Would you like me to help you into the kirtle?' Calum nodded to the bundle of homespun cloth in her arms.

She noted the lacing at the back and grudgingly nodded. It would be impossible to do on her own.

Calum put his back to her. 'Call my name when you're ready.'

His offer of privacy was unnecessary, especially after what they had shared, but it was appreciated, nonetheless. In the light of day, in the face of what she now knew, once their lust had cooled the truth lay between them like a boulder.

She undressed swiftly, her fingers trembling somewhat as she plucked free the lacing of her torn kirtle. The healer, whoever she was, had been kind enough to also include a fresh chemise. Elspeth happily traded hers, which remained scratchy with dried sea water, for the new one. The clean, soft fabric floated against her skin like a sigh and provided a good barrier to the rougher homespun kirtle.

She turned away from Calum, exposing the unlaced back towards him. 'I'm ready.'

The coarse sand crunched under his feet as he made his way toward her and gently began to lace and tighten the kirtle so it fitted her properly. Bram had still not returned by the time Calum had finished and spun her slowly to face him once more.

His lips parted slightly, as though he wished to speak, his brows drawn together over his expressive hazel eyes. He was about to say something that did not appear to sit well with him.

Elspeth held her breath, waiting to see if he might offer

some explanation that could set her trust to rights once more, to keep it from seeming so misplaced.

'The lass did a fine job stitching me up,' Bram announced from behind them. 'I can't even feel a thing.'

They turned quickly, breaking apart from one another to find Bram busily inspecting a neat row of stitches in his arm through the lowered collar of his tunic. Oblivious to what he'd interrupted, he pulled on his gambeson and grinned at them. 'Let us collect our men from the beach, then find the attackers and set this sorry mess behind us, aye?'

Men from the beach?

'The sailors?' Elspeth asked for clarification, frowning.

'Nay, our warriors from Ireland,' Bram answered easily.

She regarded Calum with such incredulity, she was rendered mute.

A muscle worked in Calum's jaw. 'I was going to tell you just now.'

Bram gave an exaggerated wince. 'I'll eh…see to the horses.'

With that, he slipped hastily from the cave and left Elspeth with Calum to explain why he'd felt it necessary to bring warriors with him when he claimed to be seeking peace.

Damn.

It had been on the tip of Calum's tongue to tell Elspeth about the men he'd had scheduled to arrive in Scotland behind them, should his plans go awry and aid be needed. He'd done it to ensure Elspeth could not be stolen away as had almost happened.

'You were going to tell me,' Elspeth prompted.

'Aye, I was, but I knew you wouldn't like it.'

'Because of how duplicitous it looks?' She crossed her arms over her chest, her eyes flashing with indignation. 'Especially on top of the men already attacking the innocent villagers of my clan.'

'Aye.' He stood his ground. 'I wanted them here in case you were taken. To protect you.'

'From my own brothers?' She glared up at him with distrust.

He could not fault her for doing so.

'I proved myself worthy of your trust before,' he said. 'Let me do it again.'

While her face was a mask of anger, her eyes blazed with hurt. Her shaken trust had cut her to the quick. No doubt she felt foolish for having put her faith in him.

He knew well how deep such betrayal could cut.

He longed to draw her towards him and kiss her hurt away, to let their passion burn away her distrust, to soften her rage until she cried out in their shared pleasure.

Unable to stop himself, he slid the backs of his fingers over her cheek in a caress and then cradled her jaw in his fingertips. 'Give me a chance to earn your trust once more,' he said again. 'Please.'

Her ire softened. 'Don't make a fool of me, Calum Campbell,' she said in a low, threatening voice. 'Or I'll kill you myself.'

Ah, there it was—that spirit he so admired.

A smile pulled at his lips. 'I'll give you the dagger.'

'I've heard as much before.' She turned from him and strode away.

If nothing else, it was a start. He knew his heart to be pure and needed only to have her see it as well.

They rode back to the beach where the ship was once more docked. The day was a fine one with a brilliant sun that glittered over calm seas. His men were already disembarking from the ship when they arrived.

It was a small band of warriors, only three dozen, but they were the finest Calum had.

Hamish stepped forward and regarded Elspeth first then nudged Calum. 'I suppose you'll not be needing us after all.'

'Aye, she's safe for now,' Calum replied, grateful the man had spoken up within earshot of Elspeth, so she would know he was truthful earlier. 'But I'll still need your aid in finding the men who are attacking the villages.'

'Campbells?' another warrior asked, a dark-haired man named Kieran.

'I hope it's not the case.' Calum squared his shoulders. 'But it's possible they are our clansmen. If so, they are most likely my father's supporters.'

Hamish looked heavenward and shook his head.

'We need to find them and keep them from wreaking havoc,' Calum said. 'If they continue, we'll never have peace. We need to cover as much of the area as we can to find them. Go through the villages, but don't make yourself known as Campbells. Meet at the cave at sundown.'

The men nodded and turned their gambesons wrong side out to hide the stitched boar's head on them as the warriors split into groups, organising themselves to carry out Calum's orders. He nodded to Bram to indicate he wanted him to stay and approached Elspeth. 'I'd like you to return to Ireland,' he said.

As expected, defiance stiffened her spine. 'You'll

never get me on that ship again,' she said stubbornly. 'And I want to see the attackers for myself.'

Because she didn't trust him. She didn't have to say it, not when it hung thick in the air between them.

'If I agree to let you stay, promise me you'll stay back, out of the way, aye?' He met her gaze.

She sighed. 'Aye.'

He nodded. 'Very well, then you'll travel with Bram and I, but pull the hood of your cloak over your head so you're not recognised.'

Having her still at his side said she at least wanted to believe him. She could have left at any moment, to race back to Ross for succour, yet she had not.

She pulled the hood over her head as he bade, hiding the wealth of her bright red hair beneath and shielding her face in the shadows.

Only last night, they had thought it would be the last time they would see one another. Now, they had a new plan. Perhaps it might mean someday they would have a future. But even to allow himself to think of such hope was too painful. Not when it could never be realised.

There was too much between their clans, too much death, too much hate.

Deep down, he prayed the men who were attacking the villages were not from his clan. For he knew without a doubt that if they were, Elspeth would never forgive him.

Even if they'd acted of their own volition, his inability to control his own volatile people would be as much a betrayal as if he'd ordered the attacks himself. And it was with that thought that he met the prospect of encountering the marauding men with heavy dread and the expectation that he would for ever lose the only lass he had ever truly cared for.

Chapter Seventeen

They went to a village that clung to the MacMillan border, too far to receive prompt aid from the warriors lodging at Castle Sween. It was the kind of place where one would expect to be attacked by marauders.

Calum led Bram and Elspeth into the small, sleepy village. The clear day had given way to the rumble of thunder as a slow drizzle sputtered from the gathering clouds overhead. It was as good an excuse as any for them to leave their hoods pulled over their heads, not that Calum and Bram would be recognised. It was Elspeth he worried after the most.

As they led their horses to the centre of the village, Calum scanned the surrounding area, looking to see if there was anything amiss. A wee lad ran by, dragging a stick through the mud so it left a line in the earth behind him, a woman was scowling up at the heavy clouds as she hurried to pull laundry from a line strung between two huts, and a man rushed by with his cloak covering a little girl who was running to keep up with him before the rain truly began.

It was a normal village scene.

And while Calum hoped to find the men responsible for the attacks, he wanted this peaceful existence to remain undisrupted by such violence. His stomach grumbled, reminding him they had not yet broken their fast.

He led the way to a tavern, so they could procure some food before journeying to the next village and on and on until they found the men responsible. It was dark within the aged tavern, exactly as Calum had anticipated between the cloudy skies and poor lighting. It would be ideal for keeping their identities from being noticed. They took a table in a far corner where no one would bother paying them any mind and lowered their hoods.

A barmaid approached them with a tired smile. 'What will you be having?' Her gaze settled on Bram and the exhaustion cleared at once, giving way to a wide smile.

'Three ales and pottages with a bit of bread, if you please,' Calum said.

'As you like.' The woman winked at Bram and swept away.

He slid from the bench where he sat on across from Calum and Elspeth. 'I'll be back in a moment.'

'See that we get our food first,' Calum groused.

Bram winked and rapped on the table twice in quick succession before departing after the barmaid.

A cold silence fell between Calum and Elspeth.

'I know you can leave to go to your brothers whenever you like,' he said. 'Thank you for giving me a chance to prove myself.'

'I don't have much to look forward to upon my arrival—particularly in regard to Ross's desire to secure an alliance by marrying me off.' She smirked. 'And I really do wish to help your people,' she said in a softer tone. 'I don't know what is going on with your men or what is happening, but I do know those women and children need food. I'll not stand by while innocent lives are lost.'

'I thank you for your consideration for them.' He ran his thumbnail along a groove in the scarred wooden table. 'I can tell you that I've only ever had good intentions with what I've done in taking you. I truly don't want any more violence.'

She looked up at him, those beautiful green eyes that had gazed upon him with such tender affection only the night before now shielded with wariness.

'I know you don't want to trust me for fear of looking foolish,' he said. 'I understand that far better than you might think. My father spent a lifetime humiliating me with merciless taunting, as though he took joy in my discomfort. I think he meant to toughen me, to be like him.'

Those memories were ones he had not shared with anyone before. They'd been too painful for too long, those mockeries of his inadequacies. The way Alexander had pointed them out in cruel humour.

'I'm sorry he was like that with you.' Elspeth's mouth pulled down in a frown. 'I was teased as a bairn too.' She gave a little wince. 'For all those things you heard about me. I wasn't a bonny lass. But it was by other children, not my own da.'

'I think in the end, his goal worked,' Calum admitted. 'But not how he'd hoped.'

Another barmaid approached the table with two ales and two pottages with a platter of bread. A quick glance behind her confirmed Bram was engaged in lively conversation with the other lass, both of them sitting cosily at a table together, sharing his ale.

'How do you mean?' Elspeth asked when the woman left.

'Alexander did make me stronger.' Calum nudged the

bread closer to her in offering. 'But it didn't make me brutal like him. I held tight to my convictions and I didn't ever let my father change the man I was inside.'

She chewed thoughtfully and sipped her ale. 'My uncle was like that as well. He thought me foolish for helping others and saw me as good for little more than seeing to household affairs.'

'But it didn't make you want to stop helping, did it?'

She shook her head. 'It made me try harder.'

He nodded as he realised she understood exactly what he meant.

She licked her lips. 'It's difficult in these times,' she said at last. 'To know who to trust, and to know why you should trust. But in the end, you can only hope that you've made the right decisions and that the people who need it most will benefit.'

'Time will show you who I am in my heart, Elspeth.' He put his hand on hers. She did not pull away, even though the worry stayed pinched at her brows.

'Now let us eat before the pottage gets cold.' He removed his hand from hers and ate his food. She did likewise, not speaking again.

When they were done, he waved over Bram who joined them once more, but only after pausing to whisper into the barmaid's ear in a way that made her smile and blush with equal fervour.

They pulled up their hoods and exited the tavern where the rain was now coming down in earnest. They mounted their horses, pausing to look over the village once more before making their way back onto the trail.

Calum breathed a sigh of relief to know this small area remained unmolested. On his next breath, however, he caught the distinct odour of smoke. He sucked in a hard inhale.

Aye, there was definitely smoke in the air, mixing with the scent of rain and wet earth. That acrid sharpness was unmistakable.

'Smoke,' Elspeth said with the same realisation.

Bram pointed in the distance. 'Over there.'

They rode hard through a driving rain that lashed at their faces. As they neared, the pitch of terrified screams rose over the noise of the storm.

A hard ball of ice formed in the pit of Calum's stomach. He didn't want these marauders to be his father's supporters. And yet a thread of fear tightening through him indicated that it was a high likelihood.

Still, he refused to believe it until he saw the men in Campbell gambesons.

The huts came into sight, followed immediately by the people who raced about between them, shrieking in terror as they were chased down and viciously slain.

This was no simple attack to frighten them. Nay, it was a massacre.

A warrior stepped into view and brought a battle axe down onto the back of a man who'd fled. But not just any warrior.

One wearing a dark gambeson with a boar's head stitched into it, so like Calum's own. His heart slid down into the mud as nausea washed over him.

These warriors were not marauders as he had hoped. Nay, they were exactly what he had most feared.

They were Campbells.

His clansmen.

The horror of the scene played out in front of Elspeth as the villager was cut down, the massive battle axe at his back causing a fatal wound. The man did not rise again, but instead lay in a puddle that quickly reddened with his blood.

His murderer stood over him, lip curling in disgust as he pulled his weapon free and straightened. He looked about, as if seeking his next victim. It was then she saw it, a boar's head stitched against the darkness of his gambeson.

The Campbell clan crest.

These were indeed Calum's kinsmen.

She gave a choked sob in disgust that his clansmen would be so brutal, so merciless. If this was what the Campbells brought to Scotland, no wonder her brothers and the other clans worked so hard to keep them out.

Tears blurred her vision. She couldn't stand by as these people were slaughtered.

'Elspeth, nay,' Calum cried out from beside her.

She ignored him, the deceiver, and pushed off her horse. She had a dagger at her side. It was scarcely even a weapon, but it was more than the people of the village had. She landed on legs she could not feel and staggered towards the huts.

Bram and Calum were at her side.

'Stay back, Elspeth,' Calum shouted as he edged in front of her. 'Go back to the other village.'

'So, your clan can kill these people?' She shoved past him. She'd always been faster than both of her siblings and now used her speed to her advantage, rushing towards a woman who had been cornered by a Campbell man with a bloody sword.

He lifted his blade high and the woman cowered back against the wall. But they were too far. Elspeth would never make it.

She stopped suddenly, aimed her dagger and held her

breath before releasing it. Exactly as Calum had shown her. The blade sailed through the air towards the attacking Campbell and sank into his arm.

He bellowed in pain and the sword dropped from his grasp.

'Cease this at once,' Calum called out to the renegades in an authoritative voice.

They paid him no mind as they continued to attack the residents of the village. Whatever else he did, Elspeth did not pause to see. Not when the woman's attacker was reaching for his sword again, his face purple with rage.

The woman tried to dart around him, but he blocked her path intent on his victim. Just two more steps and Elspeth would be there.

She cried out with the effort as she closed the distance between herself and the man's fallen sword. In a swift movement, she snatched the blade from where it lay.

While she had not been trained with the weapon, she did recall its weight and hefted it up with both hands using all the strength she had. It swung towards the man who jumped back from its path.

Elspeth put herself between him and the woman who was now sobbing. The beast of a man growled at her and pulled her small dagger from his arm, clutching it in his meaty fist. 'I'll kill you for that.'

'Are you offended that a lass can defend herself?' Elspeth demanded with disgust.

He lunged at her and brought the blade down. She narrowly avoided it as she swung the sword once more. It caught him in the side where it slid harmlessly off the thick padding of his gambeson.

Before she could lift the sword a third time, a man rushed towards them both and crashed into Elspeth's opponent, knocking him to the ground. There was a flash of a blade, followed by a cry so awful, it could only mean a man's death.

Calum pushed himself off the fallen Campbell and pulled his blade free, then bent to retrieve Elspeth's dagger.

'Enough,' he roared at the attackers. 'I am Calum Campbell, Laird of the Campbell clan, currently residing in Ireland. This is not how we will see our people freed.'

All at once, the men stopped fighting. But it was not respect for Calum that appeared to command them. A ripple of unease seemed to pass over them as they regarded one another.

Elspeth held her breath, waiting to see what they would do. To her surprise, they turned away and ran off, retreating from the village they had so brutally attacked.

She immediately turned to the woman behind her. 'Are you hurt?'

The woman was nearing middle age, as evidenced by threads of white in her otherwise dark hair. She shook her head, her eyes wide where they fixed on the body of the man who Calum had slain.

'The bloody Campbells,' she said in a horrified whisper. 'They came out of nowhere. Attacking without mercy. Killing...' Her voice broke off and she began to weep again.

Elspeth reached for her, but the woman pulled away and ran off. Elspeth did not go after her. The woman would need time to herself to reconcile what she had survived. Everyone in the village would.

Calum stood by the body, staring down at the man solemnly. He appeared to be genuinely surprised at what the men had done.

Sympathy pulled at Elspeth. He had slain his own brethren. To save her.

When she approached, he was studying the man's face.

'Do you know him?' she asked cautiously.

He frowned and shook his head, glancing about for Bram. 'That's the worst of it. I can't even recall this man's name. It's like I've never seen him before. I was certain I knew my entire clan.' He handed her the dagger she'd thrown, its blade wiped free of blood. 'Now I'm realising how many of them I may not know.' A muscle worked in his jaw. 'If I'd had a better connection with him and these other men, if I'd spoken to them more often, perhaps they wouldn't have done this.'

Calum looked around at the village, at the numerous dead laying around them, and his eyes welled with tears. 'We'll not leave until we've helped bury these people.'

'We can't stay,' Bram said as he approached.

'We can't leave.' Calum looked at his righthand man with horror. 'We have to help bury the dead.'

'Are you mad?' Bram asked. 'They don't want us here.'

'We need to find out where those men are going.' Elspeth looked in the direction where they had ridden off, on horses they had kept somewhere nearby.

Calum nodded. 'Aye, now before they get too far.'

Bram pulled him towards their steeds. 'We must make haste from here.'

Calum sucked in a harsh breath as he surveyed the fallen people. 'It's wrong just to leave.'

'It's stupid just to stay,' Bram replied.

'He's right.' Elspeth put her hand to Calum's arm and met his watery gaze as emotion swelled in the back of her throat. 'We must go.'

Calum choked out a sob, so raw and genuine with

frustration and grief that it made Elspeth's heart flinch. He turned from the dead and stalked towards his horse. 'This won't happen again.'

But despite his vehemence, she knew it was not enough. He would bear the blood of those innocent lives on his hands for ever.

And for the first time, she truly understood how much of a burden he'd accepted in taking on his role as Laird.

Chapter Eighteen

All those lives lost. And that had been Calum's fault. No matter how hard he had tried to find a peaceful resolution, some of his people had still resorted to cruelty and violence.

His father was dead, aye, but his mean spirit remained in those who followed him.

Calum should have known those men better, he should have taken them aside to have his own conversation with them after his father's death, done whatever possible to draw them into his plan for a truce. After all, what did senseless killing prove?

There was no strategy behind it. Just pure bloodlust.

Calum, Bram and Elspeth had searched the surrounding area, but could not find which way the men had travelled. The surrounding forest area was too dense, the foliage beneath too muddied with the constant raining to detect the passage of horse hooves. There was nothing for it but to wait until the next attack and follow them. But he hated that there might be another attack. With more innocent lives lost.

Finally, they turned their steeds towards the direction of the cave in defeat. They could do nothing more that day, not until they were able to track the men down.

His stomach rolled with nausea.

'Are you well?' Elspeth asked from beside him.

He didn't look at her. He couldn't. Not when his father's men had so callously slain her people.

'I know this wasn't something you commanded,' she said.

He shook his head and swallowed thickly, but the urge to retch did not abate. Perhaps his father had been right. No one would ever respect a leader who tried to be fair.

Calum's gentleness would lead to the Campbells' demise. In this instance, however, he would take a lesson from his father. He would show no mercy to those heartless men.

'We'll find them,' he said hoarsely. 'I'll ensure they are stopped no matter what it takes.' If he had to kill every last one of them himself, he would. No more innocent lives would be taken in the Campbell name. None.

After what felt like ages, the cave came into view, but the other warriors had not yet returned. No one said anything as they saw to their horses and started a cheerless fire in the small pit of stones.

Calum scarcely felt the wet chill from his clothing as he sank heavily onto a hard rock by the flames and stared into them. His thoughts were locked on the men who had committed the day's atrocities and what he would do to stop them. Perhaps make an example of them to ensure others did not follow their same violent path.

Bram settled beside him. 'Who was the man you killed?'

Calum started and looked up at his righthand man.

'I didn't recognise him.' Emotion squeezed at his chest once more at such an admission.

What kind of a laird was he to not know his own warriors?

Elspeth's arms were wrapped around herself as she stared into the fire as well. Doubtless her thoughts were on the dead too, or recalling the battle she'd engaged in and what might have happened to her.

Fear trickle down his spine like icy water. Had he not stopped the man from attacking her and the village woman, she might have been slain.

'I didn't recognise any of the men either,' Bram said.

'They're my father's soldiers.' Calum dragged his hand through his hair. 'I should have known them.'

'I know your father's soldiers.' Bram frowned. 'As do you.' He shook his head. 'I don't think those men were his.'

Calum stared at his friend. 'Are you certain?'

'I cannot say with complete certainty, but fairly damn sure.' Bram lifted his hands. 'I don't recall having ever seen any of their faces.'

'Are you saying one of the clans around here may be doing it?' Elspeth asked, taking great offence.

Bram hesitated before answering. 'I'm saying I don't recognise the men and that might mean something.'

Calum rolled the idea around in his head. Before he could focus further on it, a sound came from the front of the cave as his men entered.

Fortunately, there had been no more attacks that the others had seen. With a heavy heart, Calum shared what had happened at the village while Elspeth hung back at the rear of the cave. She was suffering too, in her own way. He would speak to her alone later, but for now, he had to confer with Hamish, whose ability to track was notorious among the Campbell hunters. And if one could track deer, surely he could track men.

Calum pulled Hamish aside as soon as the others were eating and relaxing by the fire as night swept in.

'Can you track in the rain?' Calum asked.

Hamish scoffed. 'What's the point of being a tracker in Scotland if you can't track in the rain?'

'How about tracks that are a day old?' Calum asked. 'Horse tracks.'

Hamish waggled his head. 'A mite harder, but it might still be done if there were several horses.'

'There's a small army's worth.'

Hamish's face spread into a wide grin. 'Then they might as well have left a sign pointing where they went in that case.'

'Then we'll leave at first light tomorrow to track them down,' Calum said.

Hamish nodded. 'Don't worry, Laird, we'll put a stop to them.'

Calum clapped a hand on Hamish's shoulder. 'I was hoping I could count on you.'

'Always.' Hamish lifted his skin of ale and tilted his head back to swallow the remainder.

While having his men arrive had unnerved Elspeth, Calum was glad he'd made the order. With Hamish's ability to track, they would find the men responsible for the village attacks and end their reign of terror.

Tomorrow.

That conversation done, Calum finally sought out Elspeth, who was preparing her bedroll. She looked up at him, her eyes wide in her slender face.

'Are you well, lass?' he asked.

She bit her lip and said nothing. Which was answer enough from a woman who was not the sort to ask for help.

Wordlessly, he pulled her into his arms and held her. Her shoulders shook slightly, the same as they had that day on the ship when she had nearly been washed overboard, when the horror of what might have been had caught up with her.

'That poor woman,' Elspeth said between breathless sobs. 'All those innocent people…'

'We'll find these men tomorrow,' Calum vowed. 'And we'll ensure this never happens again.'

But even as he made the promise, he hoped it was truly one he could keep. Especially with so much at stake.

Elspeth did not complain as Calum set up his bedroll near hers. Truthfully, she was glad for it.

The day's events had overwhelmed her. The memories of so many bodies, the way the woman had cowered with such fear, resigned to her dismal fate. Knowing she had been a fool to charge in with only her small dagger.

She knew that now in hindsight. At the time, she had not considered the threat, only her need to help.

Had the man not lost his sword, she would doubtless have been dead.

Had Calum not attacked her opponent, she and the woman would both be dead.

That was twice now that Calum had saved her life. But even as he offered her comfort, his own eyes remained shadowed with grief, his reaction undeniably genuine.

The other men bedded away from them that night, offering her and Calum privacy, none questioning whatever was between them to remain so close. She ought to care. The woman she was before she'd been taken would have worried what the men would think about seeing her sleeping in such proximity to Calum.

The woman she was now did not care.

She had been fashioned by the experiences that had transpired in the last weeks. The people she'd met who needed saving, the man who was ready to sacrifice everything to protect them, the times death had lapped close enough to nearly claim her, the way Calum had awoken in her such incredible passion. Aye, she was a much different woman now than she had been even a month ago and she was grateful for how her eyes had been opened to everything she'd been blind to before in life.

Perhaps that was why as they lay an arm's length away from one another, she scooted her makeshift bed closer to his and nestled against him.

Aye, the air around them was cold and damp, but he was warm. Yet the closeness was so much more than that.

It was comfort for them both.

He hadn't told her what went through his mind that day, but she could guess what anyone who saw innocent people slaughtered by their own clan would think.

'We have a tracker,' he said in a low voice so as not to wake the others. 'We'll leave at first light to go back to the village and trace the men back to where they are hiding.'

'I'll be ready,' Elspeth said.

His arm tightened around her. 'I want you to stay here.'

She pushed up on her elbow and studied him in the dim glow of firelight. 'We're not going into combat. We are tracking the men down to see where they are staying. I'll be safe.'

He opened his mouth to protest, but she put her hand

to his chest to silence him. 'I know this land better than any of you.'

He sighed, knowing what she said to be true.

'I know you want these men to not be your clansmen,' she said gently.

His heart thudded harder beneath her palm. He settled his hand over hers, holding her to him as his warm hazel eyes held hers. 'I want peace for my people.'

She nodded. 'Aye, I know.' And she did. Guilt nipped at her for doubting him and she found herself hoping as he did that the men who'd attacked the village were not Campbells.

However, if they were not Campbells, then who were they?

Calum gently stroked her face with his free hand. Her heart caught at the caress and before she could stop herself, she leaned over him to press her lips to his.

They kept their kisses chaste, ever aware of the men around them. But her body burned for Calum despite the many ways they had loved one another the night before. It had sated her appetite then, but now the memory of such passion and their simple kisses only served to whet her longing for more.

He pulled her against him, nestling down for the night with the strain of his desire apparent against her bottom. It was difficult to sleep especially when her body was on fire and her mind churned with the events of the day.

If a single evening not having Calum was so hard to get through, what would the rest of her life be like?

It was in that moment that she realised the one night she had spent with Calum would never be enough, that the idea of sacrificing her entire future would be far more difficult to put into action than she had anticipated. After experiencing such pleasure and such passion, she could never allow herself to be wed to a man like Leith.

Eventually, she did fall asleep and woke before dawn as the sounds of men rousing from their bedrolls pulled her from her slumber. She and Calum rose together and readied themselves as soft grey light began to seep into the cave.

They set out into the chilly air, their breath fogging in front of them as they mounted their steeds and returned to the village that had been the site of such needless slaughter. On this morn, they hoped to find and stop the men who had been attacking villages in such a horrific manner. And to discover if they were truly of the Campbell clan.

Chapter Nineteen

The bodies were gone from the village. Calum noted with much relief as they rode through the woods, his eyes straining to comb through the distant rows of huts and the alleys between. The day before, those narrow passageways had been littered with death. Now they were clear.

He prayed the victims and their families found peace.

For his part, he would do everything in his power to ensure the attacks ceased completely.

As Calum led their group to the spot from the day before, Hamish's sharp gaze scoured the forest floor until they reached an area Calum recognised.

'Around here,' he said, looking to Elspeth and Bram for confirmation.

They nodded, but Elspeth's gaze lingered on his.

He had been grateful for her companionship the night before, though refraining from deepening their kiss had been nearly an impossible task. Especially when her shapely bottom had rested against him through the night.

But last evening had not been for lust. It had been for comfort, for understanding. And he was grateful they could share that moment together.

'Can you see the tracks?' Calum asked. From what he could make out, there were as many broken sticks and tamped down leaves here as in the other areas of the forest they had passed.

But Hamish leapt down and knelt in the mud, first looking over it with his practised eye, then tilting his head to the side to study the surface. 'Aye, I see them.' He straightened with a nod. 'I can follow this.'

The band of tension around Calum's chest eased somewhat. He only hoped the trail would not disappear before they could find the men. They mounted their horses once more and travelled some way through the woods. As they did so, the sun rose and lit the forest around them as the birds and beasts within woke to a new day.

Thus far there had been no rain. Hopefully the weather would continue to hold.

While Hamish could track the sodden ground, no doubt it would be more difficult in the driving rain. Certainly, it would be more miserable.

They emerged from the woods onto a shore leading out to the ocean, where even Calum's untrained eye could make out the churned sand just before the lapping water. Wherever the men had disappeared to, they had gone by boat and were long gone by now.

'I don't suppose you can track over water,' Calum asked without hope.

Hamish frowned and shook his head. 'Even dogs will lose a scent in water.'

Disappointment crushed in on Calum as they all dismounted from their horses to look about more thoroughly. He had wanted so badly to either face his father's men or encounter those who were pretending to be Campbells. Ire took the place of disappointment in a flash.

He wanted retribution.

For the false representation of his clan. For so many lives lost in their brutal raids on the villagers. For his people who needed land that could yield crops so they would no longer starve.

He was so bloody tired of deceit, of being helpless to protect his people.

'I thought the lot of you left yesterday,' a voice called out to them.

Calum turned to find a young man trotting towards them, waving.

'The ship's gone.' He looked at them, confused. 'I thought you were all aboard or I'd have made them wait.'

'Made who wait?' Bram asked.

The man's brown gaze flicked to their gambesons, which were no longer turned inside out, so the boar's head stitched upon them was visible. He swallowed and looked back up to their faces.

Hamish stepped closer and cracked his knuckles. 'Who do you think we are, lad?'

The young man swallowed hard. 'Er...erm...the Campbells.'

'Who was here yesterday?' Calum asked.

The man looked around him and took a step back. Suddenly, he spun about and ran. Every one of the Campbells on the beach took off after him, but none ran as fast as Elspeth who Calum had discovered the day before to be incredibly quick when she wasn't falling in the mud.

She ran out ahead of all of them, gaining on the man before launching herself at him and tackling him into the sand. Bram was there before the man could straighten and caught him, pulling his arms behind his back, locking them into place so he couldn't flee.

Calum put his hand on Elspeth's shoulder briefly in a silent conveyance of his pride. She'd caught the lad in a matter of seconds. Had she not been there, they might have lost him.

She smiled up at him and brushed her sandy hair from her face.

Calum approached the man. 'The men who were here yesterday. Do you know who they were?'

The man shook his head, still panting from his attempt to flee.

'We're not the brutes we're being portrayed as,' Calum added. 'We don't want to hurt you.'

Hamish stepped forward and glared at the young man. 'But we will if necessary.'

'Nay.' The man flinched. 'You may not be brutes, but the men I mistook you for are. The only reason I'm not dead is because I helped them. But if I betray them...'

'It's not a betrayal of those men to tell us the truth, it's a betrayal of your people to remain silent.' Elspeth stepped forward; her ire raised as evidenced by the flush of colour to her cheeks. 'Do you know how many villagers were slain in the attack yesterday?'

The man looked down and shook his head.

'There were more dead than I could count from where I stood,' she answered solemnly for him. 'Have you seen what they do to the unarmed villagers?'

The man shook his head again, his focus still fixed on the sand.

'They kill without mercy.' Elspeth lifted his face to make him look at her. 'Men. Women. Bairns.' Her voice broke on the last word. 'Whoever these men are, they're killing your people and you're helping them. By keeping silent, you are killing them just as surely as if you had a blade in your hand.'

'The MacDonnells.' He spoke quickly as if saying the words fast minimised his culpability. 'Led by Iain MacDonnell. They've been doing it for months now. I... it started with the abbey. He just meant to scare people. I didn't...' He pressed his lips together as his eyes filled with tears. 'I didn't realise they were killing... I didn't know.'

Months.

Calum didn't believe the man didn't know about the killings. That, or he was wilfully ignorant, wanting only to collect whatever coin they doubtlessly gave him for his duplicitous efforts. Still, Calum exhaled a sigh of relief. The attackers had not been his clansmen.

'Where are they getting our gambesons?' he demanded.

'From the slain clansmen you have been forced to leave behind.' The young man at least had the sense to appear shamefaced as he replied, though the tears in his eyes had already dried.

'The bastard,' Hamish growled.

Bram released the young man, who rubbed at his skinny arms.

'Would you be willing to say at much to Ross Mac-Millan?' Elspeth asked.

'Aye,' the man replied. 'So long as you take me with you. I'll not be here when the MacDonnells find out what I've told you.'

'Aye,' Calum said. 'You can join us.'

At least until the Chieftain of the MacMillans got his hands on the man, but Calum refrained from saying as much.

Finally, they had a way to convince the MacMillans of Campbell innocence. Hopefully this time, it would be enough to stop the fighting. To earn their place back on Scottish soil.

Iain MacDonnell's involvement brought little comfort to Elspeth on the ride from the coast back to the cave.

Alan, the young man who had confessed that the Mac-Donnells were behind the attacks, had also admitted to assisting them in whatever manner they had needed, such as hiding weapons and gambesons in his own home.

His confession had proved Calum had been truthful and that her trust in him had not been as misplaced as she'd initially feared. But Iain MacDonnell was Ross's father-in-law. It was why she had asked Alan if he would be willing to speak to Ross. Otherwise, her brother would never believe that the attacks were not being caused by Calum, but by his new father-in-law.

But then, she hadn't been there to witness Ross interact with his new wife. They'd been married simply by proxy and Elspeth was sent to the abbey before Ross's bride even arrived at Castle Sween.

Regardless of whether or not they had the same happy union as Fergus and Coira, Elspeth could only assume at the very least that they respected one another. And that would necessitate the need for requiring proof of his father-in-law's perfidy.

Now they had that with Alan.

What she needed was a strong reason to compel Ross or Fergus to listen. One where she couldn't be taken to Castle Sween and made to marry Leith.

The way he had looked at her when she told him she didn't love him and would not marry him rushed forefront to her mind. He had called her a traitor. Malice had turned his warm gaze cold and made his charming smile brittle. He would still wed her despite his words, she knew that, but he would not make it a pleasant marriage. Not when she'd rejected him for another man.

She remembered the boy he'd been, the way his kindness could turn to petty spite when he felt he'd been slighted. Like the time their castle's cook had denied him a pastry and he'd had the man sacked for stealing costly spices that Leith had slipped into his own pocket.

The cave came into view and their horses all slowed to a stop.

'It's not much, but it's shelter.' Calum shrugged his shoulders and cast a hard look at Alan, as though challenging the man to complain.

'As long as you keep the MacDonnells from finding out that I talked, I don't care where I stay.' Alan leapt off the horse he shared with Bram and followed the men into the cave.

Elspeth lingered behind with Calum as their horses were led away by one of his men.

'I'm sorry I doubted you,' she said.

Calum lifted his mouth in a half smile. 'I had doubts myself. I thought I had failed my people.' A pained expression drew his lips tight. 'I thought I had failed you.'

His ready acceptance of her apology almost made her lack of trust feel worse. It would have been better if he'd been upset about the whole mess.

'Do you trust me now?' he asked.

She nodded. 'I truly think I always did. I just hated the idea that I might have been used or made to look a fool.'

He ran a hand through his hair, so it stuck up at all angles. 'Aye, I know well the fear of that feeling.'

Elspeth's gaze lingered on him for a long moment, taking him in. Not just the handsome face, the hard warrior's frame, the emotion in his sensitive eyes, but the man himself. He was a true laird. He cared for his people, sacrificed for their needs. In a position where he could have so much more, his own castle was shoddy and his meals were as meagre as those of all his clansmen.

If only Ross could get to know him, to realise the type of man he was. Elspeth knew her eldest brother well. Calum was a man Ross would admire, one whose alliance he would want to have, especially over Iain Mac-Donnell, or even Leith MacLachlan.

It was then the idea settled into Elspeth's mind; the ideal solution.

Her heartbeat thudded harder and she found herself suddenly breathless.

It seemed almost too good to be true. She could have everything she had ever wanted. Everything that she had feared she would soon be denied. And it would all be for the greater good.

They were walking slowly towards the cave, but the rest of the men were already inside, stripping off their heavy gambesons and resting by a welcoming fire. The ride to the shore where they'd found Alan and the return trip had taken the better part of the day. A golden tinge touched the sky, suggesting a sunset was soon upon them.

She stopped and put a hand to Calum's shoulder.

He turned to her. 'What is it?'

'I know how we can ensure Ross will listen,' she replied.

Calum shook his head. 'I'll not let you go to him alone.'

'Not me. Us.'

He frowned.

'He'll have to listen if we go together,' she said softly. 'If we're…'

The muscles in his neck tensed as he drew in a long, slow breath. He stepped towards her, so close the familiar smoky peat and leather scent of him pulled her back to the intimate moments they had shared. And made her crave so, so much more.

Perhaps that is what bolstered her strength, for she suddenly found herself overwhelmed with shyness.

'If we're what?' He gently ran the back of his fingers down her face.

Her heart fluttered. 'If we're already wed.'

Chapter Twenty

'What did you say?' Calum asked Elspeth, certain he had heard her incorrectly.

She bit her lip. 'If we were wed, Ross might listen to us.' Her cheeks flushed and she shook her head. 'That is if you... I mean, you don't have to—'

'Nay,' he said quickly.

His intent had been to reassure her, but clearly did the opposite as her eyes went wide with horrified mortification.

'Nay, I meant...' he shook his head. 'I meant I'd be honoured to marry you—to ask you to marry me—to wed regardless of who does the asking,' he stammered clumsily. 'But how will that make Ross listen to us?'

Looking somewhat relieved, she continued. 'It was different before when you were the enemy. Now we have proof that the attacks were not Campbells, but the Mac-Donnells. By marrying, we would be making our own alliance, joining the MacMillans with the Campbells for the first time in centuries.

'Afterwards, I'll go ahead with Alan and talk to Fergus,' Elspeth continued. 'He'll be more inclined to listen. Or if he won't, I know his wife, Coira, will—she is someone who understands what it means to care for one's husband.' Elspeth's eyes sparkled in the soft light of the setting sun even as her cheeks flushed a deeper red. 'Once we have Fergus's support, he can speak to Ross on our behalf. Perhaps he can even shelter your men at Castle Barron to ensure they remain safe while he speaks to Ross.'

Elspeth took his hands in hers. 'If we're wed and our clans are joined, your people will be safe. Once it's known that the Campbells want peace, surely your land will be restored.'

Aye, it made perfect sense. And if she was wed to Calum, she couldn't be forced into a marriage with Leith. Calum couldn't help the way that knowledge soothed the roughened edges of his jealousy. However, he wouldn't want her forced into a marriage with him any more than having her shoved into a marriage with Leith.

'Do you really want this?' Calum asked.

She frowned. 'Peace for your people?'

Unease washed over Calum at her momentary confusion. At having to say aloud what he feared most. Rejection. Not being good enough. The way he'd always felt with his father. Except he had hated Alexander Campbell.

'Me,' Calum said finally. 'I meant do you want me?'

She broke out in a smile that lit up her entire face. 'Of course I wish to be with you.' She gave a soft laugh. 'Haven't you been listening to me?'

'Aye,' he said quickly. He had not missed how she'd mentioned caring for him and how it made her blush. 'I don't want you to wed me simply for an alliance.' He studied her, trying to gauge any sense of indecision. 'I wouldn't ever want you to feel about me the way you felt about having to marry Leith.'

She shook her head. 'Never. Calum, you're a fine man, a proper laird who sees to the needs of his people.' She hesitated. 'And I hope you don't feel like you're being made to marry me either? I don't want to twist your hand...'

He chuckled at the absurdity of the idea. 'You don't need to twist my hand. I'm honoured and humbled that you'd have me as your husband.'

In truth, he had never thought of wedding her. Not because it was not an attractive thought, but because he had never considered himself worthy. First, she had been promised to Leith, then she was going to be returning to her brother for what would likely be for ever and then once more finding herself a part of Leith's future. And then, her trust in Calum had been shaken.

But now...

Aye, now there was nothing keeping them from marrying, especially when their union would bring together their clans. Especially since he'd already lain with her and at that very moment, there might be a babe planted in her womb. His babe.

He took Elspeth's face in his hands and studied her in the same way he'd done the night they lay together, when he had wanted to memorise every part of her to remember for the rest of his life. Only now he didn't need to commit her appearance to his memory to think back on later. Instead, he regarded her with relief, with the knowledge he could stare into that beautiful face every day for the rest of his life.

But first, he had to be official about it.

He took her slender hand in his and knelt in front of her. 'Elspeth MacMillan, the bonniest lass in all of Scotland and England, will you do me the honour of becoming my wife and uniting our two clans together?'

Her eyes sparkled with tears. She nodded. 'Aye, of course I will.'

A cheer erupted from the cave where they had apparently drawn an audience as the Campbell warriors had all gathered about the cave's entrance.

Calum and Elspeth looked at one another and laughed at their spectators.

'At least we will not be without witnesses,' she said, still chuckling.

Calum understood her giddiness as it matched his own, an effervescence that made him feel lighter than ever before.

Suddenly her mirth faded behind a cloud of seriousness. 'How will we find a priest to wed us? They are all loyal to the MacMillans.'

Calum knew immediately who they could go to and assumed the man had kept his loyalties. Not necessarily to the Campbells, for they had truly committed atrocities under Alexander's command, but to Calum himself. Or at the very least to Calum's mother.

'I know someone who will help.' He took her hand in his and led her to the cave. 'Let us eat something and then we can be on our way. It's not far from here.'

She faltered. 'You mean we'll wed tonight?'

'Aye,' Calum replied. 'If that suits you.'

She grinned. 'It more than suits me.'

Calum had never eaten with such haste in his entire life. When he and Elspeth finished, they rode out with Bram and Hamish, who'd offered to act as witnesses to their union. The small kirk was set in the woods, where one had to know its location to find it. Father Keith preferred it that way.

If the MacDonnells had not found it first, that is. And

even if they hadn't, there was a good chance Father Keith may not be alive any longer. He had been old when Calum had been a lad, his hair going grey against his balding pate.

The thought remained with Calum as they rode towards the edge of the forest on the outskirts of Castle Sween. Dangerous territory, aye, but necessary to find Father Keith.

It was the closest Calum had been to the castle of his boyhood since they were cast out of Scotland. The land was familiar to him, but not in a way one would fondly remember their home. Castle Sween had never truly felt like home, not with his father's constant abuse and torment. And it harboured nothing warm in Calum's heart especially when he recalled how the Campbells had been run out like vermin.

Nay, there were no good memories of Castle Sween save for those periods of respite spent in the small kirk with Father Keith.

Their small retinue now made it through MacMillan land without being spotted by any of Ross's men and discovered the stone kirk still standing where it lay nestled in a thicket.

'I'll go first,' Calum said. 'To ensure he's inside.'

'Not without me,' Elspeth said as she slid from her horse.

Calum could only smile in response to the feisty lass who would soon be his wife. There was no arguing with her, and he wasn't about to bother trying.

He approached the wooden door and rapped upon the rough surface.

Shuffling footsteps sounded from within. 'A moment, a moment,' a voice called.

Seconds later, the door swung open, revealing a withered old man, his skin like damp, wrinkled linen. But despite the man's age, his blue eyes were sharp and clear as he fixed them on Calum and broke out in a wide grin that revealed a missing eye tooth.

'Is that wee Calum Campbell?' Father Keith asked.

'Aye, it's me.' He moved towards the older man, intending to clasp arms.

But Father Keith opened his arms the way a father would to a son and hugged Calum with a full embrace that warmed his heart. 'It's good to see you, my son. Ach, the years have gone by.'

He looked behind Calum to where Elspeth, Bram and Hamish stood and waved his hand to beckon them inside. 'Come in, all of you. It's about to rain again, I can smell it on the air. Ach, this weather has been something awful, hasn't it? Come in. Come in.'

Calum led the way in, guiding Elspeth with his hand at her lower back. The interior of the stone kirk was exactly as Calum remembered—slightly dark and smoky from the tallow candles, their oily scent mingling with the damp, earthy scent of the forest surrounding them. It was a smell that brought comfort to his soul reminding him of the countless hours he had spent in Father Keith's company.

The stone walls were still bare save a silk tapestry of the Virgin Mary holding a newborn Jesus that Calum's mother had stitched for the otherwise barren building. It was a place of little wealth, but warm and always welcoming.

'How is your mum?' The old priest asked as he closed the door behind them.

Calum's mother had sought company from the kindly

priest when they still resided in Scotland, which was how Calum had come to be at the small kirk so often. 'I am sad to say that she is no longer with us.'

The priest's face withered with sorrow and he made the sign of the cross. 'She had a beautiful soul, my son. She is surely among the angels now.' His blue eyes saddened. 'I have also heard of your father's passing recently as well. I'm sorry for you to have lost both your parents.'

Calum said nothing in regard to Alexander Campbell's loss. There had never been a connection between them, not like that he had shared with his mother.

The priest put a hand to Calum's shoulder and regarded the small party. 'Now I must ask, why have you come to see me after all these years?'

Calum looked to Elspeth. 'I'd like you to marry us.'

Father Keith looked between them and beamed. 'Ach, I'd be honoured to. There's not anything I like more than young people joining in a clandestine marriage.' His eyes twinkled mischievously.

'You should know,' Calum said. 'She's a MacMillan. Elspeth MacMillan.'

He held his breath and waited for the priest's decision, one that would go against the will of Ross MacMillan, who was now Father Keith's chieftain.

Elspeth immediately liked the older man who had been so friendly with Calum, clearly someone special from his youth. It was interesting to see another side of the man she was about to marry, one who was still held in affection so many years later, though it had undoubtedly been nearly twenty years since the priest had seen Calum.

The priest turned to study her, now that he had been made aware of her identity. It would be no small infraction to marry off the only sister of a clan's chieftain to a man most would consider the enemy. Especially in the middle of a war.

'Mistress Elspeth,' the priest finally said, his face solemn. 'May I speak with you?'

Her stomach dropped. Surely this was not good. 'Aye, of course.'

He lifted his thick white brows at Calum, Bram and Hamish who moved to the other side of the small church. The priest's bright blue eyes met hers, searching as he said softly, 'Did you come here of your own volition?'

'Aye, Father, I did,' she replied.

'And do you truly wish to wed Calum Campbell?' His brow crinkled. 'Even knowing it will greatly upset your family.'

She swallowed down her fears at those words and gave a firm nod. 'Aye, Father, I do. I want to forge an alliance between our clans.' She slid a glance to Calum as joy glowed within her chest. 'And because I care for him very much.'

The priest took her fingers in his cool, dry hands and patted her. 'The MacMillans should be proud to have such a lass as yerself safeguarding their future, mistress. And I can think of no better lass for wee Calum.'

She warmed under his praise and allowed herself to be led up to the altar where a faded green cloth hung, dots of once fine gold thread winking in the dismal light. Calum joined her, standing tall and proud at her side, in front of Father Keith. Behind them, Bram and Hamish took their seats among the rows of empty pews, ancient things that groaned under their weight.

Father Keith stood before them, the psalter open in his palm. Though the lighting was poor, he recited the words without a single stumble, no doubt more from memory than reading as the cadence of immaculate Latin filled the small space, uniting Elspeth and Calum together for ever.

When it was Calum's turn to speak his vows and take her as his wife, he regarded her with such sincerity, with such tenderness, that Elspeth's eyes prickled with the threat of tears.

'Aye,' he answered, watching her with affection in his hazel eyes. 'I do.'

'And you, lass?' the priest asked. 'Do you take this man as your wedded husband?'

'Aye, I do.' She was already smiling as she replied, knowing full well what her words meant before they were even declared by the priest.

They were officially man and wife. Married.

And though Elspeth had not looked forward to marriage with any anticipation when she was younger, now she relished the idea. Especially knowing how much she cared for the man she had just joined in holy matrimony.

'You may now kiss your bonny bride,' Father Keith said.

Calum pulled Elspeth towards him. Her heartbeat skipped. Then Calum, her husband, pressed his mouth to hers, sealing their union.

'I now present Laird and Lady Campbell,' the priest said in a strong, clear voice as they faced Bram and Hamish whose excitement was shown with sharp whistles and cheers.

'Your mum would be so proud of you,' Father Keith said to Calum.

'Thank you,' Calum said reverently. 'I'm certain she would like the woman I've chosen as my wife.'

Elspeth beamed up at him.

But in this wedding celebration, there were no feasts or dances or even music. Just five people in a quiet stone kirk in the heart of the woods. There would be no wedding chamber or trunk of clothes she had been sewing for herself in the years prior to her marriage, or a bridal talk given to her by her mother. Not that one was needed now.

The union between Elspeth and Calum was to tie their clans together once Elspeth went to Fergus and Coira for their assistance in convincing Ross. And it meant a lifetime of passion, a tease of the possibility of love.

'You return to the cave,' Calum told Hamish and Bram. 'I'd like some time alone with my wife.'

Elspeth's cheeks went hot even as her body simmered with longing. It had been several days since they had lain together, though she thought of it often. The idea of consummating their marriage flooded her with a restless heat, one she could scarcely wait to have sated.

'Aye, we'll see you on the morrow.' Bram clasped arms with Calum with the plan that they would all reconvene at the cave the following day to venture to Castle Barron together.

Father Keith had disappeared while the men spoke and returned suddenly with a bundle of blankets in his thin arms. 'It's not much,' he said. 'But I've a barn if you like...'

Calum looked towards Elspeth, his expression apologetic as he seemed to be seeking her permission. He didn't have to specify the danger of trying to find an inn nearby. She would be recognised anywhere in this part of Scotland.

But a hayloft was as good a place as any for her. She would be with Calum, their future locked together, joined in their purpose to aid those in great need. And the man she had come to care for so greatly.

'Thank you for your kindness,' Elspeth said graciously to the priest. 'We appreciate your offer and happily accept.'

He gave a sheepish nod. 'Take care of this lad, aye? His mum was as kind and gentle as they come, and he's cut from the same cloth.'

'Gladly.' She gently embraced the old man, careful of his frail body. 'Thank you.'

When she drew away, tears sparkled in the priest's eyes. 'Ach, off with the lot of you. It's far too late an hour for one as old as me.'

Calum thanked him one final time before they all departed the small kirk. Outside, the rain had begun once more. Bram and Hamish took off in haste to hopefully outrun the worst of it even as dark clouds blotted out the moonlight. Calum led Elspeth to a small barn set off to the side of the kirk.

It was a modest size, to be sure, but the hayloft above was dry and smelled sweetly of hay and sunshine. Calum lay the blankets the priest had given him over the golden tufts.

'It's not the finest wedding chamber ever to be had,' he turned to her, his hands on his hips. 'But it's a far cry from a sandy cave floor surrounded by snoring men, aye?'

'All that matters is that we're together.' Elspeth went to him and put her arms around his torso. 'My husband.'

'I like the sound of that.' He grinned at her and lowered his head to kiss her lips. 'Say it again,' he murmured.

'My husband,' she said between kisses.

He growled playfully and drew her against him where

the hardness of his arousal was already evident. She grinned in delight.

'I've wanted to have you again since the night we lay together.' His body flexed towards her.

'I've wanted you as well,' she confessed brazenly. 'I think of you often, imagining your hands on me, your mouth…the things you did…'

She couldn't talk any more, not when it suddenly became too difficult to even think. Right now, she wanted only to *feel*.

He pulled the ties of her kirtle at her back and widened the homespun cloth over her shoulders revealing her chemise. Her breath came faster as he undressed her, first peeling away her kirtle and then divesting her of her chemise. His hands caressed her naked body, tracing her shape as she worked off his gambeson and her fingers found the hem of his tunic, drawing it off him.

The soreness between her thighs from the first time they'd coupled had finally disappeared early that morning. This time there would be no virgin's discomfort like before. Nay, this time, there would be only pleasure.

And now they were not dreading a future apart but anticipating one together. It had all worked out so perfectly.

So long as she could convince Fergus.

But that was a thought for another time. Not for her wedding night.

And especially not when she suspected she might be falling in love with the man she had just married.

Chapter Twenty-One

Calum couldn't take his eyes off Elspeth as his palms skimmed over her smooth skin.

His wife.

Never had he dreamed he would wed a woman as perfect as her. And certainly he'd never dreamed he would wed a MacMillan after all the strife between their clans.

'What are you smiling about?' she asked coyly.

'I cannot believe a MacMillan and a Campbell wed of their own volition.'

'And truly because we wanted to.' Her hands rested on his chest and slid upward so her hands curled around the back of his neck, as she brought her mouth to his.

Her body was like hot silk against his skin. He groaned and caught her bottom to push her more firmly against him. She moaned and deepened their kiss with the tease of her tongue against him.

He caught her breast in his hand as his thumb found her nipple.

'Aye,' she whispered, leaning her head back. 'Kiss me there, like you did before.'

With a hungry growl, his mouth trailed down her throat and over her graceful collarbone, down to the pink tip of her nipple. He parted his lips and drew the small nub between them, flicking it with his tongue until it pebbled in his mouth and her body undulated against his.

As he switched to her other nipple, his fingertips descended down her stomach to the apex of her thighs.

She whimpered, her legs parting for his touch. He stroked her, teasing a finger over her sex. She cried out and he abandoned her breasts to kiss her beautiful mouth as his finger eased into her sheath. Her hips bucked in response, but he held her in place while his thumb found her sensitive bud.

Her moans melted against his lips as they kissed. He'd meant to bring her to completion thus, but her hands were on his trews, pulling at the ties and pushing them down his hips. The cool air touched his skin, followed immediately by the heat of her touch.

She bit her bottom lip and wrapped her fingers around his length. His cock jerked to attention and her mouth lifted into a smile.

'I can tease too,' she whispered in a husky voice that made his blood simmer in his veins.

His ministrations over her sex became clumsy, less precise as the grip of her hand worked over him. His mind was too enraptured by the exquisite play of her hold on him, by the tightness building in his body. By how wet and ready she was for him.

She eased away from him, withdrawing not only her hand, but also her pelvis from his reach. Eyes still on him, she sank to her knees.

Calum tried to swallow around his dry throat. 'Elspeth…'

She took his length in her hands and licked her lips as she leaned closer to him. Her breath brushed over the sensitive head, making it jump in her light grip.

'What are you doing?' He asked raggedly.

'Loving you the way you loved me,' she replied simply.

He opened his mouth to say more when her tongue stretched out and slowly licked the underside of his arousal. Any protest or any thought whatsoever for that matter dissolved.

She stroked over him several times before pulling the tip of him into her mouth.

A groan tore from his chest. 'Aye, like that.'

With a wicked glint in her eye, she took him deeper the next time, drawing him into the warmth of her mouth. He leaned his head back as he yielded to the incredible pleasure as she licked and stroked him.

He would have liked to allow her to continue for ever, but the tension building in his body told him he would not last long with such sweet ministrations. And he wanted to claim his wife—in body as well as in soul.

'No more,' he gritted out.

But she never was a lass who did what she was told to and she gave one final, wicked suck as her tongue dragged over the base and nearly undid him. He gently caught her chin and eased her from him so he popped from her mouth. She ran her tongue over her lips in such a coquettish manner it made him tempted to let her continue.

But, nay—he wanted his wife.

'Did I not do it right?' she asked with concern.

'You're doing it too well.' He helped her to her feet. 'It's you that I want.'

She smiled and stood, gliding her body up his as she did so. His body was hard as stone, throbbing with the need to release where it nudged against her stomach.

His mouth found hers, kissing her with a passion that

left them both breathless and arching against one another.
He lowered her to the blanket covering the hay, surprisingly soft and many times better than the cold, damp
cave where they'd slept the last few nights.

Her thighs parted for him as he settled over her, so
they fit together as perfectly as before.

While she was no longer a virgin, he still took great
care as he angled himself at her entrance and slowly
pushed into her. She cried out, clinging to him as pleasure tingled through him.

With each thrust, he allowed himself to plunge deeper
inside her, the grip of her sheath squeezing him with
every slight move. Finally, he was buried completely
within her, their two bodies fully joined.

Their hips were fitted together completely, their hearts
beating as one as they continued to kiss, to touch—to
love. He remained in place for a moment, buried fully
within her, not only to allow her to adjust to him once
more, but also to savour the sensation.

She arched beneath him and he withdrew before easing back into her once more. Her cheeks were flushed
with their exertions and her eyes heavy lidded with passion.

'Faster,' she breathed. 'Like before. Harder.'

He braced himself over her and flexed his hips, driving into her so her breasts gave a tantalising bounce with
each solid joining. She cried out, her head thrown back.

Suddenly he had an idea, something that would allow
her to control the pace, to do as she wanted with him.
Holding her to him, he carefully rolled them both over
so she lay atop him.

He lightly guided her upright. 'Sit up.'

She did so, gazing down at him like a sultry goddess,

her fiery hair wild where it fell around her naked shoulders and over her breasts. He caught her hips in his hands and guided her over him, so her sex clenched around him, drawing him in even deeper. Her lashes fluttered with a pleasure he too keenly felt.

'Lean on me if you like,' he offered.

Her hands settled on his chest. Using his body for leverage, she began to move on her own. She was slow as she adjusted to the new position, but soon quickened the pace as her hips rolled over his.

She gasped in pleasure as she arched against him, every small shift gripping and pulling him in the most exquisite manner. As she did so, he thrust up into her, their bodies gliding in tandem once more, loving one another in the most beautiful way.

A familiar tension clenched within him as the need to release built. But he wanted her to climax first, to watch the pleasure play out over her bonny face as she rode him like a goddess.

Elspeth rocked over Calum, gasping at the incredible sensation of straddling atop him, controlling the speed, the depth, everything. His chest was like stone beneath her hands and he gazed up at her with an awed reverence.

She felt powerful. Beautiful.

A wife with a husband she cared so greatly for.

He grabbed her hips once more, shifting her slightly forward. As he did so, their next gyration ground the sensitive bud of her sex against him. She cried out in surprised pleasure.

He grinned back at her.

Propping herself against his chest, she arched herself over him, rubbing that spot with her body as his arousal thrust in and out of her. She was panting from her efforts, but couldn't stop. The tension building within her was too great. Too ready.

Calum kept his hands on her hips, pulling her, using his strength to help her movements while he thrust deep up into her. The tension at her core wound tighter and tighter until finally it exploded into a cyclone of bliss that left her crying out, her heat thrown back as she succumbed to its intensity.

As her crises seized her, Calum roared and jerked his hips upward into her one final time as his seed poured into her. When the brilliance of pleasure eventually waned, it took with it the little strength she had remaining. She folded forward, languid, and lay against Calum's chest, their skin slick with sweat, their hearts pounding in unison.

'I didn't know it could be done like that,' she said, still breathless.

His chuckle rumbled beneath her cheek. 'There are many ways, wife. And I want to explore them all with you.'

She lifted her head and smiled down at him. 'Is that a promise?'

'Aye, you minx.' He wrapped his strong arms around her and gently flipped them over once more, so he was braced over the top of her. His eyes locked with hers, playful and serious all at once. 'I'm going to pleasure you in all the ways a man can please a woman.'

Her breath caught. For she knew he did not only refer to the physical, but what was developing between them as well.

He withdrew from her, sending a ripple of residual delight shuddering through her. He lay at her side, his hair mussed from their endeavours, a lazy smile curving his sensual mouth. 'My wife.'

She grinned as he pushed the hair from her face. 'My husband.'

'We're going to bring peace to our area of Scotland,' he said proudly. 'Together.' His hand found hers and he threaded his fingers through hers.

'Aye, together.'

A sudden thought occurred to her now that their time together would not be limited. And now that so much had changed between them.

'Will you still teach me to fight?' she asked.

His fingertip traced a path over her shoulder. 'Why would I not?'

'I'm your wife now,' she replied.

He withdrew his hand from her shoulder and cupped her face. 'You still need to learn to defend yerself.'

'Then perhaps you can eventually teach me to use a sword?'

He chuckled. 'Aye, I can do that. We can speak more of it once we are settled in Scotland again.'

She liked the optimism of his statement, at his confidence their marriage and her appeal to Fergus would work. But a trail of unease skirted the back of her mind.

Would Calum want Castle Sween back?

'Where would you want to live in Scotland?' she asked, hesitantly.

Castle Sween had been awarded to the MacMillans by the King after the Campbells had been banished from Scotland for their brutal attacks on neighbouring clans. Surely Ross would not be so eager to be removed from his home.

'I don't want Castle Sween,' he replied, clearly understanding her fear. 'It's filled with dark memories for me, ones I don't want to relive.' His hazel eyes fixed on hers. 'Ones I don't want lingering in our new life as we have children to create a family and a life together.'

Her hand went to her flat stomach as she considered the idea of a bairn. Calum's child with his dark hair and sensitive warm gaze.

His hand covered hers and she found the idea of a family with him appealed to her more than she thought it would.

He leaned towards her and kissed her brow, the action sweet and cherishing. 'Perhaps we will build our own castle, a new one to fill with new memories.'

Tension she didn't realise she'd been holding eased away. 'I would like that very much.'

'Aye, I would too.' He drew her against him and pulled a blanket over them both.

She lay her head on his bare chest where the hairs tickled her cheek and the steady rhythm of his heart thumped in her ear. Prickles of hay jabbed through the blanket they lay upon, but it was otherwise soft where it cradled their shared weight.

Rain pattered on the roof, but inside the hayloft, they were dry and warm. And together.

In that moment, she would not want to be anywhere else in all the world.

Everything was perfect.

Their marriage had been wanted by both of them, two people who desired and respected one another. Their clans would be reunited soon, without cause for further bloodshed. No one need lose their castle to accommodate the Campbells' return. And tomorrow, she would once more see Fergus and Coira, certain she could convince them of her need for their aid. Especially once they saw that she too had found happiness in her own union.

As the pull of sleep tugged at her, Elspeth let herself slide towards it, unfettered and soothed. For with everything aligned so ideally, she was sure nothing could possibly go wrong.

Chapter Twenty-Two

Calum woke the next morning with Elspeth wrapped in his arms. They had remained thus throughout the night with no need to jump apart when the sun rose or worry who might see them.

They were wed, husband and wife, ready to begin a new journey together.

And it would all start with Castle Barron and Elspeth's meeting with Fergus MacMillan.

Calum knew nothing of the man other than what she had told him, but hoped Fergus would be as amenable to a peaceful resolution as she anticipated.

Golden sunlight poured in through the slats of the shuttered window and made Elspeth's hair shimmer like embers. There was a chill in the air, but nestled beneath the covers with her, Calum was wonderfully warm and completely at peace.

But as much as he longed to remain as they were, his men were waiting for their return. Calum reached out and gently caressed Elspeth's smooth cheek to rouse her.

She blinked her lovely green eyes open, saw him and smiled. 'Good morrow, husband.'

'Good morrow, wife.' He leaned forward and nuzzled her neck.

He'd expected her laugh, but instead she gave a little moan that left him instantly hot and hard.

In the end, they left their bed later than expected, their cheeks flushed and bodies glowing with sated pleasure. They washed with water from a wine skin, brisk in the icy morning air and packed to leave, stopping to bid farewell to Father Keith and return his bedding.

The old priest beamed with delight as they approached. 'Ach, it's a fine thing to see such a young, happy couple.' He clasped his hands in delight. 'Here, I've some bread and cheese for your journey. I know how youth can be— in a hurry, no doubt.'

Elspeth's cheeks coloured and Calum chuckled good-naturedly. 'Aye, you know us far too well, Father. Thank you for your hospitality.'

'Don't forget this old man once you're back in Scotland, aye?' Father Keith said with a wink. 'I do baptisms as well.'

Elspeth embraced the older man. 'Thank you.'

His smile widened further still as he offered them both a blessing and sent them on their way.

Elspeth and Calum readied and mounted their steeds quickly. The day was starting off fine with a bold sun shining in the sky and not a cloud to be seen. Not that such a thing mattered much in Scotland when, on a whim, the clouds could come from nowhere and turn day to night and calm to chaos.

Ever cautious, they crossed MacMillan land, only seeing guards in the distance. Certainly nothing that risked their being caught. They made their way through the clear morning to the cave where the Campbells were waiting with their gear.

They were to journey to Castle Barron and wait on the outskirts while Elspeth spoke to Fergus. If he agreed to support them, they would be at the ready to allow their forces to be aligned in the protection of the MacMillans against the MacDonnells.

Calum proudly stood at Elspeth's side when they entered the cave, his arm about her slender waist as he addressed his men. 'I'm pleased to introduce you to your new mistress, Lady Campbell.'

There were felicitations and clasped forearms all about as well as several bows of respect to Elspeth. Through it all, Calum realised he did not see Bram or Hamish.

'Where are Bram and Hamish?' He asked. 'Did you lazy things send them out for bread and cheese after they'd travelled through the night?'

'Nay, Laird,' a blond-haired warrior named Malcolm said. 'We thought they'd remained behind to meet us.'

Ice dread trickled down Calum's spine. 'Did they not return last night?'

The men looked about at one another, each shaking their head at the other. 'Nay, Laird. They didn't come back.'

'Calum.' Elspeth caught his forearm and regarded him with wide, frightened eyes.

But she didn't have to say what they were all thinking— what was likely a certainty—that Bram and Hamish had been caught crossing MacMillan lands and had been captured.

If that was truly had happened, it meant that their lives were in immediate danger.

'I can go to Ross instead,' Elspeth said hesitantly.

Calum ran a hand through his hair. Ross would need more softening to accept his sister's union to a Campbell. The marriage would not be well received. Not like it would have been with Elspeth's other brother.

Ross wanted vengeance.

But at this point, they might not have a choice.

'Let us make our way towards both castles,' Calum replied. 'I'll make a decision when we must turn to one or the other. In the meantime, perhaps we will find Hamish or Bram on our path.'

After all, Bram did lay low through the night if he thought himself being chased. But given the location of the sun in the sky, he had never shown so late in the morning as this.

It was likely Calum and his men would not find them on the journey, so Calum knew he would doubtless have to make a choice between his two most loyal warriors and the welfare of his clan.

A knot of fear sat in the pit of Elspeth's stomach as they rode over the countryside in the direction of both castles with one to the right and the other to the left. If Ross had Bram and Hamish, the two would surely be hanged as an example to others who sought to attack the MacMillan clan. Not that Ross was cruel, but he was a thorough and exacting chieftain who set the welfare of his people above all else.

Again, Elspeth wondered how his own marriage with the MacDonnell lass had worked out. Of the three of siblings, he was the only one who didn't know anything of the person he was to wed. She could only hope it had gone as blissfully well for him as it had for Fergus.

Certainly, Ross would not be pleased with her decision to marry Calum. While Ross often kept his emotions under control, she had seen how protective he was of her when he'd fought Calum. As chieftain, there were many retributions he could exact on Calum if he refused to accept their marriage. Which was why it would be ideal to go to Fergus first.

But if Ross did have Bram and Hamish, they would not live long enough for Elspeth to first convince Fergus of her plight.

It was a terrible position for Calum to be in, and Elspeth wished there was more she could do. His jaw was locked with steely determination as they rode, his demeanour sullen and quiet.

'Something is amiss,' he said to her under his breath as they rode. 'I wish you had not come.'

'You wouldn't have much to work with if I hadn't come,' she protested, unable to stop the sting of offence at his words.

'Aye, but there is something in the air.' He narrowed his eyes. 'I can smell it.'

His nostrils flared lightly, as if there truly was something in the air and he'd picked up on its scent as surely as a hunting dog. A rumbling sounded in the distance despite the uncharacteristically sunny day and blue, cloudless sky.

'Get back to the cave,' Calum said.

She frowned at him. 'I won't—'

'Get back to the cave,' he shouted as he navigated his horse in front of hers.

Elspeth froze at the urgency in his voice as the sound grew louder. It wasn't until a dark mass spreading over the hills that she understood: an army was approaching.

And quickly.

'Is it Ross?' she asked.

'Get to the cave, Elspeth,' Calum called out over his shoulder, ignoring her question.

Frustration spurred her onward. She urged her horse faster and caught up with Calum.

'If that's Ross, I can speak with him,' she insisted.

'These men are not interested in speaking, Elspeth.' He didn't even look at her as he steered the men towards the forest. 'These men are here to fight.'

'Where are you going?' she demanded.

Was he turning away from the attack?

'To the forest where we can have some cover,' Calum replied. 'I want you to leave.'

'Nay,' she replied vehemently. 'I can speak to him.'

The shadow fell over them from the thickly leaved treetops and the chirps, clicks and rustles of the denizens of the forest blotted out the rumble of distant troops. For now. Elspeth was no warrior, but she knew Ross's men would not be so easily discouraged.

Calum brought his horse to a stop and leapt down. His men did likewise.

Elspeth followed suit, but did not understand.

'We cannot afford to lose the horses,' Calum explained. 'That and Ross has more men. If we can fight in the forest, it forces most of them from their horses into the woods where we can try to hide if need be.' He pulled his sword free. 'It evens the battle.'

'Evens the battle?' Elspeth repeated in horror. 'You want peace. Not war.'

'What I don't want is you here,' Calum said. 'You need to return to the cave at once.'

She shook her head. 'Let me speak with Ross. I can—'

'You won't be able to even get to him.'

He turned to his men, issuing orders, directing the horses behind them and his stronger warriors out towards the front. Putting his back to her protests.

Anger flared up in her. He was treating her exactly like her uncle had, as a simple woman without any sense. She was more than that.

And she thought he'd known as much, that he believed in her. 'Don't ignore me,' she seethed. 'Don't treat me like an ignorant lass whose place is in the castle.'

He turned back around, his face set. 'Your place isn't in battle.'

'Then why would you teach me to defend myself?' she demanded.

'So you could protect yourself.' He shook his head. 'We don't have time for this. Elspeth...'

The way he said her name was resigned. Defeated.

As if he was going to finally acquiesce and allow her to join them.

'You're my wife,' he said solemnly. 'Not a warrior. At this very moment, our bairn may be growing in your womb. For once in your life, you must listen.'

There it was then. He did not trust her. Like all the other men in her life who did not take her seriously or think her capable.

The arrival of an army of horse hooves rumbled underfoot. Elspeth's pulse spiked. Ross was nearly there.

Her eyes burned with angry tears. 'I'm going to find Ross. I'll speak to him.'

'I want you to be safe.' He tossed a worried glance behind him to where the MacMillan men were fast approaching and pulled her to him. 'I care for you, Elspeth—I want you to be safe.'

The shouts of men came from the distance as the Mac-

Millan army approached. He pressed his mouth to hers in a fierce, protective kiss. 'Please go now.'

She shook her head. 'I need to find Ross.'

'Kieran,' Calum called out. 'Take Alan back to the cave and Lady Campbell as well.' A muscle worked in his jaw. 'By force if necessary.'

Elspeth jerked away from Calum at those words. The dark-haired warrior regarded Elspeth with a frown and took a hesitant step towards her. Calum cast one final look at her before turning away to face her brother's approaching army.

'My lady.' Kieran indicated the forest behind them. Alan needed no further encouragement and began to walk in that direction, but Elspeth remained where she stood.

'Nay,' she whispered through numb lips.

But her words were lost in the bloodcurdling war cries as the MacMillan clan, her birth clan, broke through the forest with weapons brandished. Swords rang out and bodies thudded together as the two forces collided in the middle.

The battle began in earnest, swords flashing, battle axes sinking into flesh, daggers finding weak spots in armour.

Elspeth was transfixed in horror.

Kieran's hand on her arm tugged at her. 'My lady, we must make haste.'

Calum was right. There would be no talking of clan leaders in such a situation where men were intent on fighting. He was also correct in stating they were outnumbered. Where he was wrong was in thinking she couldn't help. She was no warrior—aye, she did not claim to be. But she could force Ross to stop if she found him on the battlefield.

The only chance the Campbells had to keep from being slayed would be for Elspeth to put a stop to it all. Then Calum would see.

It may be dangerous, but she was a woman, not a soldier in a gambeson or chainmail. No one would attack her.

Or at least, she hoped not. The chance was one she would take.

There were no other options.

'Forgive me,' she said to Kieran and raced to the outskirts of battle to seek out her brother.

All she needed to do was find him and he would surely stop everything. Right now, she was the Campbell clan's only hope.

Chapter Twenty-Three

Calum was fighting a battle he knew they could not win. But there had not been enough time to run. Not with how quickly the MacMillans had gained on them. Getting into the forest had been a desperate attempt to find some way to survive. He only hoped it would be enough to spare some of his men.

Regardless, he was grateful he had sent Elspeth with Kieran and hoped she would one day forgive him. For while he would fight with everything in him, the odds were stacked against him.

They were stacked against all of his men.

Perhaps his father had been right. There was no way for a peaceful resolution. Not when one side was so fixed on vengeance.

And, really, could Calum blame Ross? What would Calum do to protect Elspeth if he thought someone had stolen her?

Calum only wished there had been more of an opportunity to talk to Fergus or Ross, to resolve it as it could have been done before this fight which few would likely survive. In truth, Elspeth's doubt in Calum gnawed at his thoughts. She had more faith in her brother than she did in him.

Heart heavy, he joined the Campbells in battle against the MacMillans, his people against Elspeth's.

He struck where he could with the MacMillan men, wounding rather than killing. There had been too much death already.

The man in front of him brought a battle axe swinging towards him, one Calum just manage to evade. Calum swept with his sword, narrowly missing the man's arm. The MacMillan man came back with a roar and whisked the massive weapon at Calum again, nearly taking his head off.

Calum pulled his dagger from his boot and plunged it into the man's right arm. The MacMillan warrior cried out as the battle axe fell to the ground. He backed up, disappearing into the mass of warriors where he would be protected.

But wars could not be won by injuring soldiers. Nay, Calum needed to seek out Ross in the melee. If he could get to him, speak to him.

It was foolish to even attempt in a battle, but he had to for Elspeth's sake. So she would at least know that he had tried.

'I need to speak to your Chieftain,' Calum cried out.

A MacMillan with dark hair and a sneer under his helm replaced the one with a battle axe.

'He has nothing to say to swine.' The warrior lunged at Calum who spun away and managed a blow to the man's back that sent him staggering.

As the warrior stumbled, Calum quickly scanned the mass of writhing men fighting behind him. But it was impossible to make out Ross.

Calum cursed under his breath. That's when he saw Kieran to the right of the Campbell men.

Alarm tingled through Calum.

If Kieran was still there, it meant Elspeth had not left.

The alarm frosted over into fear. Calum had sent her away to keep her safe, to ensure nothing would happen to her.

But she hadn't put enough trust in him to resolve this situation. His father's harsh words rushed back to him, reminding him what a weak leader her was, how he would never be strong enough for the clan.

Apparently Elspeth agreed.

Calum spun around, seeking out a flash of red hair among the foliage. Something hard thwacked him between the shoulder blades, protected by his gambeson. He was going to get killed if he didn't pay attention.

He turned once more, facing the MacMillan army to find a new warrior was drawing back a sword for another strike. Calum ducked low and swept his leg out, knocking the man to the ground and kicking away his weapon where it disappeared among the many feet of those fighting around them.

Calum straightened and frantically looked about once more. But Elspeth was nowhere to be seen.

Damn it.

Kieran didn't appear to know where she was either. He stood outside the fighting, his face turning side to side as he clearly sought her out with panic.

She was gone.

Suddenly Calum caught sight of another face he recognised. Alan.

He stood by Kieran, his face ashen.

As another man attacked Calum, he had just enough

time to see a MacMillan warrior launch himself at Alan,
his blade thrusting through the peasant.

Calum didn't have to look again to confirm the blow
was fatal. Alan wore no armour and the attack had been
forceful.

Without Alan, there would be no way to convince Ross
of the MacDonnell clan's deception. Even if Calum could
gain an audience with the chieftain, there was no more
proof save their word on the matter. And a MacMillan
would never trust a Campbell.

Apparently no MacMillan would.

Ever Calum's own wife.

Calum cried out and attacked the MacMillan man in
front of him with renewed vigour, pushing him back into
the mass of his fellow warriors.

It was then that he saw a flash of red among the green
gambesons of the MacMillan army.

Elspeth.

Calum shoved against the man who'd replaced the
other MacMillan he had been fighting. The glimpse of
red hair was gone. But he *knew* he had seen it.

She was not only in danger, she was in the middle
of battle.

He'd seen the hurt in her eyes when he'd told her to
leave. That injured expression had been followed by one
of defiance. He'd known she might attempt something
like this, that she questioned his faith in her even as he
had questioned her faith in him. And now he might lose
her for ever.

'Elspeth,' Calum shouted.

But his cry was lost among those around him, the
ones of the wounded, of the dying, of those still attack-

ing with the intent to kill. It was sheer chaos and his wife was mired in the thick of it all. In danger.

He heaved against the wall of men, trying to press deeper into the battle to get to his wife. For while she was ignorant to the ways of war, he was not and knew well that men would not hesitate to attack a woman when in the throes of bloodlust.

He called her name once more and drove harder to propel himself deeper into the fray, acting on the offensive now as he tried to fight his way into the heart of battle in search of his wife.

And hoped he would not be too late.

No matter what Elspeth thought she knew to expect of war, nothing could have prepared her for what it truly was like.

Campbells and MacMillans fought one another, each intent on killing their opponent. Men shouted and cried out amid the deafening clang of weapons clashing with one another. All around her was the stink of sweat and blood and death.

Men jostled this way and that, trapping her within the mass of bodies so that even if she had wanted to get out, she could not. Though she tried to push it away, fear grappled at her control.

The warriors were not looking where they slashed or punched. It was a brawl of survival by any means necessary, more brutal and wilder than she ever would have thought possible.

When men trained for combat in the courtyard, they did so in neat lines, their motions gone through with measured steps and a natural rhythm. There was no rhythm in this chaos. No order. No anything that made a modicum of sense.

A man in front of her was run through with a sword, its tip erupting on the other side of his body and red with bright, crimson blood. He fell to his knees, the blade still skewered through him. His eyes lifted to her, bright blue and bright with tears as he cried out in a final plea, whimpering for his mother.

Elspeth's knees went weak, her eyes hot with tears.

Calum was right. She should not have been here. She did not belong among warriors. Especially when she'd seen how much her lack of trust in him had wounded him.

A cry choked from her and she staggered backwards, but the people on all sides of her kept her upright. Someone grabbed her, jerking her around with intent.

A blade lifted in front of her face.

It snapped the terror from her and recalled her purpose. She was here to find Ross. To get him to cease this battle. To save Calum and his people.

Her dagger was clenched in her fist and she brought it up. Though the weapon shook in her hand, she had a fast hold on it and would readily plunge it into any person who meant her harm.

But the blade in front of her lowered. 'My lady?'

She blinked, suddenly recognising the face of a warrior she recalled seeing around Castle Sween in past years. Blood spattered his face like freckles.

Campbell blood.

Elspeth's stomach churned with nausea.

But now was not the time to give into such weakness. Now was for action. For putting an end to the horror of this battle.

'I need to find Ross,' she cried out.

The man nodded. 'Aye, he's there.' He pointed through the seething cluster of men towards the rear right. 'Thanks be to God you're safe.'

Elspeth tried to search through the men, many of whom were taller than her. She couldn't make out her brother, let alone which warriors were MacMillans and which were Campbells.

'Can you take me to him?' she shouted over the cacophony of battle.

'Aye, it would be an honour.' He put a hand to her shoulder, shielding her from the jostle of men fighting about her.

Tears tingled in her eyes with the profound sense of relief and finally she felt as though she could breathe again. With the familiar MacMillan warrior's help, she would get to Ross, to tell him of the MacMillan-Campbell alliance. To inform him of the MacDonnell's treachery. Then they could leave this awful place and not another man need die.

'We worried for you, my lady,' the warrior said. 'We've been trying to—'

His body jerked suddenly, and his weight fell against Elspeth with such force he nearly knocked her to the ground. She snapped her attention towards him and found his brown eyes were wide with surprise. His mouth opened, as if he meant to speak, but only a trickle of blood leaked from the corner of his mouth. He tumbled gracelessly to the ground, a battle axe jutting from his spine. He landed face first in the mud and did not move.

Elspeth covered her mouth with her hand to block her scream.

All at once, she was plunged back into the pandemonium of battle and her fear returned with a vengeance, leaving her paralysed in terror.

And then she caught sight of a familiar face in the madness of it all, through the face slit of a helm several paces away.

Ross.

His familiar face snapped her from her trance and launched her into action once more.

She called his name, but it was lost in the noise of battle, swallowed up among other shouts and cries. 'Ross,' she tried again with as much volume as she could infuse into his name.

Still he did not acknowledge her. She was too far away.

With a huff of frustration, she began to push back at the men being shoved against her. With effort, she worked her way between the backs of the warriors, keeping from facing any of them lest she be mistaken for the enemy.

Her attention fixed on Ross and remained there. She didn't want to witness any more death. Her heart could not bear to witness men's eyes as the light faded from them or be subjected to their piteous calls for their mothers in their final moments.

Just as she had passed between two men, someone grabbed her shoulder and spun her round. The warrior's face and clothes were wet with gore, his eyes brilliant with an excitement that chilled her blood.

'I'm looking for Ro—' Before the words were out of her mouth, the man slammed his fist at her, striking her with such power that her head jerked hard to the left.

She blinked, momentarily stunned. Her brain cleared and blared out a warning. She looked back to the man in time to see him lifting a two-handed sword over his head with intent.

Her muscles worked into action before her brain had time to register and she darted to the right to try to hide from her attacker. But there was nowhere to go. The man's face twisted with whatever madness it was that possessed him as he rounded on her once more.

In the recesses of her mind, beyond the panic that she only just managed to keep at bay, she remembered Calum's instructions, to attack rather than wait to defend. It would put her opponent off as he wouldn't be expecting it.

Before the crazed warrior could bring his weapon down, she rushed at him and plunged her dagger into his side. His face registered the shock of her attack as hot blood washed over her hand.

The sword slipped from his hands and fell into the forest floor behind him where it lay beside a dead soldier. The man growled at her, his teeth bared like an animal as he swung at her with his fist once more.

She tried to move away, but he caught her at the temple. Pain exploded in her head in starbursts of white that bloomed in vision. She thought she might have cried out, but could not be certain.

Her hand trembled as she brought it to her temple. When she drew it back, blood smeared over her shaking fingers.

She looked up for help and stopped short. Ross was only a few steps away. So close.

'Ross,' she called, but his name barely rasped in her throat. She tried to walk towards him, but her feet merely stumbled over fallen bodies and slid in the slippery forest floor.

Darkness lured her towards a painless abyss.

She should fight it she knew. But her body would not

do what she wanted. Ross turned away from her as he lifted his blade.

She was so close. She tried to say his name, but though her lips moved, no sound emerged.

Suddenly, she was falling, joining the dead where they littered the muddy ground. Her face hit the cold, wet mud and though she knew it would mean her death to do so, she closed her eyes and succumbed to the inky blackness.

She had failed—to save Calum and his men, to reunite the clans in peace—she had failed everyone.

And now she would die.

Chapter Twenty-Four

Never had Calum known such helpless terror as he did when he witnessed the MacMillan warrior attacking Elspeth. For a moment Calum had assumed she had a chance, when she attacked the man with the move she'd been taught only a sennight before. But the man had struck a final blow that left her reeling.

Calum had fought like a beast then, no longer caring if he killed or maimed, wanting only for his path to Elspeth to be cleared so that he could go to her. She stumbled about, dazed, blood trickling from her temple.

There had been a moment of confusion when she looked at her blood covered hand and that's when it had happened. Her face drained of colour and she sank into the sea of men, disappearing underfoot.

Seconds had already passed since she'd fallen, since he'd been delayed from going to her. Precious seconds that could mean she would be subjected to the trampling feet of men who did not pay attention where they went.

Myriad scenarios bombarded his thoughts: her skull being crushed by heavy boots, drowning in mud, being hit with a missed attack.

His beautiful, stubborn wife, whose feisty spirit he both respected and bemoaned. She didn't deserve to die for her attempt to help his clan. And she did not deserve to die like this.

Suddenly, it didn't matter where she put her faith or that she had nudged aside his concern for her to do what she felt was right. None of it mattered if she was lost to Calum for ever.

Nothing mattered but the visceral ache in his chest that told him it was more than care he felt for his wife.

It was love.

Grief rose in Calum's chest like a ball of fire, infusing him with an unnatural energy. He fought the men in front of him, not looking at who or where he struck, just hacking to get to his wife.

The man in front of Calum swung a great two-handed sword. It was a heavy weapon and moved slow enough for a warrior like Calum to easily evade. Normally. But his focus had been on the place where Elspeth had fallen.

As the sword came down, he tried to dart from its path, but was seconds too late. It landed hard on his left shoulder, knocking him to the side.

The agony nearly paralysed Calum, but he swung his sword with his good arm, dispatching the man. As the warrior fell, a space opened up, allowing Calum to fill the gap. One step closer to Elspeth.

All around him, Campbell men were dying. They were losing with no hope of turning the tide of battle.

'I'm Calum Campbell,' he shouted. 'We surrender.'

It was not his first attempt at doing such and was likewise ignored as his other previous attempts had been.

Someone knocked against his arm and the pain of it flashed through him, blinding him for a moment with its intensity. When he finally had a chance to shake his head to clear it, he could no longer see where Elspeth had fallen.

Calum's movements were clumsy in his panic as he pushed back at the men trying to attack him. He didn't want to fight. He wanted Elspeth. He wanted this whole bloody battle to be done.

Rough hands were on him, binding his wrists and calling to Ross. It seemed to all happen slow and muted as if underwater, Calum's mind reeling as he searched through the area for Elspeth. She had to be there somewhere.

Suddenly a warrior turned to face him, and Calum immediately recognised the man as Ross MacMillan. His brother-in-law.

The slow-moving world sped up once more as Calum's brain snapped into focus once more.

Ross smirked. 'We've captured you now.'

'I've been trying to surrender,' Calum said through gritted teeth, against the pain of his shoulder, of his shattered heart. 'Elspeth. She's here and has been injured.'

Ross's eyed widened with a fear Calum knew all too well.

'You brought her to a battle?' Ross asked, horrified. 'Are you mad?'

'I tried to get her to leave...' Calum shook his head. 'Stop the attack. We have to help her.'

'Enough,' Ross cried out.

All around him, the order was echoed and the clatter of weapons clashing slowly ebbed until there was only the errant clang of men who had not yet heard.

'Throw down your weapons, Campbells,' Calum ordered.

The residual sounds of war ceased and all was quiet save for the groans of the dying.

'Find my sister,' Ross said aloud.

'Here.' A man bent, followed by several others. All rose with a woman in their arms, her hair and face dark with mud, her body limp.

Unmoving.

Calum stared at her limp form, unable to see anything beyond the woman he loved. His beautiful Elspeth, so full of life, with a spirit brighter than the sun. But now she did not respond as the men held her aloft.

She was gone. Before he could tell her he loved her. Before she could realise how much he truly did believe in her. If only he had been able to acknowledge the feeling within him, to tell her the truth of how deeply he loved her.

And now he would never have a chance.

A sob choked from him.

In that instant, Calum had lost everything. Not just the opportunity for peace for his clan, but a chance for happiness, for a family.

Elspeth.

He wanted to hold her, to touch her face one last time, to whisper his love for her so that even as she was ascending into heaven, she might hopefully hear his words. Desperation and grief were a powerful combination that had him shoving against his captors.

'Restrain him,' Ross ordered.

The men holding Calum grasped him once more, their grip like iron this time.

'I have to go to her,' Calum said raggedly. 'I have to hold her, to let her know—'

Ross stepped between Calum and his view of Elspeth. 'Did you touch her?' He swallowed thickly and spoke in a low, icy tone, 'I'll ensure your death is long and slow if you harmed her.'

'Just let me see her,' Calum begged. 'Just let me—'

'Take him to the castle along with the rest of the Campbell men.' Ross shook his head in disgust. 'You'll never see her again.'

With that, Ross stalked away, slowing with reverence as he approached Elspeth, his words too low to hear as he spoke to the men holding her.

But was she dead?

The question caught in Calum's chest, locked in his heart.

And so it was, in a battle he had never wanted, he had lost everything.

The throbbing in Elspeth's skull was unbearable. She groaned and tried to turn her head, but the pain erupted with renewed agony.

'You're better off not moving,' a voice said.

One Elspeth recognised from somewhere.

Her brain whirled as she tried to open her eyes. But her lids were so heavy, making the feat a herculean effort. A whimper of frustration escaped her throat.

What had happened to make her feel this way?

She tried to recall her last memory and found only fear there.

What would make her feel afraid? In the hazy recesses of her memory, a massive wave stretched higher than the ship she was in, looming over her, her heart palpitating with the certainty that it would crash over her and she would drown. And then it did, the weight of water like a millstone dropping on her before sucking and pulling her towards the depths.

'I don't want to drown,' she murmured.

'Where do you think you are?' The woman asked, her voice ragged and husky with age.

Elspeth tried to open her eyes, but a brilliant light threatened to split open her skull. 'Ship.' The word croaked from her dry throat as she spoke with more strength. Yet even as she did so, she knew what she said to be incorrect.

Nay, that wasn't it. She wasn't on a boat. She hadn't drowned.

'Drink this.' Gentle hands braced Elspeth's head and helped her raise her chin as a mug of something warm and spiced with herbs rested at her lips.

Though it was a mite hot, Elspeth drained it, letting the soothing wet heat wash down her dry throat. She swallowed a final time in appreciation and tried to open her eyes once more.

'So bright,' she said softly.

'It's a candle,' the woman said. 'But I fear if I snuff it, we'll not be able to see at all.'

Elspeth turned away from the brilliance and slowly opened her eyes. Though the glow was far less brilliant now, the light still seemed to scrape deep into her skull.

'You're at Castle Sween.' The woman appeared before her, an old woman, grizzled and stooped, that teased at Elspeth's memories.

'Castle Sween,' Elspeth repeated it to herself as she tried to discern why she would be there. She hadn't been there before. Of that she was certain.

'You took a knock to the head as I understand it,' the woman said.

Elspeth frowned. 'I think I know you.'

'I hope you do, lass.' The woman smiled. 'I'm Morag, the healer.'

The woman's name was one Elspeth did recognise, but though Morag said she was a healer, Elspeth could not summon any association with her aside from a vague familiarity. Her thoughts were too thick, shifting too slowly, as though mired down in congealing mud.

The events trickled back as she tried desperately to make sense of her unwieldy recollections. Slowly it all began coming to her in broken pieces that made little sense.

A battle. Witnessing horrible things. So many dead and injured. So much blood.

She had been struck. Aye, in the head like Morag had said.

Now the difficulty of focusing made sense. Elspeth had been hit in the temple. Perhaps that had addled her. But she'd been trying to get to Ross. To let him know.

'Ross,' she muttered.

'Aye, the chieftain is here as well. Hale and hearty, so don't you trouble yerself over him.'

But Elspeth couldn't relax. A restlessness shifted through her body. She wasn't worried about her brother. There was a reason she needed to see him.

'You're safe now.' Morag put a gentle hand to Elspeth. 'You'll be sleeping soundly soon when the herbs take effect and when you wake, your head will feel better.'

Elspeth frowned. 'Herbs?'

'Aye, they were steeped in the mug I gave you,' the old woman replied. 'I'm the healer. Morag. Do you recall now?'

Had they had this conversation already?

Elspeth nodded, placating, but even as Morag explained about the herbs, a wave of exhaustion blanketed over Elspeth, making her mind feel as though it was weighted down. There was something she had to say.

Calum.

The single thought of his name broke the dam of her confusion as memories rushed back to her then. She gave a soft choking sob.

'Calum,' she whispered.

'You need not worry,' Morag said furtively.

'Where is he?' Elspeth asked, fear spiking through her. She wanted to get up, but her body was too heavy.

'Shush now, lass.' Morag ran a soothing hand over Elspeth's brow. 'He cannot hurt you now.'

'He never hurt me,' Elspeth protested. She tried to shift, to sit up, but her body did not want to cooperate, her limbs too numb to move. 'Why can I not get up?' The question came out in a whimper.

Morag shushed her again. 'It's the tea, lass. I made it stronger to help you heal faster.'

A tear leaked out of Elspeth's eye and trailed down her face as she finally acknowledged the depth of her true emotions. 'I love him.'

'What did you say?' A chair groaned as Morag leaned closer.

'I love him,' Elspeth said, her words slurring as her speech became as thick as her thoughts. 'We're wed.'

'I can't hear you, child,' Morag said gently.

Elspeth could scarcely think as the urge to sleep overwhelmed her. 'MacDonnells attacking... Married... Alliance...'

'Ach, my lass, what you've been through.' Morag's cool, dry hand ran over Elspeth's brow. 'Don't you worry, he'll be dead by dawn.'

Elspeth shook her head and protested. Or thought she protested. The darkness of sleep swept over her like an oncoming storm she was powerless to stop, and she could no longer discern the real world from the dream world.

But she hoped she had protested. That Calum would be saved. That they might be reunited soon.

Chapter Twenty-Five

Restlessness had Calum in a hard grip. He paced his small cell, unable to stay his agitation. The wound at his shoulder ached, but its discomfort was pale by comparison to the awful twist in his chest.

His men were there with him. The ones who had survived.

Bram and Hamish were in the dungeon at Castle Sween as well, in a cell across from them. They'd been captured on the way back to the cave. Trackers had been set on their trail after they were taken to the dungeon, which is what had led to the attack.

But thankfully Bram and Hamish had been spared.

For now, at least.

Uncertainty hung in the air as they all waited to discover their fate.

But it was not Calum's fate on his mind. Nay, it was that of his people, who would be left abandoned in Ireland with no word as to what became of him and the men who were supposed to save them. And, as always, Elspeth remained forefront in his thoughts.

His heart gave a painful squeeze.

He'd seen her go down after the blow to the head. It

played over and over again in his mind, the way she had stumbled about and then slid to the ground. He'd been in enough battles to know what awaited those who fell.

Men trampled those underfoot, their focus fixed only on what was in in front of them, on survival, lest one be slain. They were not considering who they might harm or whose face might be shoved into mud to drown.

If such a fate had befallen Elspeth…

All at once, the agony of it was so great that Calum found it hard to draw breath. Emotion clogged his throat and hammered about in his skull.

'I failed you.' Kieran looked away, his shame evident in the hard clench of this jaw. 'Forgive me, Laird.'

Calum shook his head and clasped the shoulder of one of his strongest warriors. 'You could not contain lightning any more than you could my wife.'

He still spoke of her if she was alive. In truth, he did it because he could not reconcile himself to the idea of her death. Aye, he'd seen the way her body hung limp in the men's arms, unmoving.

Yet he could not give up hope.

Footsteps approached and Calum straightened.

He was a man in love, a man locked in fear for the wellbeing of his wife to whom he had never been able to profess the extent of his true feelings. But he was also a laird. If he could do anything to protect his men, he would.

Light preceded the man's arrival, creating a warm glow on the dirt floor and nearly blinding Calum and his men with its brilliance in contrast to the pitch black they'd adjusted to.

By the time the MacMillan guard stopped in front of their cell, Calum had done what he could to push down his grief over Elspeth. But when the guard turned to face him, he could not stop the desperate words from tumbling from his mouth.

'Where is Elspeth?' Calum demanded. 'Is she...?'

The man narrowed his eyes.

Calum gripped the icy bars of his cell. 'Damn it, man. Tell me, does she live?'

The guard sneered. 'You need not worry after the lass, after all, you're the reason she was on that battlefield. Whenever happens to her is a stain on your soul.'

Bile rose in the back of Calum's throat. The guard's words were correct. It was all Calum's fault.

'She's my wife,' he said. 'We married to unify our clans, to bring peace. Because...because I love her.' His voice caught. 'I want an audience with Ross. Now.'

The man stared at him for a long moment, then scoffed. 'You're a fool if you expect me to believe your lies. Whatever you forced her to do isn't anything I care to repeat to Ross. Nor can you expect an audience with him. He'll not waste his time on the likes of you.'

'Bring him to me,' Calum demanded.

'It's true,' Bram said from the opposite side of the dungeon. 'I was a witness to the wedding.'

'Well, if you were indeed a witness, it will not matter after tomorrow,' the guard said. 'When the lot of you will be hanged.'

Hanged.

A chill spread over Calum that had nothing to do with the damp, icy air of the dungeon.

'Well, not you.' The guard gave a malicious grin and slid his finger across his neck and began to stalk away, taking the flickering light of the torch with him.

'The MacDonnells are behind the attacks,' he shouted after the man.

There was no reply.

'See the MacDonnells for your villagers' deaths,' he tried again. 'It wasn't us.'

Still there was no reply, save the slam of a heavy door that sealed them all in the dungeon, relegating them to their miserable fate.

Desperation pressed in on Calum, clogging his throat and leaving his chest tight.

If he was dead, his people would have no champion and no way for them to get their land back in Scotland. They would be abandoned in Ireland where they couldn't farm and be left to slowly die due to famine and disease from lack of proper care.

He had failed them.

Emotion clenched at him, dragging him into desolation. Elspeth…

He could see her in his mind's eye, those flashing green eyes and her lovely bright red hair, the way she looked at him as her whole heart lit her face. For him.

And he had repaid that love by bringing her into battle, not protecting her, leaving her vulnerable to being attacked. He should have been there at her side.

He couldn't stop the image of her after battle from surfacing in his mind again. The lovely flush of her cheeks now pale, the light of her eyes shielded behind closed lids, her ferocity extinguished.

He had failed her too.

His wife.

The woman he loved. Who he would always love.

He tried to swallow away the thickness in his throat,

but it stubbornly remained, intensifying the ache already lodged there.

His torment would be over soon, the next day he would be beheaded, and then they would be reunited in death. He only hated that his men would be there with him. And that his people would suffer for it.

'Forgive me,' he said in a gravelly voice. 'I have failed you all.'

Thundering blows rained down on Elspeth's brain. She groaned and rolled over in her sleep, but the thudding did not abate.

Footsteps clicked over the floor, mingling with the awful bangs.

'What is that?' Elspeth asked as she blinked her eyes open. Daylight limned the shuttered windows.

A blonde woman stood by her bed, her curling hair trimmed short and uncovered. She was a petite lass with blue eyes and a heavy shawl around her shoulders. Her mouth stretched into a smile when she saw Elspeth looking at her. 'Good morrow, sister.'

Sister?

Who was this woman?

'I'm Ilysa,' the blonde said. 'Ross's wife.'

Ross's wife. Elspeth toyed in her mind for the memory and found it right away.

She sucked in a gasp. The thudding of drum beats continued.

'What is it?' Ilysa asked. 'Are you unwell?'

Elspeth stared at the woman she did not know, the woman whose father had been attacking the villages and putting the blame on Calum and his men.

'Calum,' she said in a strangled voice as she recalled

the strange dream she'd had with Morag. Fear shuddered through her that perhaps it hadn't been a dream after all.

Ilysa's face softened with sympathy. 'I cannot imagine how awful an experience this has been for you.'

'Where is Calum?' Elspeth sat up in bed and her head spun, making dots of white dance in her vision.

'Don't get up,' Ilysa rushed to her and put a hand to Elspeth's shoulders, steadying her.

'Ach, lay back down now, lass,' Morag's familiar voice filled the room, followed by her clipped footsteps.

Immediately Elspeth knew the dream was indeed reality. That on this morning, Calum was set to die. But it was now morning.

He might already be dead.

The drum beats. They hammered on still, thudding over taut leather, marking the seconds before men were to die.

'Calum.' Elspeth pushed out of bed, ignoring the women trying to guide her back onto the mattress.

Ilysa cast a sympathetic look at Morag. 'Calum is…'

'I told you, lass,' Morag said in her no-nonsense tone. 'He's to be put to death. You don't need to worry after him.'

Elspeth cried out, her knees nearly losing their strength beneath her.

Calum.

Dead.

It couldn't be.

He was too big a man in her mind, his convictions too powerful, his determination too great, his love too vivid. How could a man so potently alive be so readily snuffed out?

'I love him,' she said passionately.

Ilysa and Morag looked at one another sharply before turning their attention back to Elspeth.

'What did you say?' Morag asked, her voice a shadow of a whisper.

'He's my husband.' Elspeth could not keep the tremble from her voice. 'We wed to align our clans, to end this war. Tell me now, is he dead?'

'Why didn't you say something last night?' Morag asked, her eyes wide. 'I'm not certain…the hanging is scheduled to begin right now.'

No sooner had the words left the old healer's mouth, Elspeth raced from the room. Her steps were unsure, and the corridor seemed to swing about around her, but she did not slow her pace.

She knew this castle better than any other after living in it for so many years. Every turn, every corner, and the exact location where death sentences were carried out in the courtyard.

Footsteps sounded behind her.

'You're in your night rail,' Ilysa called out.

Elspeth wouldn't have cared if she was naked. She had to get to Calum, to see if she could stop the execution before it was too late. As she approached, the drum beats became louder, faster, thundering in time with her own heart.

She was running out of time.

Sunlight dazzled her vision as she pushed outside to find a massive crowd of villagers and clansmen gathered together. The gallows had been erected on a platform, and the five men stood waiting with nooses strung around their necks. And standing in front of the hooded executioner was Calum, his hands bound, a gag tied round his face.

Elspeth cried out, calling his name, but the drumbeats were too loud now, too close together. They drown out her pleas as she ran with all the strength left in her body.

Her bare feet slapped against the cobblestones as she raced towards the crowd. As she did so, Calum sank to his knees and the executioner picked up his axe.

She was out of time.

Chapter Twenty-Six

The Lairds and Chieftains of the MacLachlans, Mac-Donnells and MacWhinnies had come to see Calum put to death in the courtyard of the castle which had once belonged to his family. Beheading, an honour they no doubt did not feel he deserved. Yet still it was to be granted.

The clan leaders sat high at the parapets, looking down on him as they always had since as far back as he could remember.

It was his father's need for violence which had been the Campbell downfall and now it was Calum's botched attempt at peace which would ultimately seal his clan's fate.

His men were lined up on the gallows, five at a time as they awaited death. After them would come five more. And then another five. On and on until his small army was all dead.

Calum would be put to death first, his rites already delivered by the aged priest now muttering those same words to Calum's clansmen.

The drumbeat was a steady thrum, too neat and even to match Calum's own pulse, which leapt with an erratic thrum that left his hands trembling. A breeze swept through the courtyard, carrying with it the crisp hint of an upcoming freeze.

He closed his eyes and pushed aside the pain in his arm from the wound that had not bothered to be tended to. Instead, he savoured the brush of wind over his cheeks, the way it ruffled his hair. This was life and he had only a few seconds left to live it.

Linen bound Calum's mouth to still any of his protests. His enemies did not care to hear his final words. Not when the offence of so many deaths left them already so enraged.

But in Calum's heart and mind he said his own farewells. To his people who he would leave behind as he prayed to God that they might somehow be saved. To his soldiers who would die alongside him that their deaths would be swift and their souls readily accepted into heaven. To Elspeth…

He recalled her with vivid clarity and how she fitted so perfectly in his arms, how her spirit was both bright and stubborn all at once, how she always summoned strength in the most trying times. His throat clogged with emotion when he remembered how she looked at him, her eyes soft with affection, her expression one of supplication, yielding to the passion between them.

Regrets assaulted him in these painful final moments of his life—the regret that he had not made time to teach her more, that he would never again have the opportunity to hold her to him. That he had never told her he loved her.

'Lower your head.' The executioner's deep voice broke through Calum's memories.

Calum lay his head on the executioner's block and opened his eyes, gazing out at the sea of faces, of those

who had arrived to see his death. But that was not where
his mind was.

Nay, he was lying in a hayloft with a blanket beneath
him with Elspeth at his side, her hair flecked with bits
of hay, her cheeks flushed from their coupling and her
eyes bright with love.

For him.

He smiled softly to himself behind the linen pulling
at the corners of his mouth, scarcely hearing the drumbeats any more.

All at once, the pulsing thud stopped and a sudden
quiet descended on the courtyard. Calum tensed, waiting for the executioner's blow when all at once the still-
ness was shattered by a scream.

'Nay,' Elspeth cried out again.

No one paid her any mind. The executioner's blade
was lifted high overhead with intent. Calum's head lay on
the chopping block, his mouth bound with a strip of linen
as his gaze stared out over the heads of the masses who
had been led by bloodlust to watch his execution that day.

She shoved through the crowd. Strong arms grabbed
at her, but she broke away with a strength she had never
had. Freed, she leapt up the small dais, taking the stairs
two at a time. She didn't think as she raced towards the
executioner whose axe was beginning to swing down towards Calum's tender neck.

Nay, her only thoughts were on Calum, on saving the
man she loved.

As the axe lowered, she screamed once more and
threw herself over Calum, blocking him from the deadly
blade with her body. She tensed, waiting for the blow

to cleave into her. And in that tumultuous second, she breathed the words she had longed to say. 'I love you.'

Air whooshed past her, sending a shudder rippling over her skin as the blade sank into the wood, missing her little toe by a hair's breadth. Calum snapped upright in that instant and swept his legs over her to push her further from the axe.

He looked at her and tears filled his eyes, his mouth working with incomprehensible words mumbled around the cloth in his mouth. She quickly untied it so it fell into his lap, freeing his lips and desperately pressed her mouth to his, savouring the feel of him being alive.

'Elspeth,' he said in a broken voice between kisses. 'You're alive.' His shoulders wriggled and she realised they were bound behind his back. She'd paid so much attention to the axe she had not even noticed.

She reached around him now to untie the rope binding his wrists.

'I love you.' The rope uncurled from his wrists before dropping to the wooden platform and he pulled her into his arms. 'I should have told you that before, but I didn't know—'

'I didn't know either until I almost lost you.' Her voice broke.

'I thought you were dead.' Emotion clogged his throat and he cradled her against him. 'My God, you're alive.'

'And so are you.' Tears streamed hot down her cheeks as she held onto him so tightly that her body trembled. 'I thought I would be too late. I thought…' She broke off, giving way to her sobs.

He pulled away and met her gaze, his own cheeks wet with tears. 'You shouldn't have risked yourself for me. Elspeth, you could have been killed.'

'I couldn't bear to lose you,' she whispered.

He drew her towards him again in a fierce hug. 'I love you, Elspeth. No matter what happens, I want you to know that. I *love* you.'

'I love you too,' she said against his chest, the fabric of his tunic damp against her cheeks.

'What is the meaning of this?' Ross demanded.

Elspeth looked up to find her eldest brother no longer along the parapet with the other noblemen, but standing over her, his expression hard.

It was then she also remembered everyone else around them—the crowd that was watching in fascination, the nobles up on the dais at the parapets, the Campbells set to be hanged and the executioner in his black hood at their side.

'Elspeth,' Ross said in a low warning tone. But she had never been afraid of Ross. She knew him too well and knew how greatly he loved her.

Calum got to his feet and helped her to hers. He immediately released her once they were both standing, doing so out of respect. But she didn't give a fig for respect. She would readily sacrifice it to save him.

Instead, she clasped his hand in hers, refusing to let go.

'Calum Campbell is my husband.' She looked up to where Leith sat with his father. Beside them were Fergus and Coira who now leaned forward, their gazes fraught with concern. Surely, they would recognise the depth of her love.

'He is the man I have chosen for love,' Elspeth declared loudly.

Leith's face darkened, but Coira's broke out in a smile.

'What is the meaning of his?' Ross asked in a low

voice. Despite his anger, he swept the cloak from his shoulders and put it over hers to cover her.

She stood proud, not modestly clenching the cloak about her shoulders as she might once have. 'I've come to know Calum these last few weeks. I've also come to know his people and how they are starving in Ireland. Good people, many women and children. People who don't deserve to die, especially when we have land enough here.'

'You wed him to save people who are not your own?' Leith demanded.

'To unite our clans, aye.' She looked out on those gathered around them. 'I married him to save all our people from experiencing any more death. We have all lost enough fathers, sons and husbands. Our union unites our people in peace.' She looked at Calum, who stood with his chest squared as he watched her with affectionate pride. 'And I'm married to him because I love him.'

'You say he wants peace, but what of the continued attacks on our people?' Ross demanded.

This was what Elspeth dreaded the most. When she finally spoke, she did not do so aloud for all to hear, but quietly for his ears only. 'Forgive me, but your own father-in-law is behind those attacks.'

Ross's brow furrowed.

'We have a witness outside of ourselves,' she said quickly. 'A villager.'

Calum shook his head. 'Alan was slain in the battle.'

A knot of grief for the young man tensed in Elspeth's chest. If she had gone with Kieran, he would have lived.

'A witness is not necessary,' Ross said at last. 'I trust you, Elspeth. And it doesn't surprise me that MacDonnell is involved. He has already betrayed us all once. He wants control of Castle Sween, and a few weeks ago he tried and failed to get it when Ilysa foiled his plan to kill me. I didn't want him anywhere near Sween, but he's still a clan chieftain and the others insisted on him being here today.' He waved to his guards who withdrew the nooses from the necks of Bram, Hamish, Kieran and two other warriors whose names Elspeth did not know.

'Iain MacDonnell,' Ross bellowed. 'You are accused of attacking my people in the name of the Campbells to ferment trouble and undermine my leadership. What say you to these claims?'

The Chieftain of the MacDonnells rose from his seat alongside the other Chieftains, Lairds and nobles. His broad shoulders did not sag under the weight of the charge. Instead, he lifted his chin defiantly as he faced those he was alleged to have wronged.

'We have witnesses,' Elspeth said, knowing they did not. But she could not stomach the idea of the MacDonnell's lies.

MacDonnell hesitated, then gave an arrogant smirk. 'Aye, it was my people who attacked under the guise of the Campbells, starting with the damned abbey. The lot of you were too damn foolish to see through the ruse. All my men did was wear the gambesons of fallen men and you saw what you wished.'

The crowd behind Ross roused to life in outrage.

'You don't even try to deny it?' Laird MacLachlan asked incredulously over the roar of the rabble.

MacDonnell barked a harsh laugh. 'What does it matter? I'll not be punished for my crimes. You wouldn't dare cast me from Scotland like you did Alexander Campbell and his whelp. I'm not a mere laird, but a bloody chieftain.' He cast a derisive sneer on them all. 'I'm untouchable.'

'You forget that I too am a chieftain,' Ross said. 'One whose clan you have mercilessly slaughtered. One who has more than one qualm with your treatment of people.' He strode towards the stairs leading to the parapet of noblemen, his eyes narrowed with intent. 'One whose castle you tried to steal even though your plot to kill me failed. One whose wife you spent a lifetime mistreating.'

Ross paused in that moment to look through the crowd to where Ilysa stood with Morag on the outskirts. There was a flash of emotion in his expression as he gazed upon his wife. Her right hand went to her chest, pressing upon it as though she were trying to contain her heart. In that one glance shared between Elspeth's eldest brother and the petite blonde who had toiled at her bedside, Elspeth knew in her heart that Ross too had found love.

The crowd had grown restless, shouting encouragement to their chieftain, crying out for revenge.

But Elspeth knew nothing could truly come of Ross's threats. He could not slay MacDonnell or he would be the one to face the King's wrath. Sadly, MacDonnell was right; he was untouchable.

And while she wanted to stay her brother's hand, it was not her place to do so.

Especially not when Ross gave a determined growl as he scaled the rest of the stairs. MacDonnell gave a cocky grin and stalked closer to the landing to wait for Ross, cracking his knuckles like a brigand.

Elspeth tightened her hold on Calum. Whatever came of this battle, it would not bode well for Ross.

'All will be well,' Calum said gently.

'How?' she asked, her heart caught in her chest.

Fergus came to the rescue, leaping from his seat to stand between MacDonnell and Ross.

'He has much to atone for,' Ross's declaration echoed through the silence. 'And today he will finally pay for what he's done.' He put a hand to Fergus' chest. 'Sit down, brother.'

Fergus slowly backed away and stood by Coira, and Elspeth's heart sank in her chest. At least Fergus would be at the ready should Ross need him. She only hoped he might step in before Ross killed the other chieftain, before irreparable damage could be done.

Ross flew at MacDonnell, sending his fist into the man's jaw. The older chieftain's face turned to the side with the blow and refocused on Ross with a swift recovery.

The crowd roared to life with jeers at MacDonnell and encouragement for Ross.

MacDonnell tried to strike at Ross, but her brother ducked away, his body young, strong and battle hardened. Despite MacDonnell's arrogance, he didn't stand a chance against Ross.

That was what worried Elspeth. And Fergus shared her concern as evidenced by his tense expression.

Elspeth had always been known as the one with the fierce temper, but it didn't mean Ross didn't have a vicious streak of his own, no matter how deeply he tried to bury it. But especially when provoked and whatever hurt it was that had gleamed in Ilysa's eyes when her gaze locked with that of her husband had clearly uncovered that streak.

MacDonnell swept an arm at Ross. 'He's got a dagger,' a woman in the crowd screamed.

Ross evaded that strike as well as the one following it before catching MacDonnell behind the knee and sending him landing on the ground with a thwack that echoed out over the courtyard. Moving with the speed of a hunter, Ross was on MacDonnell, twisting the dagger from his hand.

He remained over the fallen chieftain, the weapon in his hand, his chest rising and falling with his frantic breathing. His wrist jerked, flicking the dagger from blade to hilt against his palm. Ready to plunge it into MacDonnell.

Elspeth gripped Calum's arm. 'Don't do it,' she whispered to her brother under her breath.

No sooner had she made the quiet plea, than Ross backed away and tucked the dagger in his belt. 'You've gone too far this time, MacDonnell. The King will deal with you when he hears about the extent of your crimes. Perhaps we can convince him to send you to Ireland as you deserve.' With that, he put his back to MacDonnell.

The other man scrambled to his feet. 'That's it?' The older man scoffed. 'You never were worthy of being chieftain. Why do you think I sent you my weakest child? You didn't deserve my prize daughter so it's a good job the King made you give Lilidh back to me.'

Ross spun around and faced the other man, his face a mask of rage unlike anything Elspeth had ever seen on him. 'Ilysa is a greater prize than you'll ever know.'

'She's a deformed weakling.' MacDonnell spit on the ground near Ross's feet.

Before Elspeth could even pull in a sharp breath at such an offence, Ross launched himself at the other chieftain, his fist smashing into MacDonnell's face.

Blood gushed from the older chieftain's nose, saturating the pale blue tunic he wore. His hands flew to his face in astonishment and he staggered back several paces, eyes wide with surprise.

It was the staggering back that did for him. The low crenellation groove of the parapet caught him behind the legs and his arms windmilled. For a brief moment, he appeared to have caught his balance, but then he disappeared, sailing over the edge. He shouted in surprise, a sound that was abruptly cut off a second later.

The entire crowd in the courtyard went still. Ross stepped to the edge of the parapet and peered over, MacLachlan and Fergus joining him. When Ross turned back to his people, his face was grave.

A cheer broke out among the people.

The reign of terror imposed by the MacDonnell clan had come to an end.

And thankfully the act of a fall could not be blamed on Ross. After all, it had been MacDonnell himself who had staggered backwards.

Elspeth breathed a sigh of relief for her brother's sake. For the sake of the Campbells. For the life they could all now live in peace. She lowered her head to Calum's chest and realised for the first time, he did not hold her with his right arm.

'What's happened to you?' she asked.

He shook his head. 'A flesh wound.'

Ross hurried down the stairs once more, pausing only to speak with one of his warriors before quickly rushing through the crowd towards the castle where Ilysa had disappeared.

'Come,' Elspeth pulled at his left hand. 'Morag will look after it for you.'

'Only if you put on some proper clothes and slippers.' He indicated her bare feet.

Now she did wrap Ross's cloak more tightly about her as she led him towards Castle Sween, eager to get him inside, to have his wound tended to. Her hand tightening on his, reassuring herself that he was truly there with her. Alive.

A smile broke out on her face. And he always would be.

Chapter Twenty-Seven

Calum allowed Elspeth to pull him towards Castle Sween. The people parted for them as they passed, their faces still wary as they regarded him. Not that he blamed them. His father had exacted many atrocities on the Mac-Millans, not only in the past, but more recently as well.

The Campbells would still have much to atone for in the coming years. Calum's union with Elspeth was merely the first step in healing wounds, both old and fresh alike. And he would see to it that his people did everything in their power to help and offer support to the surrounding clans.

Elspeth strode in front of him, her gait slightly unsteady. It had been impossible not to notice the bruise at the side of her face where she had been struck. She cast an impatient glance back at his arm where the wound throbbed. It didn't matter. The only truly important thing was that she was alive, his warriors would be freed and his people would now be safe.

Gratitude welled in his chest.

She had survived the battle. How, he did not know, for truly it was a miracle. And despite the injuries she had suffered, she still managed to save him and his people.

He stopped suddenly and pulled her towards him.

Her brow creased with worry. 'We need to see to your arm.'

But he was concerned about her as much as she was about him. He ran his fingertips gently down her brow, hovering just over the bruise. 'You're not well either.'

'I will be soon,' she said. 'We both will.'

He pulled her into his arms, not wanting to let her go as he reassured himself that she was really alive, there with him. That the future they had hoped for might actually become reality. That in a life where everything seemed as though it always went wrong, a shift had occurred and now it was all going perfectly right.

'I love you, Elspeth,' he said with so much emotion that a knot thickened at the back of his throat.

She drew away and looked up at him, cradling his face between her palms, appearing even lovelier than he remembered. 'And I love you, Calum Campbell.'

Together they strode through the entrance of Castle Sween, the place he had lived for the first six summers of his life, before his clan was cast out of Scotland and forced to try and survive in Ireland.

When Calum told Elspeth he did not wish to live in Castle Sween and preferred to establish themselves in a new castle, he was entirely honest in that admission. There was naught here for him now.

'We'll build better memories wherever we go,' Elspeth said gently.

He looked down to where he cradled her at his left side and smiled. She understood him better than anyone. The same as he did her.

Aye, once they were fully recovered, they would begin

their new life together with a fresh start where his people could live in peace and their love could continue to grow.

A fortnight later

Elspeth had never seen so many tents in her whole life. They stretched out over the area of Tarbert like white birds settled against the landscape. Between them were the partially built huts where the families living in those tents would eventually settle.

For ever.

'It's good to be home.' Calum put his left arm around her, still favouring his right as the deep gash healed.

Morag often said how lucky he was that the wound had not become infected in the time he'd spent locked in the dungeon. But luck seemed to be on Elspeth and Calum's sides.

It had been a considerable undertaking to relocate the Campbell clan from Ireland to the lands north of Tarbert, including Tarbert itself and the rundown castle upon its craggy shores. The clans that had once united against the Campbells now came together to offer gifts of grain and other food stores to see them through the relocation from Ireland to Scotland, saving many lives that might have otherwise been lost during the arduous transition.

Even the rain had somewhat abated, offering the Campbells an opportunity to set up their temporary tents while huts were being built.

Elspeth fingered the golden necklace at her throat, the small sunburst with the smooth ruby stone at its centre. Alison had brought it to her on the day the Campbell clan returned to their land.

Calum's eye caught her caressing the piece of jewellery and a whimsical smile touched his lips. 'This truly is a symbol of everything we have gained.' His expression sobered somewhat. 'I didn't know my mother as well in her later years as I'd have liked, but I believe she would have loved you. I know for certes she would be proud of what you've done.'

'What we've done.' Elspeth released the necklace to pull him close. 'Together.'

'Mistress Elspeth,' a little voice called.

Elspeth turned round to find wee Jamie running towards her. He was still a slip of a thing as he'd been when he'd first met her in Ireland when he'd begged them to help repair his mother's home. But at least now he wore proper clothes that were absent of tears and dirt.

'It's Lady Campbell now.' Sorcha peered out of one of the tents and waved at them apologetically. The colour had started returning to her cheeks and though she was still thin, she was not painfully so now.

Jamie paid his mother no mind as he ran up to Elspeth with his hand outstretched. 'I found something for you.'

'Ach, what do you have?' Elspeth opened her hand under his and a small stone fell into her palm. Bits of crystal showed against the grey rock, so her skin was visible through clear areas.

'It's a diamond.' Jamie's blue eyes went wide.

'So it is,' Elspeth exclaimed.

'It's perfect for a lady like you.' He smiled up at her. 'So, I saved it to give to you.'

She put the small stone into the pouch at her side. 'I shall treasure it always.'

Calum ruffled the lad's hair. 'You're a fine lad. One of these days, I'll have you come train with us if you like.'

'Aye, so I can be a warrior like my da.' Jamie looked

behind him and grinned at the man cutting wood near the tent.

Elspeth's heart warmed to see the families whole once more. No more men needing to go from one country to another nor fearing that they may never return home again.

With his gift delivered, Jamie darted away towards his family's tent, leaving Elspeth and Calum smiling after him.

'Speaking of training,' Calum threaded his hand through Elspeth's. 'With everyone settling in so swiftly, we'll be resuming practices again soon. If you know someone who would like to join.'

She grinned at him. 'You know I do.'

'Riders,' a guard shouted from where he stood on a recently repaired parapet.

There was still much work to do on the castle. Time had done its worst to the old structure, but the other clans lent not only materials, but also men to offer their assistance. For now, it could at least be lived in with all the leaks repaired and the living quarters sealed so they were no longer draughty.

The horses stopped before the castle and two riders dismounted before the warriors riding up behind them. Ross and Fergus.

Elspeth approached her brothers, trying to quell the flare of nerves in her stomach after their visit with Laird MacLachlan to smooth things over. She had intended to go too, but Ross had said he preferred to speak with Laird MacLachlan and not his son, Leith.

'Well?' she asked with great hesitation. 'Did I ruin the alliance with the MacLachlans?'

Fergus scoffed. 'Laird MacLachlan is sore about sending guards to help here when he's trying to build a new curtain wall himself, but he doesn't care about the wedding as you were never officially betrothed. And…' He looked to Ross as both their lips curled up in mirth.

'And what?' Elspeth pressed.

'Leith is wed.' Ross lifted his brows.

'A wee slip of a thing that dotes on him and loves him almost as much as he loves himself,' Fergus added with a snort of laughter.

Elspeth gave him a chastising look, but could not stop her own laughter at the comment. 'She must be enamoured if that truly is the case!'

And if Leith was well married, he would no longer seek her hand.

'We were going to write you a missive when we returned home, but knew you'd be on pins waiting to hear back.' Fergus winked at her.

'You know me too well, brothers.' She hugged them each in turn. 'Thank you for coming to tell me directly. Now, off to your wives. I'll not keep you from your families, but do give them my love.'

Her brothers needed no more encouragement and were once more on their steeds, heading towards home and the women who loved them.

'Do you feel better?' Calum slid his arms around her waist and drew her towards him.

'Aye.' She gazed lovingly up at her husband. 'Now I don't have to worry about being abducted again,' she teased.

'Not that it ended so very badly when I took you.' His eyes twinkled.

She playfully pushed at his chest. 'If someone were to do that now, I'd stab them with my dagger.'

He quirked a brow. 'Would you?'

'Aye, I've learned a bit from a certain warrior.'

'A fine one?'

She laughed. 'Ach, a very fine one.'

He puffed his chest out with pride.

'Those lessons saved my life on the battlefield,' she said, mentioning it for the first time. 'And you were right. Being in battle was not what I expected. I don't think I would have survived if I didn't know how to fight just a bit.'

'I didn't mean to doubt your strength on the battlefield that day,' he said gently.

She nodded. 'I know that now. You sought only to protect me.'

'The same as you did for me in trying to go to Ross to end the battle.' He smiled in understanding.

It was the first time they had discussed that fateful day, but it was nothing that had driven a wedge between them. Deep down, they both realised the actions of the other for what they had been motivated by: love.

His hand moved over her back in quiet strokes, understanding her need for comfort. But then, he always seemed to sense exactly what she needed when she needed it. 'I can teach you to wield a sword now too, if you like,' he offered.

She considered his offer. 'Perhaps I'll learn a bit more of the dagger first. I feel there's much more to know still. And then the sword.' She rested her hand on his strong chest and revelled in the strong beat of his heart beneath her palm. 'After all, we're not limited on time any more.'

He put his hand over hers, sealing it against his heart. 'We've all the time in the world, my love.'

She smiled at those words, at what they meant to her

soul as she imagined what the future would bring. A new home, aye. And a new life. Perhaps bairns?

All she knew was that they would do it together and she'd have it no other way.

Chapter Twenty-Eight

Tarbert Castle, April 1364

Calum stood on the parapet looking out over the Scottish land he had been given, the deed signed by the King's hand within the first year of their living there.

The years in Tarbert had been prosperous for the Campbell clan, with bountiful harvests providing enough food that famine was a thing left to their bitter past. As time wore on and the people of Argyle lived a peaceful existence beside the once-feared Campbells, their trust had begun to return.

It brought Calum great pride to see his clan embraced among their neighbours once more, to see them prosper with well-built huts that fended off rainy seasons and cold winters. But his people were not the only ones to prosper.

'It's a sight,' Elspeth said quietly as she appeared beside him. The babe in her arms nestled close as a breeze stirred the downy fluff of red hair at the crown of her head. Wee Catriona had been born only a few days before and was named after Calum's mother.

'This was the life I'd always dreamed of.' Calum put his arm around Elspeth, cradling mother and child at once.

Several horses approached with a wagon rattling behind it. 'It appears Fergus and Coira have arrived.' The giggles of children followed Elspeth's announcement, bringing them both down the stairs to the courtyard to welcome them.

Gregor and Ailis, Coira's children from her previous marriage, raced over to Elspeth. 'Can we see the new bairn?' little Ailis asked, popping up on tip toe for a better vantage point.

Elspeth leaned over gently to let the children see. Calum tensed like a nervous nursemaid. While the delivery of Catriona was what Morag called 'easy,' there had been enough screaming and blood to make Calum think otherwise despite everyone's reassurances that Elspeth was well. Including from his wife.

Ailis cooed in delight, but Gregor swiftly lost interest as lads his age do when it comes to bairns. Within seconds, they were both racing past Calum, through the courtyard to the newly constructed stables to feed apples to the horses.

Coira was immediately behind them with Mhairi on her hip, the lass born to Coira and Fergus who had recently celebrated her first summer. 'Ach, let me see the wee babe.' Coira leaned closer, but Mhairi squirmed in her arms.

Fergus came up behind her and plucked Mhairi from his wife so she could better peer at Catriona.

Calum clasped Fergus's free forearm in welcome. 'We're glad you could come.'

'Yer wee lass is a bonny one.' Fergus grinned at him. 'You know Elspeth will be making you teach her to fight as well.'

Calum laughed. 'She told me that before we'd even named her.'

Fergus chuckled and readjusted Mhairi on his hip. 'Aye, that sounds like Elspeth.'

Another horse and cart approached as Ross and Ilysa emerged with their son, Cormac, who had seen three summers and was ready to take on the rest of the world.

Ilysa did as Coira had, pausing by Elspeth to croon over wee Catriona as Ross joined Calum and Fergus.

'You know you'll have to teach her to fight?' Ross lifted his brows.

Calum could only laugh in reply. 'So I've been told.'

Elspeth approached him, her face glowing with a joy that warmed Calum's heart. 'Since we're all here, we had best be on with it before she wakes.'

'She'll wake when the priest puts salt in her mouth,' Fergus said, and Coira nudged him with a chastising shake of her head to quiet him before she rushed off to the stables to reclaim Ailis and Gregor.

But Elspeth only smiled and stroked Catriona's downy red hair. 'I imagine she will.'

The babe nuzzled closer to her and gave a little grunt in her sleep. Calum couldn't resist doing as Elspeth had and gently stroked their daughter's soft head. The smell of her was unlike anything he'd ever encountered before, powdery, new, and it touched a place in his heart, staking a claim in a spot that would always belong to Catriona and her alone.

'Ach, Cormac howled something fierce when the priest put salt into his mouth,' Ross said, earning a similar silent rebuke from Ilysa.

The men all shared an innocent look as the families made their way to the newly completed chapel.

The castle had taken over two years to repair, but was finally completed. The chapel had been the final bit with the rich, coloured glass being put into place on the day of Catriona's birth.

The heavy wooden doors parted to reveal Father Keith waiting for them, a smile stretched on his aged face. He greeted them and gazed down at Catriona.

'She's a bonny lass like her mother.' He smiled kindly at Elspeth who embraced him.

In the last two years, Father Keith had assumed a place in the castle, becoming part of their clan and part of their family. Tears sparkled in his eyes. 'Your mother would be so proud.'

It was something the old priest said to Calum often, and something that always warmed his heart to hear.

'Aye,' Calum agreed as he smiled at his beautiful wife and child. 'I know she would be.'

Elspeth gently handed their daughter to Father Keith who took her in careful hands and approached the alter.

The scent of fresh wood from the newly constructed pews mingled with the smoke from the candles as Father Keith began to speak in Latin. In that new church on restored Campbell lands, enemies were now family, a war that had torn them apart for so long was now completely at an end and all had found happiness in true love.

And that love provided the very best end to the feud between the Campbells and the MacMillans who were finally, blissfully, at peace.

* * * * *